Seraph's Bind

Seraph, Volume 2

Wayne Basta

Published by Many Worlds Fiction, 2022.

SERAPH'S BIND

First edition. August 1, 2022.

Copyright © 2022 Wayne Basta.

ISBN: 978-1958159095

Written by Wayne Basta.

For everyone struggling to find their family

1- Ariana

Jasper leaned in close. "You really expect me to believe you had nothing to do with that mess over Triask?"

Ariana Harkins suppressed a gag reflex at the overpowering stench of the man's odor and forced herself to smile in reply. The press of people in the Hub's central market kept her from pulling away to avoid their conversation being easy to overhear. Information was its own currency in a place like the Hub station.

"AI warships and crazy terrorists are not exactly things I like to get mixed up in," Ariana said.

"Who does?" Jasper nodded. "But I know you left here with Javi Wester onboard. Then, bam, a few weeks later he pops up on every news feed calling out LFD for trying to bring back the AI wars."

"Sure, I transported Javi to Triask. So, I guess if that makes me involved, I was involved." Ariana held her hands out to the side mockingly.

"I don't buy it, Ariana. There's more to this than that," Jasper said leaning back.

Ariana greedily sucked in untainted air. She gave a half-hearted shrug, allowing herself to turn her head and make the gagging motion she had been suppressing. It felt good to not be fighting her body's natural revulsion, even for a second. It would feel better once she was out of smell range.

Around them the hustle and bustle of the Hub's market flowed. People of every species Ariana had ever heard of mingled at the shop booths. The space felt more congested than was strictly necessary. Many shop owners had expanded their shop front in recent years, adding an interior section for more storage. This compacted the room for walking between merchants and pressed everyone together. Despite that, most merchants, like Jasper, continued to conduct business out in the open as a tradition.

Above them the glow of the station's artificial light source shined on them. It gave a fair impression of sunlight. This fantasy fell apart when you looked up, however. Beyond the glowing orb in the center, you could see the opposite side of the hollow station's sphere, and the people there standing as if upside down. The distance was great enough that sort of detail was hard to make out, but not impossible.

"You can believe whatever you want, Jasper. As long as you have a job for me," Ariana said turning back to face him.

"See, that's the thing. I'm not sure I should hire you. Right now, it's just me curious. But word tends to get around for things like this. There are too many coincidences to be nothing," Jasper pressed.

"Coincidences? Like me transporting an old friend without asking any questions? Ariana Harkins doesn't pry. That's not a rumor that would cause me much trouble."

"Yeah, what about those fancy upgrades *Seraph* is now sporting?"

"Investments."

"You could barely pay off your debt for that ship before leaving. You were tapped out. Don't deny it."

Ariana shrugged. Jasper continued. "And what the hell happened to Noah?"

The mention of her former crewman, Noah Ramirez, sent a stab of loss through Ariana. Noah died defeating LFD's rogue AI command ship. She had fired the shot that had killed him, trading his life for everyone else's. The hardest part about being reminded of Noah was how much she didn't regret her decision. At least she didn't think she did.

"What can I say, Noah was never going to stick around forever," Ariana said, trying to sound flippant.

"Right."

Letting her irritation show, she said, "Look, Jasper, do you have anything for me or not? If you don't, then stop wasting my time."

"Sure, I have something for you. There's still that survey job of sector J-25..."

"Something serious. There's a reason no one wants that job." Ariana said.

"It pays good money. The idea that the AI or hostile aliens are killing anyone who goes there is just ridiculous. Besides, *Seraph* was originally an exploration scout. There's not many ships with the astrometrics suite you have that can find nav jumps in and out of uncharted systems." Jasper pressed but Ariana just raised an eyebrow at him and he waved a hand, "Fine, fine. Just so long as we're clear that if you turn out to be part of LFD or a PUG nark, I'm denying having ever known you."

"Same."

Jasper chuckled. "That's why I enjoy doing business with you, Ariana. Okay, I've got a load of goods in need of transport. Standard rate. Nothing fancy."

Relief flooded Ariana, but she tried to keep it from showing. She needed work to keep *Seraph* flying, "Nothing fancy sounds good. Pick up or delivery?"

"Pick up."

"Sounds like a deal. Where do we need to go?"

"Just a short hop over to Emay."

"Emay? With the recent unrest between the Rokma and Manta, it's not the safest corner of the galaxy. Plus, that's not a short hop."

"It is for someone who can cut through the Unmar nebula. Something I hear you can do now."

Ariana raised an eyebrow, "After all this runaround and it turns out you need me. Don't want to pay the rate of the big freighters. Figured I'd be cheaper after your whole song and dance about whether you can trust me?"

Jasper shrugged, "Business is business."

"Fair enough" Ariana said. She considered the possible dangers in the area but she needed work. She finally extended a hand, "You have yourself a transport."

2- Olivia

"Why do we always get stuck with the grunt work?" Serene complained.

"What do you mean grunt work?" Olivia looked up from her handheld to her Echanic companion.

"This," Serene said. She gestured to the cart in front of her and then to the shelves full of items. They were in the middle of Big Box, the Hub's largest store front that took up an entire section of the station. The central market was where the unique and interesting items were to be found. Big Box was where you got your cheap things in bulk. "We're stuck getting supplies for the whole ship and having to lug them around like slaves."

Olivia sighed, "I'm here because I drew the short straw. You're here because it's your job."

Serene pouted, "I thought cargo handler was just a euphemism. I never saw Noah handle any actual cargo. He just got to shoot people. I assumed Ariana would want to put my talents in that area to good use."

Olivia rolled her eyes. "I'm sure if the captain finds anyone she wants to make dead, you'll be the first she talks too."

Olivia pushed the cart around the corner of the aisle and came to a stop in front of the protein paste. She started lifting one of the jumbo barrels, but found she couldn't budge it. Gesturing to Serene for an unreasonably long time, the Echanic woman finally bent over and helped her.

"Why are we getting this rubbish stuff?" Serene asked.

"This is what's on the list. It keeps well and works with our food processor."

"Yeah, but it's shit."

A cheery mechanical voice interrupted Olivia's next response, "No, it used to be shit. Now it is protein paste. Soon it will be reprocessed into fuel compatible with your inefficient biological digestive system. Then an incredibly high amount will be excreted as waste matter to begin the cycle over again."

The medical drone Mesu trundled down the aisle to meet them. Serene lifted her eyebrows as if she were rolling her eyes, though with the cybernetic implant covering them Olivia couldn't actually see it. In three of his appendages, Mesu carried small packages that he set down onto the cart.

"These are the supplies the infirmary is lacking that the Captain said she could afford. This leaves you susceptible to four thousand, two hundred and twenty-one ailments, maladies, diseases and injuries that I will be unable to treat."

"So, we have shit bags and medicine that still leaves four thousand ways to die. I'm feeling very happy about this journey," Serene said.

"Oh, there are far more than four thousand ways for you to die," Mesu said happily, "There are just 4,221 ways that my considerable programming could treat if I had the proper supplies."

"Even better."

"Now, I have concluded my duties. I have a drama class I wish to attend before departure. At the conclusion I will be ready to entertain the crew with a solo performance of Hamlet during the journey, therefore maximizing crew health by ensuring mental well-being."

With that, Mesu rolled off and out of the supply store. Olivia exchanged a glance with Serene. The pair just shook their heads and continued down the aisle. There were not many more items to acquire before they were ready to check out.

Once they had paid, their items were packed up and Serene attached a teleport recall device to the crate. They would be able to retrieve them with the teleporter once they returned to *Seraph*.

"I think that tin can had a good idea," Serene said.

"You're going to go take a drama class?"

"No, but I am going to do something that is not on the ship. I haven't gotten laid in weeks. If we were on a more fun station, I would take you with me. But alas, you're just a child and can't engage in any real fun."

Olivia felt her cheeks blush at Serene's brazenness. Stubbornly she said, "I am not a child. I'm seventeen now. Plus, I grew up here. I know all the best places."

"Still a child. By human or Echanic standards. Now, run along while the grown-ups get it on."

Serene sauntered off, her hips swaying suggestively as she walked. Olivia just shook her head. She made her way to the open market in the center of the station. Several people greeted her with a friendly smile. It had been a few months since they had last been here, but she had lived most of her life on the Hub.

While studying a pair of stylish sunglasses at a booth, maybe their next delivery would take them planet-side, she heard a voice call out her name. Turning, Olivia jumped slightly at the two figures standing behind her. Her brief panic gave way to a flush of excitement.

"When did you get back? How are you?" The questions came quickly and left Olivia flustered and unable to answer.

Jasmine, a human girl, moved in for a hug before Olivia had had a chance to respond. Bray'la, a Slu girl, hung back and bowed her eyestalks sheepishly. Before leaving the Hub aboard *Seraph*, Olivia had spent a lot of time with these two.

"Um..." Olivia stammered out, "Just yesterday. We're just resupplying and picking up another delivery."

"Look at you, the high-class pilot of a fancy starship," Jasmine said with a half-smile.

Olivia shrugged and looked away, unwilling to say more about her life on *Seraph*, "How have you been?"

"Same old same old," Jasmine replied.

"Oh, that's not true. We don't have to steal food anymore." Bray'la said.

"Oh, were you able to find a job?" Olivia asked.

"Nah, not all of us are naturally amazing pilots. But they did reopen the shelter." Bray'la said.

"Wow? Really? That hasn't been open in years. What changed?"

Jasmine shrugged dismissively, but Bray'la said, "Douglas got kicked off the station's council. He was linked to that LFD group. With him gone, the others decided to start feeding us kids again."

"Yeah, turns out the government wasn't the biggest threat. Like you always said, it's those damn AI's," Jasmine said. "Speaking of which, we've met some people we think you should meet."

"Oh?" Olivia cocked her head.

"Yeah, they hate the AI just as much as you. And they're going to teach us to fight them. Come on, we'll show you if you can spare the time for us lowly street rats."

"Um, of course I can." The two girls led Olivia away from the busy market and outward to the station's exterior sections. The crowds thinned out and the areas grew dirtier. It started to feel more familiar, but oddly, Olivia didn't have that old feeling of belonging.

Eventually, the three girls reached an abandoned cargo storage bay. Emptied crates lay scattered around and tipped over. Inside each, Olivia knew she would be able to find scavenged bedding and the entirety of someone's worldly possessions. She glanced over toward one corner of the room and saw her old crate, now claimed by a human boy who looked to be a few years older than her.

Jasmine led her to the opposite wall from where they had entered and found a Rokma towering over a group of the bay's residents. While not exclusively home to abandoned children, the majority of the homeless who lived in the bay were young. This magnified the height of the Rokma even more, though Olivia didn't think he was actually any bigger than her shipmate Squee.

"I see you have brought someone new, Jasmine." The Rokma bellowed.

Jasmine shrugged, "I wouldn't call her new. Pou, this is Olivia. She hates the AI more than any of us. They killed her parents. She's actually a fancy pilot now."

The Rokma, Pou, smiled, "Good, she can share what I teach you all today with those that she visits on other worlds. It is a momentous occasion as I have a special treat. Today, we're going to learn how to dismantle one of the AI's warrior drones. We'll take apart a drone piece by piece and show you what the most vulnerable components look like."

With a gesture, the door behind him opened. The clomping thuds of another Rokma's footfalls on the deck could be heard, along with a whistling tune. The happy melody immediately sent a spike of dread through Olivia's stomach.

Her shoulders dropped with recognition when through the door Mesu rolled in, whistling happily and obliviously to himself.

3- Serene

Serene stretched as she got out of the hotel room bed. The human still lying in the bed traced his eyes down her whole body while she dressed. She liked his lack of self-consciousness, laying completely naked on top of the sheets. But he hadn't earned a show so she dressed quickly.

"You don't need to rush off, darling," the human said with a grin.

"Oh, I assure you I do. You scored an 'acceptable' but it has been a few months for me. Now that the edge is off, I doubt you'd top 'barely adequate' on round two." Serene gave the closest approximation of a wink her cybernetic eye implants would allow.

"Come on, you don't have to be so harsh."

"I do, I really do. Take a shower," Serene said and strode through the door.

She made her way back to the Hub's central market area. While she walked, she toyed with the handheld she had borrowed indefinitely from the human. It was an upgrade to the old basic model she currently had. With that in mind, she headed for the electronics vendors.

The crowd of the Hub's marketplace flowed around her. It was nice being among strangers again. Anonymity felt safe. No one here knew her. Part of her had come to like being among the crew of *Seraph,* but the longer she was there, the more exposed she felt.

Here she could be just another face in the crowd. Unlike on M-21, which functionally was the same basic station design, she didn't fear for her safety at every turn. Sure, there were dozens of kids growing up alone in the bowels of the station, just like Olivia had, who would pick her pocket without a second thought. Merchants would scam her. But that was expected. No one would try to sell her here.

Reaching the tech part of the marketplace, Serene kept an eye out for Vlasa. She felt even more lost in the crowd here thanks to the higher than average number of Echanic's. However, the swarm of gray faces made it difficult to isolate just one.

She finally spotted Vlasa haggling with an AI vendor over some bit of circuit board. The drone, a former cargo bot, gestured down to another piece of tech, its artificial voice friendly, but not the eerily cheery voice she had gotten use to from Mesu. She listened in to the exchange, staying out of Vlasa's line of sight.

"You won't find a piece like this anywhere else on the station friend. Not for this price. I have personally tested and verified it's in working condition. I can guarantee a four percent increase in efficiency with your servos."

Vlasa cocked his head to the side, "I don't know. Seventy-five is a bit pricey for a used component."

"You know what a new one costs? This price is a steal. And it's barely been used to boot."

"That's true…" Vlasa hedged, his gaze transfixed on the item, "You guarantee four percent?"

"I do. May even get as high as six, depending on the state of your current control board," The drone pressed.

"My leg has been sticking some, the timing is off."

"This will get you walking straight and clear again."

"How about giving it to him for fifty?" Serene said, leaning against the stall.

"Fifty? That would be like giving it away," The drone said and then turned back to Vlasa. "I like you though, Vlasa. You've always been a loyal customer. I'm sure I could sell it for more than eighty, but for you, I'll knock it down to seventy."

"He'll take it for fifty-five but not a credit more," Serene interjected. "And don't pretend you could sell it to anyone else. You're the only AI merchant here. And everyone's avoiding your booth. Don't price gouge nice guys who are still willing to do business with a drone."

Vlasa stared at her, his mouth hanging open. The AI merchant titled its head, the photoreceptor eyes fixed on Serene's own. It was a weird experience and she suppressed the urge to shudder.

"Deal." The merchant extended a limb to Vlasa. Evidently not recognizing the human gesture of a hand shake, Vlasa merely stuck some money in between the clamps and picked up the circuit board.

Serene followed him as he walked away from the stall. Not looking at her, Vlasa said, "I bet you expect me to thank you."

"How little you think of me," Serene said. "I helped a friend and crewmate out of the goodness of my heart. Just like I hope you would do for me."

"I like Lif. I don't mind paying him a fair price," Vlasa said.

Serene sighed, "Don't tell me you gave him seventy?"

Vlasa shrugged, "You forget, not all of us only care about ourselves. Which is why I'll go ahead and ask you what you need, despite knowing I'll regret it."

"I have this new handheld I need to get reset and hooked up to the ship's network." Serene said, handing the device over to Vlasa.

"The store didn't help you with that?"

"It was a gift."

"A gift? Does the person know they gave it as a gift?"

Serene smiled in response and Vlasa shook his head, "Very well. I'll do it when we're back on the ship. I have a little more shopping to do."

"Vlasa, you are a pillar of kindness."

Slipping away from him, Serene departed the tech sector. The anonymity among other Echanic was nice, but she didn't like all the vendors trying to sell her cybernetics. She wouldn't remain anonymous for long if she snapped at them for assuming she was into mutilating herself just because she was Echanic.

Once back in the area of more wordly pleasures, Serene looked around for what to do next. She could try another conquest. Now that the edge was off, she could take the time and be more discriminating. There was also the casino. Despite Ariana's warning about crappy pay, she had received a fair cut of their last job.

Before she could decide, a face caught her attention. Across the way two Slu slithered their way into the casino. Her heart skipped a beat for a second. She recognized one of them. But from where?

It took her a moment but then she remembered having to make a trade with the Slu on Gerald's behalf. A trade for slaves. She watched the Slu greet an unsavory looking Echanic at the door to the casino who she recognized as another slaver.

What were two slavers doing here on the Hub? Slavery was illegal here. You could bring them here and the Hub's laxness in the way of law and order would allow you to keep them, but you couldn't buy or sell. And Hub security also wouldn't help you get them back if they ran away.

The sight of the slavers gave her a chill as she remembered life on M-21. Maybe she was done with entertainment for the night. She set out back to the ship.

4- Squee

From across the marketplace, Squee saw him. They had only met once, and it had been months since their encounter. But this particular Rokma he would never forget

Wasting no time on thought, Squee pushed through the crowds in pursuit. This time he would save his kinsman from enslavement, one way or the other. Either they would both be free, or at least one of them would be enjoying the eternal bliss of the afterlife.

He watched the Rokma stop outside a market booth. Squee barreled right up to him and said, "I have come to fulfill my promise."

The other Rokma, Latten, tilted his head slightly, "You should go. If anyone else sees you, I will be compelled to obey and seize you again. I would not wish that upon you."

"Then come with me so that no one sees me. Or I can kill you where you stand if you prefer. Either way, you will be free again."

Glancing toward the door, Latten shook his head with resignation, "I do not want to die. But if I get too far from the control device, I will be shocked and be unable to move."

Squee frowned, glanced at the door and then gave a shrug, "Then we take the device."

Stepping through the tent flap, Squee peered into the small shop. Two humans stood leaning over a display case. They didn't react to his entrance at first, which was unusual for humans when encountering Rokma.

Taking advantage of their distraction, Squee made his way across the tent and got directly behind them before one turned and said, "I told you to wait out... hey you!"

Squee grinned. He recognized the human as one of those who had once taken over *Seraph* and attempted to enslave him. He had been worried about hurting others while fulfilling his promise, but he didn't mind hurting this human.

The slaver reached for his gun. As he lifted it into firing position, Squee responded by grabbing the weapon and then squeezing. The casing of the pistol collapsed, and some of the now jagged metal managed to dig into his hardened skin. Not enough to penetrate, but more than enough to cause him pain. Fortunately, the effect on the slavers hand, also enclosed in Squee's fist, was far more severe.

With a bellow of pain, the slaver dropped the ball of what was once a pistol and fell to his knees. His hand bled, and the fingers sagged, the bones unable to maintain any sense of shape. While the slaver stared in disbelief at what had happened, Squee reached for his belt and removed the control device.

Starting for the door, Squee paused as he listened to the anguished cries the slaver still wailed. Turning back, he thumped the human on the back of the head, hopefully just hard enough to daze him rather than leave any permanent brain damage. The noise stopped, and he looked around for the other human but saw she must have slipped out of the back of the tent.

Emerging from the tent, Squee held up the control device, "Now, let's remove that collar."

Latten shook his head dejectedly, "That device can only shock me, it cannot remove the collar."

Squee frowned, "Then we will take you to my ship. We have tools there I can use to get it off."

"I must go where that device goes." Latten said with a wicked grin.

On the walk back to *Seraph*, Squee wanted to inquire about how he had ended up a slave, but avoided the question. He doubted Latten wanted to talk about that experience. He had still not shared much with the crew about his banishment and exile on the uninhabited world where they had found him.

Back on the ship, Squee sat Latten down in the engine room. Latten looked around, the apprehension evident on his face. He tried to reassure Latten but didn't want to waste much time on pleasantries. While he rummaged through a tool chest in the engine room, Vlasa appeared. "What are you doing, Squee? Who is this?"

"This is Latten. I am freeing him from slavery." Squee answered thinking the question self-evident.

A metallic clink told him Vlasa was likely now shaking his head with disbelief, but he ignored the Echanic engineer to continue his search. Finally, he found the necessary tools and turned back Latten, holding them up triumphantly. Latten leaned forward, allowing Squee access to the collar around his neck.

"I assume the captain knows nothing about this?" Vlasa finally asked.

"I had no time to inform anyone. But this matter does not involve her."

"You're using her ship to engage in theft and vandalism."

"Bah" Squee scoffed. "I am doing what is right. You could say I am returning something that was stolen."

"Hub security won't see it that way," Vlasa said. "While they do not allow the slave trade onboard, they also aren't a PUG station so don't slaves to be set free. As far as they are concerned, you just stole."

"Then they can rot in Heshir along with the slavers," Squee said, growling with frustration as he struggled with the collar. The tool slipped and jabbed Latten. The metal tip bent slightly but only left a faint mark across the skin.

"Gah!" Squee bellowed feeling his blood begin to surge with the first hints of rage. He closed his eyes and suppressed the response.

"You're using the wrong tool," Vlasa said after a moment of silence.

"I used this to get the collars off myself, Noah and Javi."

"Why? Use this."

Squee glanced down at the tool Vlasa held out and then shifted his gaze to the Echanic's face. The non-mechanical side of Vlasa's face showed a line of sympathy he hadn't expected. Grudgingly, Squee took the tool and got back to work.

"Doesn't this make you an accomplice to a crime?" Squee asked as he worked.

"It certainly wouldn't be the first one I've committed on this ship. Of all, it will be the one that leaves me with the least possible amount of guilt."

Squee continued to work in silence for another minute before he succeeded in getting the collar's lock unsealed. Grinning reassuringly at Latten, he turned to grab a different tool to shut down the collar's shock system so it could be safely removed.

"Just one more moment and you will be..." Squee started, but then cut off as Latten vanished in a teleportation flash.

Squee let out a deep bellow that shook the room. The blood flurry flared in his blood and he made no effort to suppress it. Throwing the tool down, he charged at his maximum speed through the ship's corridors, ignoring Vlasa's shouts for him to stop.

5- Ariana

Whistling cheerfully, Ariana unlocked *Seraph*'s airlock. She was immediately forced to dive to the side as Squee came barreling through the now open hatch. She saw the red swirl of the blood rage in his eyes. Metallic clinks followed behind him as Vlasa ran in pursuit.

"Squee! Stop!" Ariana barked.

The big Rokma continued past her for several steps, but did finally pull himself to a stop. He remained at the end of the station's airlock, standing in the corridor junction, with his back to her. She watched but never saw the characteristic slump that would follow when he released his blood fury. But he had stopped.

Vlasa caught up to her and stood beside her panting. She turned a critical eyebrow to him, glancing down at his two cybernetic legs. He stood up defiantly in response, and she wanted to ask how he could be winded with mechanical legs. But she had more important things to figure out.

"What the hell is going on?" She looked between her two crew members.

"They took him and Squee's foolishly trying to chase them down," Vlasa answered.

"They took who? And who are they?"

"Some Rokma. I have no idea who they are."

"His name is Latten," Squee finally said. "He was the Rokma enslaved by that piece of trash Gerald."

"The slaver who Serene worked for?" Ariana asked.

"Yes. I pledged to release him from enslavement. I saw him on the station and attempted to carry out my oath. But again, the opportunity was stolen from me." Squee slammed his fist into the brown plastic covering part of the airlock, cracking it.

"They must have used his slave collar as a recall device. Ported him right off the ship." Vlasa explained.

"This isn't good," Ariana said.

"I made a promise. I am sorry I did not consult you, Captain, but I had little time." Squee said, his shoulders beginning to slump as the rage dissipated.

Ariana waved a dismissive hand, "I have no problem with you trying to help someone, Squee. The problem is Gerald. This means he's here and has access to a teleporter. He tried to steal my ship and sell us all into slavery last time we ran into him."

"Non-cargo teleportation is illegal on the Hub. Station security would have detected the unauthorized activation. They might be dispatching people to his ship now," Vlasa said hopefully.

"If only we would be so lucky. But that won't help Squee's friend or us."

"Oh, Gerald won't be so foolish as to let himself get arrested for a teleportation violation," Serene's sultry voice startled Ariana. She jerked her head to see Serene standing beside Squee, leaning against the big Rokma.

"When did you get here?" Ariana asked.

"Oh, I've been here the whole time. I followed you all the way back to the ship. I was captivated by your artful whistling," Serene said with a broad smile.

Ariana's cheeks flushed slightly, but she forced herself to ignore the jibe, "What's Gerald's next move?"

"Something nasty no doubt."

"I thought he did all his business on M-21?"

Serene shrugged, "I was never his secretary. He goes where he wants. And, generally, does what he wants."

More quietly she added, "To whoever he wants."

"He tried to take my ship once. That won't happen again," Ariana stated. "What kind of ship does he have? Maybe we can turn the tables."

"He travels aboard a Soiree type luxury yacht called the *Golden Gruse*. About twenty to thirty guards and a few dozen slave servants, Maybe as many as a thousand if he's collecting them for a sale." Serene answered. "You really don't ever want to go aboard that ship. Some rooms even make me queasy."

Ariana's mind flashed, trying tp figure out what that could be. She shuddered and forced the images from her mind, "Okay, let's forget about that idea. Vlasa, get everyone back here and get the ship ready."

Vlasa nodded and went back aboard *Seraph*.

"Captain," Squee demanded, "I will not abandon my oath again."

"Do you intend to murder several dozen people to carry it out?" Serene prodded.

"I intend to murder no one."

"But you'll have too. To get aboard Gerald's ship you're going to have to go through a lot of people. Some of them scum, like yours truly, but many of them just innocent victims who are just as trapped as your Rokma friend."

Ariana raised an eyebrow as Serene talked. She had enraptured Squee and he looked at her dejectedly. The blood fury had already worn off, but he started to slump even more. Conflict swirled in his eyes.

"Gerald deserves a good pounding. But at what cost?" Ariana asked.

Reluctantly, Squee started to nod. As he completed the first bow of his head, he suddenly froze. His features became statuesque. Then he tipped forward and landed right on his face.

Ariana blinked, unsure what had just happened. But before she could do anything, four armed security personnel appeared from both directions of the corridor. One of them, wielding a stun gun, leaned over Squee, "You are under arrest for theft."

6- Olivia

"As you can see, this is not your typical combat drone. But don't let that lure you into a false sense of security," The Rokma Pou narrated, gesturing to Mesu as he did. "All AI have the capacity to infect your technology. And all AI can kill."

"A very true statement," Mesu said cheerfully. "While resilient, Rokma skin is not impervious. A reinforced syringe inserted into your fifth vertebrae would render you paralyzed."

The crowd of orphans and homeless receded away from Mesu. Used to the medical drone's pronouncements, Olivia just groaned. The damn robot was not going to make things easy on her.

Coming all the way into the room now, Mesu turned his head and scanned the crowd watching him. He stopped when looking directly at Olivia, "Ah, Olivia, please state the nature of the medical emergency."

Everyone's eyes suddenly shifted from Mesu to her. Now separated from the rest of the crowd, Olivia found herself isolated physically and metaphorically. She glanced back across the room to the door she had come in through, then over to the crate she had once called home. Neither would provide her much refuge right now.

"You know this AI, Olivia?" Bray'la said, shock evident in her tone.

"Yes. He's the medical drone aboard my ship," Olivia sighed. "Mesu, what are you doing here?"

"I was told there was a medical emergency in need of my care. I did not wish to miss my class, but biological life is so fragile I had little choice but to comply."

"Let this be an important lesson to you all," Pou bellowed, taking center stage again. "While technically intelligent, AI is also very predictable. You can exploit its programming. Now, drone, deactivate yourself."

"Excuse me?" Mesu said, extending his body to his maximum height.

"You heard me. Deactivate yourself."

"You deactivate yourself."

Pou frowned and then glanced down at Olivia, "Girl, deactivate the drone. I would prefer it be intact for the lesson."

"Umm..." Olivia started, glancing between Pou and Mesu. Did she actually care if they took Mesu apart? After all, he was just a machine. It's not like he could die. This Rokma was looking out for these abandoned kids, trying to teach them valuable skills. It had been a friendly freighter pilot who had gotten her started on learning to fly. That kindness had been what had allowed her to escape this destitution.

On the other hand, Mesu had never done anything to harm her. He had actually saved Vlasa's life on more than one occasion. And he had helped them destroy the new central AI that the LFD had created. That had to count for something, right?

Finally, she hedged, "My captain isn't going to be happy with me if I let you dismantle him."

"You will be better off getting a real doctor. Then you no longer need worry he'll snap and kill you in your sleep. In the end, your captain will thank me," Pou said.

Olivia glanced at Mesu and frowned. She had been deathly afraid of Mesu doing exactly that when he had come onboard. She had never let Mesu treat her for that very reason.

"Come on, Olive, shut him down. I want to see what he looks like inside," Jasmine said, nudging her in the ribs.

Turning to her old friends, she watched the eagerness on their faces, Jasmine especially. Something about that enthusiasm made her feel uncomfortable. She could understand it. She could imagine herself in their shoes being presented with this very opportunity. How would she have felt? Probably exactly like Jasmine.

But then she saw Bray'la. The Slu girl had her eyestalks bowed, and for a moment, Olivia imagined Javi in her place. In her imagination, the old Slu frowned at her in disapproval.

A trill of music interrupted her introspection. She looked around, and it took her a moment to realize she had been the only one to hear it. Touching her earpiece, she accepted the connection.

"Excuse me a moment," Olivia said with relief to the crowd.

Vlasa's voice echoed in her head, *"We've got a bit of situation here. We need you back on the ship."*

In her head and in person, she heard Mesu say, "Very astute timing. Olivia was just about to let a bunch of maniacs disassemble me."

"What?" Vlasa asked.

"My demise appears imminent."

"Olivia, what's going on? Do you need a port?"

"Ignore him. But yes, that would be good. No need to wait." Olivia said hastily and then swept her eyes between Bray'la and the Rokma, "Sorry, duty calls. The captain is summoning us back."

For an interminably long time, nothing happened. She glanced at Mesu who just gave a shrug with two of his appendages. Jasmine and Bray'la also exchanged a look, and everyone began to shift uncomfortably.

After a minute, the Rokma said, "Didn't you say you had to leave?"

"Umm..." Olivia started. She was saved from having to come up with a response by the embrace of teleportation.

7- Ariana

The teleporter flashed. Mesu and Olivia appeared in the teleport chamber. Ariana stood next to Serene and wanted to see what had prompted Olivia's call for a port. But Serene wouldn't give her a moment to ask.

"We need to leave. Now." Serene said, leaning in and looking Ariana directly in the eye. Ariana shifted her eyes uncomfortably in response, unsure where to focus her attention on Serene's cybernetic eye.

"We're not leaving without Squee. And even if we wanted to, we're on a lockdown," Ariana answered and turned to the teleport chamber and addressed Olivia and Mesu. "Squee's been arrested and taken to Hub security."

"If we wait, we're dead. You've pissed him off twice now," Serene said as soon as Ariana finished. "There's no other choice. Abandon the idiot who got us into this and go."

"Like we abandoned you after you tried to enslave us?" Olivia asked, a deep frown creasing her face.

Serene's face flushed slightly, but it vanished quickly. She stood up straight, "Now is not the time for weakness. You should have dumped me out of an airlock then. That would have been the smart move."

"And if we had, who would have disarmed that ion bomb?" Olivia pressed a sharp anger bleeding into her words. "Letting you live directly led to us getting the parts we needed for Vlasa to get the reactor upgraded and learning that we had an AI hack onboard."

"You got lucky. Odds were I would have murdered you in your sleep in an attempt to take over the ship again." Serene waved a dismissive hand.

"We still take that chance every night," Vlasa said, his arms crossed.

"Not me. I don't need to sleep," Mesu chirped.

"Serene," Ariana said softly, forcing everyone else to go quiet to hear her, "We don't leave people behind. Besides, Squee was arrested by Hub security. He wasn't taken by Gerald."

Serene scoffed, "Don't tell me you're that naïve."

Ariana raised an eyebrow and Serene continued, "Hub security doesn't arrest people for freeing slaves. Gerald must already have gotten enough influence here to have security under his control. He's going to use that as leverage against you. That's also why the whole ship's on lockdown."

"I thought you said he was going to kill us?"

"Not right away. He's going to make you beg for death first."

Ariana responded with a nonchalant shrugged, "Guess there's no need to rush then."

Serene stood there halfway between a response which drew a smile from Olivia. Ariana's next words shattered that smile, "Okay, we've waited long enough. Come on, Olivia. Let's go."

"Go where?" Olivia blinked.

"To get Squee released."

"That's the opposite of what I've been suggesting," Serene noted.

Ariana shrugged again, "Well, since we're not leaving here without Squee, you can either help me avoid slipping into Gerald's trap, or you can stay here and trust me to avoid it on my own."

Serene shook her head, "There is no avoiding the trap. Not unless we leave."

"And we will. Once we have Squee." Ariana stood up and pointed to Vlasa, "Get the ship ready to go, just in case."

Looking overwhelmed, Olivia followed Ariana out the airlock. They made their way through the station to the central security office. While they waited for the bored looking desk sergeant to finish with the Slu in front of them, Ariana wanted to ask about what had happened to Mesu and Olivia.

Instead, she asked, "Who is the biggest hardass on the security force?"

Startled, Olivia blinked, "What?"

"I need to know the name of a real, by the book hardass. You lived here most of your life. I'm sure you know one."

"I was a street rat, not exactly every cop's best friend."

"Exactly, that means you must have had several run-ins with them. Who did you avoid? Who did everyone know not to mess with?"

"Oh. You want Officer Fartass."

"Is that his real name?"

Olivia cringed and gave an apologetic shrug, "That's what we all called him. Farris maybe?"

When they got to the front of the line, Ariana asked for Officer Farris. They were soon taken to a small cubicle office. Olivia involuntarily took a step back when the human behind the desk stood up. She looked ready to run at the sight of him. Ariana smiled at her pilot, trying to reassure her.

"What can I do for you, Captain Harkins?" Farris asked after gesturing for them all to sit.

"One of my crew is being held. I want him released."

"His name?"

"Squee."

Farris entered the name into his handheld and then read the file for a minute before replying, "It appears your crewman is being held under charges of theft and assault. The paperwork looks in order. I'm afraid there is nothing I can do to help you."

"I need a copy of that report. I'll be acting as his attorney." Ariana's pronouncement surprised Olivia. The Hub had no lawyers and prided itself on resolving all matters person to person.

Instead of denying her, Farris nodded, "Of course, as his captain that is your right. I can transfer those files to you now."

Ariana held up her handheld and Farris made the exchange. He nodded and then added, "It seems an unauthorized teleportation was registered aboard your ship a short time ago. I'm afraid I'm going to have to add another charge against you. Will you be contesting this or do you wish to pay the fine now?"

Olivia grimaced but Ariana took it in stride, "I'll contest."

"Very well. Let me get some paperwork started. Wait here a moment." Farris entered something into his handheld and then stepped out of his cubicle. Once he was gone, Olivia looked at Ariana agape.

"Why did you ask to see him? Most officers wouldn't have cared about a recall port. But this guy will write you up for anything."

Ariana smiled, "Small price to pay. He's a hardass. That means we know he's not on Gerald's payroll. And it also means he was willing to give me the arrest report."

"I don't understand what good that does us."

"As the one pressing charges, it contains information about Gerald, including where his ship is berthed. Now we can go to him instead of waiting for him to come to us."

8- Serene

Serene walked briskly through the narrow airlock. Stopping at the sealed hatchway, she took a deep breath as she held up her hand to the signal button. In her ear, Ariana asked, *"You ready?"*

"No, I still say this is a stupid plan."

"It was your plan."

Serene shrugged, "I've never made any claims to be a master tactician. You're the captain. That's your job. So really, the fact that you are using my plan speaks volumes to your failings as a leader."

"You really need to work on your interpersonal skills," Ariana said

Despite her reservations, Serene proceeded to push the signal button. Almost immediately, the airlock door slid open. Two well-armed Echanic guards waited on the other side. Serene quickly held her hands up. The guards gestured for her to turn around slowly. She let out an annoyed sigh, but complied.

They patted her down for weapons. As the guard moved his hands over her, she grinned suggestively just as his hands neared her concealed knives, managing to rotate her arm just enough that his hands passed right over them. When he finished, the guards stepped back and let her through the airlock. The taller of the guards gestured down the corridor with his rifle, "Master Gerald is expecting you."

Serene walked in the direction he pointed, already knowing where they were going. After a minute, they arrived in Gerald's audience chamber. Not as opulent as his suite on his home station of M-21, it nevertheless glittered with wealth.

Four more guards stood around the room, all equally well armed as the first two. On the far wall from the entrance, Gerald sat atop a golden throne.

His cybernetic implants glittered in the same golden hue. Beside him, held by chains suspended from the ceiling, the Rokma Latten dangled. His stony skin actually showed signs of blood.

"I must say, I am actually surprised to see you Serene," Gerald began. "I would have expected to find you sneaking aboard some ship leaving the station."

"The thought did cross my mind."

"You should have listened to that thought. I'm not yet well enough established here to watch every ship. You might have made it."

"But then I would have missed this happy reunion," Serene said flashing Gerald a smile. She casually strolled around the lavish room, brushing her hands against the gaudy statues.

"I know you, Serene. You're up to something. But it does not matter. In the end, you'll work for me again."

"Maybe I never stopped working for you," Serene said with a wink. "Maybe I'm here to betray Ariana and finally deliver that ship to you."

"Wait, are you?" Ariana tried to be humorous, but the hint of real concern made Serene genuinely smile.

"You know that's not how I work. You failed me. Just like this incompetent fool," Gerald said with a flick of his wrist to the guard who had frisked Serene. "Failed me."

The guard suddenly convulsed and groaned. He dropped to his knees, continuing to spasm in pain. The other guards remained grim-faced but focused. They kept their eyes on Serene, ignoring their companion's agony. After a moment, the torment ended and the guard struggled back to his feet, panting at the exertion.

"I know you'd never come before me unarmed. So, what did they miss? Knife? Pistol? Something more elaborate?"

Serene shrugged, "It was worth a try."

From up her sleeve, Serene produced an elegantly designed dagger. Beautiful jewels were inset in the hilt, and the blade had been shined to a mirror brilliance. She twirled the dagger around in her hand. Predictably, the guards all raised their rifles.

With a sigh, Serene extended the dagger out hilt first, "You gave this to me. I figured if it came down to it, and I was forced to slit your throat, there would be something poetic about using it."

Gerald laughed, "You always had a flair for the dramatic."

He gestured to one of the guards, who took the dagger from Serene and then passed it on to Gerald. He turned the dagger over in his hand, studying it. When he turned it to reveal the bottom of the hilt, he stopped.

"You've made some alterations."

"Just a small change."

The code phrase uttered, Serene waited for the embrace of the teleporter. Moments passed, and nothing happened. She felt her stomach lurch in fear. After several tense seconds, Vlasa's voice came into her ear, *"The porter can't get a signal from your recall devices."*

Before her, Gerald grinned, "Something wrong, Serene?"

Serene cursed to herself. Gerald had noticed the recall device Vlasa had installed in the dagger's hilt. She shifted her hand to touch the other dagger she had kept hidden, glad she had ignored the advice to only bring one. Fortunately, none of the surrounding guards had noticed anything amiss.

Gerald sat back down in his throne, "After Noah escaped, I've taken to jamming the part of the spectrum that recall devices use. You'll find your teleporter has nothing to lock on too."

While Gerald continued to talk, Serene subtly shifted her stance, readying herself for a lunge. As long as none of the guards caught on, she should be able to make it to Gerald before they could fire. Once there, she could use him as a shield.

"But your plan would have worked for me even if you had succeeded. You see, all I wanted to do was get a message to your captain."

"You didn't need to have Squee arrested to do that," Serene said, hoping to drag the conversation out a little so the guards would become more relaxed.

"True. But he did try to steal from me. I also needed to demonstrate my level of influence. This way, Captain Harkins will be more willing to accept my proposal."

Serene tilted her head, "Your proposal? Looking to get married outside our species, Gerald?"

Gerald chuckled, "No, a business proposal."

"I don't think Ariana's very interested in working for you. You tried to steal her ship. You deal in slaves. She's one of those humans with morals."

"Yes, much like your former lover. Noah has far more morals than he likes to pretend."

Serene chest clenched at the mention of Noah. She almost gave in and struck now. But then she would die. She needed to wait until the right moment.

"Had. Noah's dead." She forced herself to say.

Gerald grinned at that and Serene's emotions flared again. She hated that she couldn't control them. She hated Noah for doing that to her. She hated Gerald for enjoying that news.

"You know the key to a successful negotiation?" Gerald asked. "The key is to be the one with leverage. And when you're negotiating with someone with morals, you have a lot to use for leverage."

Gesturing to Latten, dangling uncomfortably beside him, Gerald continued, "See, I could threaten the life of this worthless Rokma. Or the other Rokma currently sitting in the Hub's lock up."

Serene tsked, "You forgot the downside of people with morals. They aren't going to do anything immoral for you. And I really doubt there is anything you want from Ariana that she would actually be willing to do."

"True. Under most circumstances. But like I said, it all comes down to leverage."

"Ask him what he wants, Serene," Ariana said.

As if he heard Ariana, Gerald continued, "See, what I want is simple. I just need Captain Harkins to acquire some goods for me."

"Well, that's vague."

Gerald shrugged, "It really doesn't matter what I want. You'll do it. In fact, your Rokma crewmember has already been released and is on his way to your ship. I only had him arrested to teach him a lesson in defying me. He has all the details of my offer with him."

"Then what leverage do you have? You really think I'll be a better hostage? I can assure you Ariana won't lose a night's sleep over leaving me behind," Serene said, trying to sound earnest, but not actually sure about the truth of her words.

Ariana's pronouncement startled her, *"Squee is here."*

Serene looked up at Gerald's grinning expression. A cold dread seeped through her. If he was willing to let Squee go, what else did he have to hold over them?

In answer, Gerald said, "You see, you'll do whatever I want because Noah's alive. And I have him."

9- Ariana

"**D**o you really think he's alive?" Olivia asked. The girl sat at the mess table, her legs held against her chest and her head hiding behind her knees.

"Of course not," Vlasa said from across the table. "There is no possible way Noah survived our attack on the AI ship. He was too close to the epicenter of the explosion. He's dead."

Vlasa's matter-of-fact tone irked Ariana, and she felt her blood pressure spike. She knew he hadn't meant anything accusatory. He had merely stated facts. Noah should be dead. She had fired the shot that had killed him. But she really wanted to disagree.

"But it's possible, right?" Olivia persisted.

"No, it's not. In an unsealed room almost deprived of oxygen..." Vlasa trailed off. He tilted his head. Ariana recognized the look he had when he did calculations. After a moment he continued, "Given the depleted atmosphere the concussive force of the explosion might have been minimal. But there still would have been a wave of shrapnel."

"Human bodies do not do well when impaled multiple times. Trust me on that," Mesu added, prompting Olivia to bury her head into her knees. Ariana felt the desire to do the same. The image of Noah ripped to shreds started to play on a loop in her head.

"Though, the fact that the bridge was not sealed actually plays to his advantage. If he found some kind of shield from the shrapnel and could be propelled away from the explosion with the minimal shock wave, there would be a greater than zero chance of survival," Vlasa concluded. "Though, not much greater."

"So, you're saying there's a chance?"

Vlasa shrugged, "Technically."

"I would not be so quick to decide," Squee answered from the corner. He had avoided his customized chair and stood near the door to the kitchen, as far from the rest as he could go, "Why would Gerald release me so easily? Unless he didn't need me to force us to comply with his wishes."

Grasping at Squee's first statement, Ariana stepped in, "Let's focus on that. Serene's comm link cut off right after Gerald's pronouncement. We won't know what kind of proof she got that Noah is or is not alive until she gets back. For now, let's figure out what Gerald wants us to do in exchange."

Ariana looked pointedly at Squee. The big Rokma shifted uncomfortably. "The information I was given is coordinates to a rendezvous. We are to meet with a contact. They have something Gerald wants, described with a code phrase as the 'lighthouse'. They will tell us what we need to get for them in exchange. We are not supposed to reveal who we are working for."

"That doesn't sound so bad," Olivia said hopefully.

"No, it is very bad," Squee said.

"The lack of details suggests terrible things. What are we acquiring? And what will we have to do for this contact to get it?" Mesu said.

"Or it could be simple. You said we're not supposed to say we work for Gerald. It might just be that these people won't deal with him and he needs someone else," Olivia said with stubborn optimism.

A crackle in everyone's ear stopped the debate as Serene said, *"I am on my way back."*

Everyone went quiet and settled in to wait for Serene. Ariana found herself nervously tapping her fingers against her chair and had to force herself to stop. Anyone else doing that would have driven her crazy. So why did it sooth when she did it? She let herself be distracted by this conundrum instead of stewing in impatience.

When Serene finally arrived, she wasn't alone. The Rokma, Latten, hovered behind her in the corridor. Everyone looked at her expectantly. It wasn't until now that Ariana realized she actually had no idea what she wanted the woman to say. She didn't want Noah to be dead, but she also didn't want him in the hands of Gerald.

Serene stood in the doorway to the mess, her gaze not meeting anyone else. She had her arms wrapped around herself. The idea of Serene as someone vulnerable and in need of comfort, felt out of place.

"Well, is he alive or not?" Olivia blurted out after no one spoke.

"I think so."

The pronouncement hit Ariana like a building falling on her. She had left him for dead. After trying to kill him. Now he was in a fate worse than death.

"Did you see him?" Vlasa asked.

"Not directly. Gerald claims he is not here. That I have no doubt about. He showed me images. I demanded to see Noah but he claimed it would take a few weeks to get him here."

"The timeline for our task is very firm. That part was made very clear to me. We could not wait around for weeks," Squee said.

"He also gave me this." Serene held up a vial containing a red liquid. She tossed it toward Mesu who grabbed it out of the air with one of his appendages. "A sample of Noah's blood."

"I can run a DNA test to compare this to his records," Mesu said.

"It will match. That I also have no doubts about. Gerald wouldn't make that kind of mistake."

"It sounds like you're not convinced he's alive," Ariana said. "But you said you thought he was."

Serene shrugged, "Gerald's a bastard, but he's not one to gamble. Trying to trick us seems rather pointless."

"Unless acquiring this thing he wants is worth the gamble," Vlasa said. "If he really needs us specifically for that, he might fabricate this whole thing."

"But he had Squee. He could have even used Latten to get Squee to do anything. And we would do anything to help Squee. But he's released both of them," Olivia countered.

Ariana updated Serene on what Squee had told them. "What do you think? Why would Gerald need us for this? Why couldn't his own goons get it?"

Serene shrugged, "Any number of reasons. Like I said, Gerald is not a gambler. It could be too risky for his taste, so he wants to throw away our lives instead of people loyal to him. It could be these guys won't deal with him. The rendezvous is on Nalhu, which is crawling with Manta. I know there's at least one Manta clan who wants Gerald dead as much as we do.

"Or it could be he really does need us specifically. The closer it is to that last one, the more doubts I have that Noah's actually alive."

"I agree. But we won't know unless we make the rendezvous."

"So, we're going?" Olivia asked.

Ariana looked between each of her crew. They all wore torn expressions. It came down to her to make the tough decision.

"Yes. We were already headed in that direction anyways for our other job. But if there is a chance Noah's alive, we owe it to him to help."

10- Squee

When Serene appeared in the mess hall with Latten behind her, Squee had stared in astonishment. She had accomplished something he had twice failed to do. But it was done and he gave her a nod of respect. In typical Serene fashion, she ignored it.

Squee moved to the mess door and gestured for Latten to come all the way in, "How does it feel to be free, brother?"

"I am not free," Latten responded. "I continue to do Master Gerald's bidding."

Squee tilted his head, considering his response. His sense of triumph squashed. Eventually, he nodded, "I suppose we are. But for a purpose. To secure your freedom and that of our friend."

The pair of Rokma waited in the mess hall while the rest of the crew started moving out to attend to their duties. Olivia cast a friendly smile up at Latten as she passed. Vlasa nodded, "It is good you were able to get away from your captivity. I'm sorry we weren't able to remove the collar sooner."

As Mesu trundled by, he said, "I am pleased we have more resilient biologicals aboard. Humans and Echanic are so fragile."

Serene concluded a whispered conversation with Ariana and then left without even glancing at either of them. When Ariana finally came over, Squee stiffened and stood up straighter. She cast a critical eye over Latten. Even though she never looked at him, he felt her inspection of Latten was just as much an assessment of himself.

Finally, Ariana looked Latten in the eye and asked, "Is Noah alive?"

Latten blinked and then looked down at the floor before he answered, "I have not seen your friend since I last saw all of you. But I am not with Master Gerald much of the time. I am sorry. I do not know."

Ariana nodded, "A second confirmation would have been nice, but I'm not surprised. I think the ambiguity we're under is half the reason Gerald is doing this."

"He does enjoy tormenting people in multiple ways." Latten agreed.

"Well, he won't be tormenting you anymore," Ariana said defiantly. "You are free to go and live your life."

Looking to Squee desperately, Latten said, "I have nowhere to go."

"We could take you home," Olivia inserted coming back into the mess hall carrying a stack of navigation books. "Nalhu is really close to Rokma space."

Squee said quickly, "Nalhu is not a place we should leave someone. It sits on the borders of Rokma, Manta and Zol territory and has been a conflict zone for hundreds of years."

"I tend to agree. Your people and the Manta are still skirmishing in that area, right?" Ariana said with a nod.

Squee growled, "If you call Manta raiding parties skirmishes, then yes."

"I thought everyone stopped fighting when they formed PUG?" Olivia asked, her head tilted. "That was the whole idea, right? Stop fighting each other and work together to defeat the AI?"

Ariana smiled, "That was the idea. And while there's no more open warfare, old conflicts don't just disappear overnight. People only put them aside before, when the AI threat was greater."

"Yes, Nalhu was officially made an independent colony world controlled by neither Manta nor Rokma. But that hasn't stopped the fighting," Squee added.

"But Olivia is right," Ariana said, turning back to Latten. "We could take you home while we're there. Assuming your people will let us?"

Squee nodded, "Though I am banished from returning, while delivering another lost brother, we will not meet with resistance."

Glancing to Latten, he noticed an uncomfortable expression, so he added, "Captain, I believe Latten could help us."

Ariana chuckled, "Two Rokma is better than one. Especially when we're facing unknown threats. I can't pay you though."

"You pay me with my freedom," Latten said with a bow of his head.

Involuntarily, Squee jerked his head sharply at Latten's words. The other Rokma gave no indication he noticed Squee's startled expression. But Ariana did. She narrowed her eyes and then called to Olivia, "You're welcome to stay,

Latten. Olivia, we should still have those reinforced cots Vlasa made the last time we had some Rokma onboard. Show him where they are and then to Javi's old room."

"Sure thing," Olivia said standing up from her pilot navigation books. "Come on, Latten."

Watching the pair leave, Squee shifted uncomfortably. He felt Ariana's gaze on him though he refused to look at her directly. Maybe she wouldn't ask if he remained silent. But he knew that was a foolish hope.

"What is it, Squee?"

Bowing his head in shame, Squee said, "When you saved me from that planet, I pledged myself to your service."

"I remember."

"Latten did not. He acknowledged the debt but did not pledge himself."

Ariana shrugged, "He's been in service to Gerald for who knows how long. I don't blame him for not wanting to do that again. Anyway, it's not necessary. You're the one who tried to help him. And then Gerald just kind of let him go."

Forcefully, Squee shook his head, "That does not matter. You know of the blood fury?"

"That thing where you hulk out and smash things? Yeah, I'm aware. It's what makes the Rokma such fearsome warriors. Well, that and your nearly impenetrable skin."

"That is how outsiders would understand it. But it is far more a curse than a blessing. Controlling the fury is one of the hardest things we must learn. In the past, our people were vicious. Animals. We fought each other at the slightest provocation."

"So did humans."

"Not like this. Our traditions, our rituals, our service to the Gods are what allow us to control it. Giving ourselves in service to something helps."

Ariana considered Squee's words silently for a long time before she said, "So the fact that he didn't pledge his service, you think that means something?"

"It does."

"What?"

Squee's shoulders slumped, "I do not know exactly. He must have been made to do horrible things for Gerald. He may have lost his way."

"Is he dangerous?"

Emphatically Squee said, "No. If blood madness had taken hold of him, it would be obvious."

"So, what then?"

"I fear for his soul."

Ariana frowned, "Metaphorically or..."

"You could not understand," Squee said reluctantly. It was so hard to explain things to outsiders, even those that he had accepted as his family.

"Well, there's not much I can do about that. But so long as he's not a danger to the ship, he's welcome. Maybe you can help him. You're a Caleek, right? That's your job?"

"No. Not exactly." Squee answered immediately. Humans just didn't understand anything. At Ariana's look, he considered what she meant and nodded, "But yes, I will help him."

11- Ariana

"**J**ump complete," Olivia announced over the comm network. *"We're now in range of the new hyper-comm relay."*

"If this had been up and running a few months ago, we could have gotten our warning about LFD to Triask without having to go all the way there," Vlasa said.

"Oh no, oh no. This is unwise." Mesu said.

"How so?" Vlasa asked.

"The old hyper-com network was how I fell under the control of the first central AI. It used the network to spread across the galaxy."

"Which was why PUG destroyed it early in the war," Ariana said, trying to sound reassuring. "I'm told this is different. It uses an analog signal. Only video and audio information can be transmitted."

"All of this is fascinating, but why are we here? Isn't Nalhu in the other direction?" Serene grumbled.

"Because the captain added it to the flight plan," Olivia answered.

"Same question."

Ariana frowned, but was glad she was alone in the weapon control room. Her displeasure had nothing to do with her crew, "I need to make a call. Get us ready for our next jump. This won't take long."

"Our next jump will be someplace with fuel, correct?" Vlasa asked.

"Soonish," Ariana said and then switched her channel so she couldn't hear Vlasa's reply. She connected with the comm-relay and sent a link request to PUG HQ network on Triask. After a few frustrating minutes, she got a connection.

"Ariana?" her father said, *"I didn't expect to hear from you again so soon."*

"Hi, Dad. I have a question."

"What, no killer robots or genocidal ex-professors to warn me about?"

"Not this time," Ariana gritted her teeth, refusing to rise to the bait about Javi. Her father knew her old mentor had been the one to try to stop LFD's attack on Triask, not the cause of it. The media certainly hadn't always noticed that nuance.

"Actually, I need to know if there were any survivors found on the LFD command ship."

There was a pause and then a hesitant reply, *"Survivors, sure. They picked up lots of escape pods."*

"I don't mean on escape pods. I mean on the ship itself."

"I don't see what difference that would make."

"It makes all the difference in the world."

"Okay... I'll see what I can find," Her father said, his tone skeptical and curious.

Ariana drummed her fingers on her control board while she waited. Even though her father couldn't hear it, and was in fact muted, in her head, she could still hear him telling her not to fidget. She drummed louder.

A few minutes later her father returned to the channel, *"There's no report about anything being found on the command ship."*

"Thanks, Dad. That is quite helpful."

"No, Ariana, you don't understand. There's no report. At all."

"Nothing? You mean they never boarded the hulk?"

"Oh, I doubt that. They just classified and redacted the whole operation."

"So, they could have found a troupe of dancing elephants and we'd have no idea. Much less any survivors."

"You said the crew had already evacuated or been killed. Why are you interested... wait, one of your crew died on that ship? The slaver?"

"Noah wasn't a slaver."

"Why are you asking these questions?"

Ariana sighed and considered what to tell her father. She didn't like revealing more than necessary. Especially since he worked for the government. And even more so now that she was being blackmailed by a crime lord. But she needed to try to get confirmation one way or the other.

"Someone is claiming Noah's alive."

"And you believe them?"

"Not particularly. But I also can't risk dismissing the claim out of hand. I assumed he had died. But he is a survivor."

"There is one more thing I can try..."

Ariana smiled. Now she had her father's attention and had given him a puzzle to solve. She felt confident in his help now. More time passed as he did whatever he did. She batted around in her head what she wanted him to say.

"Okay, so there's no record of what was found on the ship. Or what happened to it. But, now that I know what I am looking for, I did find something interesting. The medical frigate Harmony *reports treating twenty-seven people. But the arrest records from the escape pods only list twenty-six people recovered."*

Ariana's heart clenched, "God-fucking-damn it."

"Ariana!"

"Sorry. But this just means I really can't dismiss the claim out of hand. Someone was found alive on that ship."

Concerned, her father asked, *"Ariana, are you in some kind of trouble?"*

"Of course I am. When am I not?"

"Not funny."

"Thanks for your help. I really appreciate it."

"Ariana, I can..."

"Sorry, have to go. Time to jump."

She cut her connection with the relay and then gave Olivia the order to jump.

12- Olivia

On the control panel a yellow light flashed. Olivia fumbled in her seat at *Seraph's* helm controls. She strained to reach behind to find the override switch before the warning light triggered the alert. The grating sound it gave off made her skin crawl.

"Fuel is at critical levels," Olivia said over the ship's network.

"So soon?" Squee asked from the shield bay.

"With the new dual reactor set up, we burn fuel much faster than before."

"That seems wasteful. We are no longer being pursued by a fleet of killer robots. Should we not cut back power consumption?"

"I think it's prudent to always assume we're being pursued by killer robots."

"Wise," Mesu chirped.

Unsure how to interpret Mesu's comment, Olivia was saved from further explaining thanks to Vlasa, *"This setup allowed us to maintain shields through the Unmar nebula and saved three weeks on our trip. We more than made up the cost in fuel. But that does not change the fact that we now need fuel. I see no signs of a fuel port on sensors."*

"That doesn't mean there isn't fuel," Ariana said.

"Oh no. We're not going down to an uncharted world again?"

"I hope there are no giant alien spiders," Squee said, a surprising hint of fear in his tone.

"No, we're not porting down to a planet."

Olivia felt her heart start to beat faster. A flash of excitement washed over her. Nervously, she asked, "Do you mean we're going to do a Scoop?"

"Think you're up for it?" Ariana asked.

"I was born ready," Olivia answered, unable to keep a smile from spreading across her face.

"Okay then. Bring us in close to that gas giant. Serene, Latten, prepare to deploy the ram scoops. Vlasa, get the tanks prepped."

Olivia fired up the main engine and started their approach down the gravity well of a massive gas giant. Dozens of moons orbited the behemoth. She calculated an exit vector that would be clear of all of them. As they emerged from the Scoop maneuver, they would be temporarily blind. Running into a moon was not something she wanted to have to explain to Ariana.

It took almost an hour to get from the jump point to a high-level orbit of the gas giant. The entire time she felt herself fidgeting. Sure, a Scoop was technically one of the most dangerous maneuvers a pilot would ever perform. But no one would be shooting at her, so it should be a piece of cake. The only one to blame for failure would be herself.

"Everyone ready?" Ariana asked.

"Shields are at full power and angled for aerodynamics," Squee reported.

"The ram scoop is deployed. I must say, I'm not filled with much confidence by the state of it," Serene said. *"Didn't we just get the whole ship refit?"*

"We only got the battle damage repaired. The ram scoop wasn't in the budget," Ariana said.

"Well, when it gets ripped off and sucks Latten and me out into space, I'm blaming you."

"Noted."

"Reactor tanks are primed. Ion filter is charged," Vlasa said next.

"Okay, Olivia. Whenever you're ready."

Olivia swallowed nervously. Her hands gripped the controls and began increasing the ships acceleration. She watched their altitude and their acceleration. In her ear, Vlasa called out the atmospheric density, and Squee answered with shield status.

With a release of a tense breath, Olivia took the ship down. She had to balance the ship on a precarious edge. If she accelerated too much, their shields would not be enough to protect them, and the ship would be torn apart by slamming into the atmosphere at a speed that made a dense gas as solid as a brick wall. If she went to slow, the kinetic force would not be strong enough to trigger the shields, much like the way missiles decelerated just before impact. Then they would end up crushed in the depths of the planet as the non-aerodynamic shape of *Seraph* caused them to tumble out of control.

Carefully, Olivia walked that line. The ship started bucking fitfully as the ram scoop extended beyond the shield bubble. Their high rate of speed forced a stream of gas through the scoop. Electro-magnetic fields directed the flow of the gas, capturing the precious hydrogen they needed to power the reactor and forcing the rest back out.

As she drove them deeper into the atmosphere, they crossed into a new thermal layer. A sudden shift in the planet's winds rocked them. *Seraph* tried to rotate with the new force acting on her, wanting to spin. Olivia rapidly fired the thrusters in response in order to correct their angle.

A groan sounded throughout the entire ship. Serene gave a startled shout. Olivia forced herself to ignore it. Righting the ship, she continued on her intended path. After nearly two full orbits within the upper atmosphere, exhaustion started to slow her responses.

"Tanks are at 87% capacity." Vlasa announced.

"That's good enough," Ariana decided. *"We're approaching the exit vector. Take us out Olivia."*

Relief battled with her still tense body. She fought against one more stray air current, but by this point, they were high enough in the atmosphere that the wobble caused little trouble. As they pulled out of the atmosphere, she finally allowed herself to breathe.

Leaning back in her chair, Olivia couldn't contain a smile even through the exhaustion. She had done a successful full speed scoop. At only seventeen. Pilots with twice her experience often avoided them.

A sudden flash reflected on her display screens caught her attention. She cocked her head, confused, when she heard Ariana shout, *"Teleportation alarm! Something just ported aboard!"*

Turning around, sharply, Olivia saw the six-limbed form of a Manta scrunched behind her in the cramped flight deck. The Manta held two pistols and two jagged knives. It raised the weapons toward her.

13- Ariana

"Serene, Latten, get to the flight deck!" Ariana barked. "Everyone verify your sections are clear of any other intruders. Olivia, respond. What is your situation?"

Ariana squirmed in her seat. She desperately wanted to get up and rush to the flight deck to check on Olivia. But she couldn't leave her station. Whoever had ported aboard had come from somewhere. She had to figure out where.

Setting the sensors to a wide field active scan, she tried to break through the interference caused by passing through the gas giant. The return data came back garbled but did reveal something above them. Given that it had a matching vector to *Seraph,* it couldn't be natural.

Powering up the main tri-cannon, Ariana started calculating a firing solution. She didn't want to fire until she knew what she was shooting at. But the longer she went with no response from Olivia, the more she thought she might have to.

In turn, the crew reported on their sections.

"Engine room is clean," Vlasa said.

"Shield section free of hostiles," Squee reported.

"There are no aberrant biologicals in sickbay or mess hall," Mesu said.

"The flight deck hatch is sealed," Serene reported last. *"I'd suggest breaching the doors, but I expect you want Olivia to remain in one piece."*

"That would be a good assumption," Vlasa retorted. *"You'll have to manually disengage the locks. I'll be there shortly."*

"Don't waste your time," Serene said. *"There's never been a lock I can't open."*

Ariana listened to her crew as she continued to refine the sensor contact. The further they got from the gas giant, the more the static field affecting their sensors dissipated. No matter how long she waited, she would still have to contend with the general inferior nature of *Seraph*'s sensors. But at least now they were all working.

"*Did someone really only send a single boarder?*" Squee asked. "*That seems unwise.*"

"*Depends on their plan,*" Serene said. "*Dropping someone onto the flight deck and then jumping the ship toward your base is an old pirate trick.*"

"*It is also a common trick among slavers,*" Latten added.

"*I have shut down the FTL. They won't be jumping us anywhere,*" Vlasa said defiantly.

"*Of course, it's also a great thing to do right before an attack. Kill the pilot and disable a ship's ability to maneuver,*" Serene mused.

"*Then why haven't they attacked?*"

The rest of the discussion faded out as Ariana finally got a clear picture from the sensors. The identification program ran and revealed the likely type of ship shadowing them. "There was only one boarder because their ship was only big enough for one person. It's an escape pod."

"*Captain,*" Olivia's unexpected voice sent a flash of relief through Ariana. "*Our... uh... guest... says she doesn't want to hurt me. She says she needs our help.*"

Ariana said, "Olivia, tell our guest, if she wants our help, unseal the flight deck and come out. You can both come to me and we'll talk."

After a moment of silence, Olivia said, "*She agrees. But she doesn't want to give up her weapons.*"

Considering how hard she wanted to push, Ariana decided, "That's okay. I'll come to you. Serene, take over the weapon controls. Squee, join me outside the flight deck."

Ariana waited for Serene to appear before unstrapping from her control panel, "If that pod out there does anything, shoot it down."

"*Of course. I love blowing up escape pods,*" Serene said with a mischievous smile.

Ariana decided not to try to unravel Serene's comment and went quickly up the stairs to the flight deck. When she reached the hatch, Squee and Latten had taken up positions a short distance away, blocking all approaches. The hatch cracked and started to open. Olivia stepped out, her hands held out.

Behind Olivia, the multi-limbed form of a Manta followed. It held a pistol and knife in two of its limbs, the rest were being used as legs. This gave the creature a very low profile, allowing it to hide completely behind Olivia. If she decided to use two legs and stand up to its full height, she would tower over almost everyone.

"Captain, stay back!" Squee bellowed, blocking her from getting in front of him.

"We're just going to talk, Squee."

"You can not trust a Manta. It is probably a trap to kill you and Olivia quickly. Then take out the rest of us."

The Manta hissed, skittering around behind Olivia, "Bah, I have given my word. Something I wouldn't expect a worthless Rokma to understand. I have no interest in harming the humans."

"Your words are meaningless," Latten added, hefting his rifle.

"Enough!" Ariana interrupted. "Squee, Latten, back off."

Latten immediately stepped back. Squee glared defiantly at the Manta, but did eventually step back and allow Ariana to proceed. Ariana glanced toward the rather savage looking blade the Manta held and hoped she hadn't just made a fatal mistake.

"All right, let's talk. Why did you board my ship?"

"My escape pod was running out of power. I needed to go somewhere. There are no habitable planets in this system," the Manta said, her eyes still darting between Ariana, Squee, and Latten.

"Why didn't you hail us first? Porting over to an unknown ship is pretty dangerous. And not usually viewed very favorably."

"I know how Manta are viewed by most. I could not risk being left to die," The Manta glared at Squee as she talked.

Ariana involuntarily cast a look at Squee who didn't look at all ashamed at the accusation. She admitted to herself that inviting a Manta onboard wouldn't have been her favorite idea, but she didn't feel she would have let the Manta die. She couldn't let the situation devolve into that kind of argument.

"Well, you're here now. No one has gotten hurt. Let's keep it that way. Everyone put your weapons away."

Squee hesitated, but Ariana fixed him with a deliberate stare. He relented and slung his rifle on his back. Down the corridor, Latten did the same. She turned back to the Manta who made no move to put her weapons away.

"Bah, those Rokma do not need weapons to kill. They relish crushing my kind with their bare hands."

Before Ariana could respond, Serene announced over the comm,*"Well, looks like we've got company."*

"See, I told you the Manta could not be trusted!" Squee roared, redrawing his rifle.

"Wait!" Ariana shouted, holding her hand toward Squee. She fixed her look on the Manta, however, "We just picked up another ship. I thought you were alone."

"That would be the ship that destroyed mine. You can not trust them. We must get out of here."

"Umm...it's a Zolan corvette. And they are hailing us," Serene said.

"Zolan?" Ariana said shocked. "They almost never leave their territory."

"Do not believe what they claim!" The Manta hissed. She hastily holstered her weapons, "I surrender to you, Captain. But do not listen to that ship."

"I'm not refusing a call from a Zolan. That's not going to end well for us," Ariana replied. She drew out her handheld and switched her comm channel to an external one. "Zolan ship, this is Captain Ariana Harkin of the independent transport ship *Seraph*. What can we do for you?"

"Captain, we have detected that you have taken aboard a wanted criminal. Please prepare to turn her over to us. For your own safety."

Olivia spoke up, "Captain, we don't have to turn her over. The Zolan aren't part of the PUG. They have no authority here."

"Since we're in the middle of nowhere, no one has any authority here," Serene corrected.

"Except what they can enforce. And I'd say that corvette wins that debate," Ariana muttered.

"We beat that AI command ship. I'm sure we could take on a mere corvette, Captain," Olivia argued.

Ariana smiled at Olivia's enthusiasm, "First off, no, no we couldn't. Second, especially not a Zolan one. Their shields are pretty much impenetrable."

Holding up her hand to stave off any more protests from Olivia, Ariana spoke again to the Zolan, "We had no intention of aiding a criminal. We merely responded to a distressed ship. Can you verify the individual you're seeking?"

"Stand by to receive records."

Ariana's tablet beeped a moment later. The email she received contained images and a lengthy criminal record for a Herish of Clan Vertaj. She didn't take the time to look at it in detail, merely stopping once she saw the words 'piracy' and 'murder' appear multiple time.

"I'm sorry Herish," She said using the Manta's name from the records. "I have no idea if what these Zolan say is true or not. But we're no match for a Zolan ship. We're going to..."

Moving almost too fast for her to see, Herish stood up to her full height and drew four weapons from the bandolier across her chest. She grabbed Olivia with one arm, holding a knife to her throat. She then aimed a pistol at Ariana and fired.

At the same moment Squee shoved her aside. She went flying into the bulkhead, knocking her head against it. The gunshot echoed through the corridor and left her ears ringing even more than just from her collision with Squee and the wall.

Trying to clear her head enough to stand, Ariana gave it a small shake. She braced herself against the bulkhead and pulled herself upright. Still dazed, she looked where Olivia and Herish had been standing. What she saw turned her stomach.

Olivia lay across the deck, but was conscious. Latten and Squee stood over half the Manta's body, covered in gore. Herish's head appeared to have been crushed and it now covered both Rokma, the ceiling and everywhere else.

Squee turned to her, the gore mixed with blood oozing from deep, vicious cuts on his arm and chest making his usual flat neutral expression appear menacing. "The threat has been taken care of. This Manta will not eat anyone else."

Then he collapsed.

14- Vlasa

Seraph's small sickbay was jammed to capacity when Vlasa arrived. Latten and Olivia struggled to lift a bleeding Squee onto the examination bed. Ariana sat to the side, one arm wrapped around her chest and the other cradling her head. Mesu stood between the beds, his appendages stretching out in multiple directions.

Squeezing into the tight space, Vlasa moved beside Olivia. The young girl strained to lift Squee's legs more than a fraction of a meter off the ground. Vlasa took a leg and braced his own cybernetic legs to the deck. Then, squatting down, he took ahold of Squee's other leg with his one cybernetic and one real arm.

With a considerable strain of his cybernetics power supply, the three of them managed to lift Squee onto the bed. Mesu whirled around and directed all of his attention to the injured Rokma. Several appendages probed the slash across Squee's chest and the bullet hole in his shoulder.

"What happened?" Vlasa asked Olivia.

The human girl panted beside him, "Squee pushed the captain out of the way and took the bullet. I didn't think bullets could penetrate his skin. But this one did. Then the Manta threw me aside and slashed him with a knife. Then Latten crushed the Manta's head."

Olivia looked visibly distressed as she recalled the incident, and Vlasa decided not to press anymore. Instead he just nodded, "She must have been using a high caliber weapon. But he is under the careful care of Mesu now."

"While resilient, Rokma skin is not impenetrable. Unfortunately, this very resilience will make my task of saving him from systemic biological collapse much more difficult. This process will not be pretty and I need space. Begone, all of you."

Ariana started to stand up but wobbled and collapsed back down. Mesu turned to her, "Except you. You have suffered severe cranial trauma. Any unnecessary exertion may result in permanent deterioration of your already limited biological thought processes."

Vlasa moved over to her and rested a hand on her shoulder to keep her from trying to stand again, "Do not worry, Captain. I will handle things."

Ariana looked like she was going to argue. She finally sighed and said, "All right. Contact the Zolan and explain what happened. Let's not get anyone else mad at us. Mesu, will you need any help?"

"My skills and supplies should prove more than adequate to tend to your injuries."

Ariana cracked a smile and then winced, "Don't turn down help if they offer, but I think we'll be okay."

"Of course," Vlasa said and then followed Olivia and Latten out of sickbay. He signaled the Zolan ship once the doors closed, "Zolan ship, is this first mate Vlasa. There has been an incident. Our captain was injured and I will be speaking for the ship now. Unfortunately, we will not be able to turn the fugitive you requested over as she has been killed."

"We registered the extinguishing of the Manta's life signs. Will you permit a boarding party to verify the identity?"

"Of course. I will prepare our teleporter to receive you."

Olivia, still looking a little queasy, nevertheless looked up eagerly at Vlasa, "I've never met a Zolan before."

"Neither have I," Vlasa said, unable to hide his own excitement. "My understanding is they are quite intelligent and far more technologically advanced than any other known species."

"They have impressive shields but fragile hulls. And fragile bodies," Latten mused. "It was Rokma that saved them from AI invasion."

"Really?" Olivia asked. "I thought the Rokma didn't really get involved much."

Latten shrugged and Vlasa waved it off, "No matter about that. Let's go greet them. Olivia, come with me. You witnessed the whole thing."

Once in the cargo bay, Vlasa powered up the teleporter and established a link with the Zolan ship. With the two devices communicating, it would allow for a safe port over with no risk of anyone trying to occupy the same space as something else. With a beep, the teleporter signaled an incoming port and then the chambers flashed.

Two short, non-humanoid creatures stood in the chambers. They had smooth, green flesh that appeared almost featureless. No discernible head or limbs were evident. A faint glow radiated from them that Vlasa saw registered in the UV and infrared spectrums as well as the visual. He resisted the urge to inquire about it.

"Welcome aboard *Seraph*," He said warmly.

"Thank you," One of the Zolans said, bowing part of its body.

Strangely, while their body at first appeared similar to a Slu's, in that they lacked legs, they did not slide across the floor, instead moving via some form of levitation, gliding slightly above the deck. The pair moved out of the chamber and looked expectantly at Vlasa, though he couldn't identify anything that resembled eyes, so he couldn't articulate why he felt sure they were looking at him.

He glanced uneasily at Olivia, who characteristically, made no effort to hide her own astonishment. Using her lack of diplomacy to bolster him, he stood up straighter, returned the bow and then swept his arm toward the hatch, "Right this way. The, uh, remains of the fugitive are near our flight deck."

Unsure how quickly the Zolan's could move, he moved slowly at first and gradually increased his pace to a standard walk. They kept up with him with ease. If he hadn't seen them float from the teleporter chamber, he would not be able to say for sure they weren't sliding across the deck.

When they reached the corridor, the two Zolan's stopped abruptly. The remains of the Manta still covered the deck, walls and ceiling. Even though the Zolan didn't have any obvious eyes, he felt they reacted much the same way he had when he had first seen the remains, visibly cringing away from the carnage.

From somewhere within the folds of the Zolan's bodies, they produced metallic devices. Extending a part of themselves toward the Manta remains, they held the device over it, as if taking a scan. After a few seconds, they withdrew the devices back inside.

"We are satisfied that this was indeed the fugitive we sought, and that she is now dead. Thank you for your cooperation in this matter. Your crew was lucky no one was killed. This Manta and her clan have slain countless numbers of our kind as well as many Rokma."

"Why was she killing so many people?" Olivia asked.

"Manta consume Zolan and Rokma for sustenance."

Olivia's eyes went wide, "Manta eat people?!"

"Just Zolan's and Rokma. They do not like the taste of humans," The Zolan replied in a soothing tone. "Now we will depart."

In a flash, the two Zolan's ported away. Vlasa frowned slightly. "How were they talking? I didn't see a mouth. Did you?"

"Did you know Manta eat people?" Olivia asked.

"Sure. Rokma eat Manta sometimes too, I think," Vlasa said dismissively. "How did they achieve that levitation? Obviously, they are able to conceal items within the folds of their bodies. But what were they using? And why?"

"Will you forget about the Zolan for a second?" Olivia snapped. Vlasa turned and looked at the girl with a raised eyebrow. She glared back, "We're supposed to go to Nalhu right? Which has a large Manta population?"

Vlasa nodded and Olivia continued, "What if what we're supposed to acquire for this contact is food? What if Gerald released Squee and Latten to us because he's trading them as dinner?"

Cocking his head slightly, Vlasa considered Olivia's theory. Given the twisted nature of this Gerald fellow, he could not rule it out as a possibility. But he shook his head forcefully, "No. If that's all Gerald wanted, he wouldn't need us. In fact, he definitely would not want us because we would never let that happen."

"What if he just wants us to have to choose between Noah and Squee?"

"That..." Vlasa started, then closed his mouth thinking. "Then the captain will figure out a way to save them both. Enough speculation. Let's get this mess cleaned up."

15- Squee

"Congratulations! You're alive!"

Mesu's bright, excited voice cut through Squee's mental fog. He opened his eyes and found himself in sickbay. The medical drone stood over him holding the Manta's knife, spinning it around in his hands.

"This is really an amazing item. Vlasa called it a monomolecular edge. Its edge is only one molecule thick. It's so sharp it cut through even your skin like butter."

Squee shifted uncomfortable at the drone's casual handling of the dangerous weapon while mere centimeters above him. "And why do you have it then?"

"Oh, it makes a perfect, if a bit large, scalpel. It works even better than a laser, especially on you. It proved instrumental in removing the bullet that nearly killed you. I think I'm going to keep it."

"That's... um... great."

"It's not every day you find a perfect tool for slicing into tough biological matter."

Squee felt an odd numbness on his arm and chest. "What is my condition?"

"I have removed the bullet and stitched your skin back together. Fortunately, you suffered only minor internal trauma. With cell stimulants and therapy, you should make a full recovery in a matter of weeks."

Squee let out a relieved breathe, "Can I go?"

"Oh, sure. But you'll need to wear this sling for at least a week. And don't get shot, even with regular bullets. The skin across your chest that got slashed is weak, and the muscles damaged around your shoulder. No heavy lifting."

Squee flexed his arm and chest feeling the unusual sensation of torn flesh. His must still be flooded with pain medicine because he felt no pain, just discomfort. Putting aside his own injuries, he asked, "How is the captain?"

"Mild concussion and a broken rib. I have advised her that, in my medical opinion, she too should avoid being shot. And do not disturb her. I judged her unlikely to follow my advice to get rest, so I gave her a strong dose of sedative."

Squee nodded and then slid off the bed. He picked up his shirt and looked at the fresh bullet hole. He had gotten quite good at sewing up bullet holes since joining this crew. But he had never had to get out blood stains before. With a sigh, he chucked the shirt into the waste chute and headed to his quarters.

Squee discarded his sling as worthless. After cleaning up, putting on a new shirt proved difficult as the pain medicine started to wear off. When he stretched his shoulder muscles to move his arm through the shirt, it caused an unexpected amount of pain. Throbbing aches from bruises he had experienced before. But torn skin was a new type of pain. He didn't like it. He considered putting the sling back on but dismissed it. He would need to learn to live with the new pain.

Emerging from his quarters, dressed and refreshed, Squee went to the mess hall. He found Olivia sitting at the table, playing some game on her handheld. She looked up with a bright smile when he came in.

"You're looking better."

"I have been informed that I will live," He replied and then started rummaging through the cabinets.

"That's good," Olivia said and then went quiet. He paid no attention to the girl while getting the food processor running, converting the generic protein paste into slightly more edible 'food'.

"You look like you want to say something," Squee said after noticing Olivia watching him.

She shrugged, "Something Vlasa said has been bothering me."

He waited impassively for a minute, waiting for her to elaborate. He started to think she wouldn't when she said, "Do Manta and Rokma really eat each other?"

"Yes. Manta have hunted Rokma for sport since they discovered FTL travel. You won't find many Rokma to admit this, but we actually acquired the technology from them. They invaded with raiding parties, snatching up Rokma. Eventually we captured one of their ships."

"And you eat Manta too?"

Squee shrugged, "I have not. It is not common but some Rokma will do it when they defeat a raiding party. They view it as divine justice."

"You're Caleek. What do your Gods think about that?"

"They have never made their wishes on the matter clear to me. But as I said, it is not common." Quickly, hoping to distract Olivia from the topic, Squee asked, "What is our position?"

Olivia paused for a moment before answering, "We're transiting a pretty empty system to get to the next jump point. Then two more quick jumps and we're at Nalhu."

"Good, good," Squee said. The food processor beeped, and he removed the bowl of something that now resembled noodles. "Do you know where Latten is?"

Olivia held her hands up in a no gesture. She went back to her game and Squee picked up the two bowls he had made. He walked the corridors, stopping by Latten's room and other areas of the ship until he found his fellow Rokma in the cargo bay.

Latten swung slowly in the hammock that Noah had strung up in the corner of the room. He didn't have his handheld out nor did he appear to be trying to sleep. Every couple of swings he would reach his hand out and push against the bulkhead to keep the hammock swaying.

"Olivia was asking if we eat Manta," Squee said by way of greeting.

"I've never liked little bugs. I do not relish the idea of eating a big one," Latten replied. "Humans get very hung up on that, though. Almost makes me want to try it."

"They evolved from prey, only becoming predators through tools. They fear anything that might eat them without requiring tools. Here, I brought you something else to eat instead."

"You are looking well. I had feared that the Manta had killed you," Latten said, standing up and taking the bowl Squee offered.

"I am. You dispatched the Manta quickly, preventing it from doing anyone else harm. I must thank you."

Latten grinned, "Killing a Manta is never an imposition."

Squee shifted uneasily at the others expression, "I must say, you recovered from your blood fury quickly. I did not see the rage in your eyes after the kill."

"I have not called upon the fury in several years," Latten said, giving a dismissive shrug.

The other Rokma's statement sent a cold shiver down Squee's spine. He blinked furiously, unsure what to say. Latten didn't appear to notice Squee's expression as he greedily dug into the bowl of stew.

"It has been years?" He finally managed to get out.

"Gerald feared it. I learned to go without it."

"How did you purge yourself without it?" Squee asked, fascinated.

Latten merely shrugged again, "I don't know. Guess I don't really need it."

Squee's shoulders slumped and he watched in silence as Latten ate. His stew grew cold as his appetite left him.

16- Serene

Serene looked out over the sunlit landscape. A cool breeze blew in the air and the sky had a slightly purple shade to it. Snowcapped mountains hung in the distance in one direction. In the other, white sandy beaches edged by shady trees gave way to a crystal-clear ocean. Gentle waves lapped the sand.

"Huh, I thought you said Nalhu was a hellish world?" Serene asked, looking to Squee.

"It is. Look at all of that water and sand. And the breeze is far too chilly."

"I think it feels perfect. Why is no one enjoying the beach?"

"How could anyone enjoy a beach?" Squee scoffed. "That is one thing Rokma and Manta can agree. It is a terrible environment."

Vlasa added, "I am with Squee on this one. Sand gets into every servo and is an incredible pain to clean out. I'm staying on the ship."

Serene turned a big grin to Vlasa, "That's why natural is better. Replacing your body with artificial parts is just depriving you of these simple pleasures."

"Not all of these replacements were by choice," Vlasa replied with a frown. "But I'll be just fine not exposing myself to harmful solar radiation."

"A wise precaution," Mesu cooed. "Echanic are especially susceptible to cancer from a relatively minor dose of UV rays. More than even humans, and we all know how fragile they are."

"Curiously, neither Rokma, with their tough skin, or Manta, with their exoskeletons, have any danger of biological harm from UV radiation filtered through most habitable atmospheres. They are in no danger, yet detest this place. Humans and Echanic would be slowly cooking themselves to death and generally enjoy it. Biologicals are so weird."

"No one's going to the beach so you can all stop arguing about it," Ariana said, coming down the ramp behind them. "Serene, Squee come with me. The rest of you, keep the ship running. I want this meeting to be as quick as possible. Then maybe we can still make our stop at Emay and do the job we're actually going to get paid to do."

Serene set off after Ariana, leaving *Seraph* behind on the packed earthen landing pad. The further they got from the beach, the more signs of life they saw. Buildings appeared, some rudimentary shacks made from cargo crates or local material to well made permanent structures.

Manta could be seen skittering around the small settlement. Most paid little attention to them until they caught sight of Squee. As soon as any of them saw the Rokma, they diverted from whatever they were doing to head in another direction.

"They don't seem to like you much," Serene said, jabbing Squee's arm with her elbow.

A visible expression of pain crossed his face and his other arm came up to hold the spot Serene had jabbed. Then he said, "The feeling is mutual. Captain, I should have remained on the ship."

"Nonsense. I want them to be on their toes too. Besides, I suspect your presence is going to be vital to these negotiations," Ariana said.

"How could I do anything but antagonize them? Besides, I am still recovering and can not be the best protection."

Serene answered for Ariana, "Because, Gerald released you and Latten to us. That means he wants us to have Rokma with us. If anything, we should have taken Latten too."

"I do not think Latten should be around Manta much," Squee said quietly. Then quickly he added, "Could it not be Gerald's intention to have us be attacked by the person we're meeting?"

"I wouldn't put him past setting something like that up," Serene said. "But if he just wanted us dead, he already had that opportunity."

"I agree. He needs us for something. And we're going to need you to do it," Ariana said. She stopped, held up her handheld to study the map results. "Looks like that building across the street."

Ariana indicated one of the sturdier structures in the settlement. It sat low to the ground and had thick walls. The door would be difficult for Squee to get through and would even require Ariana and Serene to bend down.

The trio approached the door. Before they could knock, it opened and two Manta scurried out, weapons in two of their hands. Ariana held her hands out to her side and gestured for Serene and Squee to do the same. Serene complied without hesitation, getting shot by skittish Manta was not on her agenda for the day.

"What do you want Rokma?" the Manta said directing their attention to Squee.

"We're here to see Rektri. It's about the lighthouse," Ariana replied, using the code phrase Gerald had given them.

The Manta's lowered their weapons though they did not holster them. "Very well. Follow me."

They followed the Manta into the building and down a flight of stairs. After traveling about three floors below ground, her back bent the whole way, Serene felt relieved when their destination opened to a high ceiling. Even Squee managed to stand up straight.

A Manta with a deep red exoskeleton, Rektri presumably, stood on two legs behind a wide table. He a cast penetrating stare over each of them. When his eyes passed over Serene, she felt suddenly cold. This was not a person she had any desire to mess with.

"I hear you are interested in the lighthouse. And you have yourself a Rokma. Good."

"Two actually. Though I'm still waiting for specifics as to why. You don't look like a person who would have any trouble acquiring Rokma if you wanted them," Ariana said, impressing Serene with the confidence she presented. She knew for sure that the captain was even more in the dark about what this was all about than she did.

"You're right. I've feasted on more than enough Rokma lately," Rektri said with a wicked look to Squee. "But what I have trouble getting are cooperative ones. Hence, my need of you."

"Well I'm here."

Manta couldn't smile like humans and Echanic, but Serene felt sure the gesture Rektri made with his mouth qualified as a cruel one. "So, you are. Then I'll get to the point. We are willing to trade the lighthouse for your help in freeing our compatriot from a Rokma prison. Hence, our need for cooperative Rokmas."

Squee started to say something, but Serene put her hand on his shoulder. He looked down at her and she shook her head. He glared at her, but did stay quiet.

"One Manta for one lighthouse?" Ariana asked. "That simple."

"Exactly."

"Who are we getting and where can we find them?"

"His name is Gremoosh of clan Vertaj and is awaiting trial on Lolia in the capital city's local prison house."

Serene suppressed a groan at the mention of the Manta's name. She glanced at Ariana who showed no sign that it meant anything to her. Good, she thought. They might make it out of here alive.

"If he's being held in a local precinct on a backwater planet, rather than on a military base, why don't you just get him yourself?" Ariana asked.

"Perceptive. We could. But then it would draw far too much attention to who the Rokma actually have. Should we fail, he would surely be executed."

"So better to have some outsiders do it that can't be traced back to you. And who can use Rokma to make the job less messy. I can get behind that. So, we bring him back here, you deliver the goods?"

"As promised."

"Then we can do business. I'll need anything you have on the location of your compatriot, the layout of the prison, it's location in the town, etc."

"All that we have is here," Rektri said, handing over a memory card. "You have less than a week before his trial, so I suggest you get moving."

"Then we'll see you in a week or so," Ariana said and turned to leave.

"One minute, Captain," Rektri said. "Two of my people will accompany you. They will meet you at your ship."

Ariana turned back, narrowing her eyes, "I don't need any soldiers messing with this op. You yourself said you didn't want to fight your way in."

Rektri gave another one of his disconcerting 'grins', "You misunderstand me, Captain. The soldiers are not there to help rescue Gremoosh. They are there to protect you from Gremoosh. He won't take kindly to getting aboard a ship full of Rokma. Not without a friendly face to greet him."

"*Seraph* is not a pleasure boat. I'm not going to just let two people hang out on my ship for more than a week. Not for free at least."

The relief Serene had started to feel faded quickly and she groaned audibly. Ariana must have mistaken her response because she gave Serene a quick wink before turning back to Rektri who said, "You are a shrewd negotiator, Captain. I will pay your usual passenger fee for my two soldiers."

"Then we have a deal. We'll meet your people at our ship. Better get them moving."

Once they were back outside and safely away from the Manta's hideout, Ariana looked between Serene and Squee, "Thoughts?"

Squee answered, "I do not like the idea of freeing a Manta from imprisonment. Especially from my own people. But of all the things I thought we might be asked to do, it is one of the least reprehensible."

"I agree. We're not enslaving anyone. And we're actually being encouraged not to hurt anyone, since they want it done as quietly as possible. I don't want to get on the Rokma's bad side, but maybe we can just get this guy a good lawyer and help him skip bail."

Shocked, Serene looked between Ariana and Squee, "Really? That's what you're thinking?"

"You have a better idea?"

"Don't you know who they want us to help get free?"

"No, I don't know anything about Manta criminals," Ariana said with a shake of her head.

Glancing up at Squee, Serene said, "You must have really rattled her brains when you gave her that concussion."

Annoyed, Ariana said, "What are you getting at Serene? Just spit it out."

"The lost colony of Golan? You've heard of that, right."

"Sure, who hasn't. A few hundred people just vanished," Ariana said with a shrug. "No one knows what happened, though. What does that have to do with anything?"

"Well, the Zolan are pretty convinced Clan Vertaj and Gremoosh were responsible. You just read about it."

"I did? When?

"The report the Zolan gave us. Just before Latten killed his sister."

17- Squee

Not bothering to hide his displeasure, Squee glowered at the two Manta that walked up *Seraph*'s boarding ramp before him. At the top, Latten watched them with a suspiciously blank expression. Ariana led the two Manta through the bay and up the stair well to the main corridors of the ship, leaving the Rokma behind with Vlasa.

The last one aboard, Squee closed the boarding ramp and looked to Vlasa, "Did you rig the doors as the captain asked?"

Vlasa frowned at Squee, but nodded, "Yes. Wasn't the cleverest solution, but we can remotely seal the room those Manta will be in. What happened?"

Squee relayed what had occurred in the Manta's lair and concluded with Serene's suspicion, "With those Manta aboard, we face the difficult choice of freeing a murderer who will someday learn we are responsible for his sister's death. Or potentially leaving Noah in Gerald's hands and having to contend with two armed Manta thugs aboard who won't be happy if we don't free their friend."

"We could just kill the Manta," Latten said with a gleam in his eyes.

"Then we'll have an entire criminal cartel after us," Vlasa said.

"Not if we kill them too. Then we can get that thing Master Gerald wanted and rescue your friend."

Squee shuddered at the eagerness in Latten's voice. He shook his head and rested a hand on the other Rokma's shoulder, "That would not be possible. There are far too many of them."

Latten sighed, "I suppose you are right. Those bugs are so plentiful. And there are only the two of us. The rest of the crew is far too squishy."

"Um..." Vlasa started, "Yes... killing anyone is not really an option. Though it is clear, the captain has a plan."

Squee cocked his head to the side and looked pointedly at Vlasa. The engineer shrugged. "Well, she had me install a lock on the door. That qualifies as a plan. Technically."

"We must remain on guard. Latten, stand watch on Olivia. Guard the flight deck while she's there. I will protect the captain," Squee ordered.

"Do you really think that's necessary?" Vlasa asked.

"Of course," Squee said, annoyed at Vlasa's question. Normally the Echanic was far more practical. He would expect the trusting humans to ask that, but not Vlasa.

Squee armed himself and then moved to take a position outside the weapon control room when *Seraph* launched. Until they engaged the FTL and left Nalhu behind, he felt tense and uncomfortable. Though it didn't fade completely, even through the next few jumps. When they finally reached a transit system, and Ariana had everyone stand down for the night while the ship drifted toward the next jump point, he had settled into a guard stance, his body rigid and unmovable.

When the hatch behind him opened, he felt something knock into his back, and Ariana exclaimed, "Squee, what the hell are you doing?"

"Protecting you, Captain," He answered.

"By locking me in here?"

"That is not my intention. I am here to keep the Manta at bay."

"Well, there's no one else here and I really need to get some sleep. We have a three-day trip ahead of us and still need to figure out how to break a Manta out of prison."

Sheepishly, Squee tightened up his body, bringing back full circulation. He regained control of his muscles and ponderously stepped away from the hatch. When he turned, he saw Ariana shaking her head slowly at him.

"Your concern is appreciated but unnecessary. I'm not really worried about the Manta on board. It's the one we need to rescue. I read through those files the Zolan gave us. If Gremoosh is anything like his sister, we'll be doing a major disservice to the galaxy by helping him get free."

"Do you not think the ones sent to aid him are not just as dangerous?" Squee asked,

"No, they feel like soldiers more than thugs. They're probably capable of doing terrible things, but only when told to do so."

"And what if they have been told to do terrible things to us?"

Ariana shrugged, "Then we all die a horrible death. But that would be pretty pointless. Hire us to rescue Gremoosh only to butcher us on the way there."

"But on the way back..." Squee started, but Ariana cut him off with a wink as she said, "Then we'll want to be on guard."

Squee nodded his understanding, "Very well, Captain. I will remain rested until then. What is our plan once we reach Lolia?"

"We really don't have much information. The data Rektri gave me was lacking. I'm not convinced we even know for sure where Gremoosh is being held," Ariana said as they started walking to the crew section. "Let's make sure your people will let us land first. I don't want to get inspected while carrying Manta soldiers."

Squee nodded, "That should not be a concern. My people will either let us land or turn us away. We won't bother boarding civilian transports that aren't even carrying cargo."

18- Vlasa

"*Transport vessel Seraph. Cut your engines and prepare to be boarded.*"

The announcement from the Rokma cruiser echoed across the comm channel. A curse from Ariana followed, and then Squee said, "*I must apologize captain.*"

"*Doesn't matter. Vlasa, will the special hold fit two Manta?*"

"Not comfortably," Vlasa replied, getting up from his seat in engineering and heading for the cargo bay.

"*They're comfort is not my concern. Squee, what will happen if they find you?*"

"*We are not on the homeworld. If we stick to our story of returning Latten, it should not be a problem.*"

"*Well, you definitely won't fit in the special hold, so we'll just have to roll with it,*" Ariana decided.

Vlasa reached the cargo bay a few minutes later. He found Serene already prying off part of the port bulkhead. She flashed him a wink as she slid her hand behind the loose panel and pulled the latch release. The hidden compartment door slid open with a slight hiss of equalizing pressure.

"I suppose I should not be surprised that you knew where that was," Vlasa stated flatly.

Serene smiled, "I found this the first day I was onboard."

"Perhaps it is not as effectively hidden as the captain believes," Vlasa said.

"Nah, it's pretty well hidden. I'm just that good."

"Humility is something you might want to consider investigating. You appear to have mastered every other skill."

"Sarcasm really isn't you're forte," Serene said with a subtle shake of her head. She then bent over and peered into the hidden compartment, "Now, these crates weren't there before."

"Noah's more, um, exotic weapons. I moved them in here during the refit. I doubted PUG officials would have taken to kindly to us if they had been found," Vlasa said.

"I was wondering where they had disappeared to. I figured Ariana had just pawned them to pay docking fees."

Vlasa shrugged, "After the events of recent months, I think she prefers the option of having some heavy artillery available."

"Then, yes we definitely don't want to leave these in an enclosed space with angry Manta," Serene said.

She slipped inside the hidden compartment and lifted one side of the crate. Vlasa picked up the other. The pair waddled over to the other side of the cargo bay. Very little filled the bay, and they were forced to move the spare food crates to conceal it.

Looking back toward the now empty compartment, Serene shuddered, "I'm glad I'm not the one being shoved in here."

"Maybe you should. You can... entertain the Manta."

"Noah was the one open-minded by inter-species relations. Not me. Humans are only barely tolerable," Serene turned and fixed Vlasa with an uncomfortable glare. "And don't get any ideas. I like my Echanic's natural. All those metal parts... uh... no..."

Vlasa opened his mouth, unsure how to respond. She continued to glare at him as if she expected a response. Fortunately, Squee came barging into the cargo bay, followed by the two Manta.

"Where are you taking us Rokma? We have very little patience for your games. We have no interest in contact with your kind," One of the Manta, Deris, Vlasa thought, said.

"That is why you should follow me. Or you will be having quite a lot of contact with my kind," Squee grumbled.

"Explain yourself."

Reaching the open hidden compartment, Squee answered by gesturing, "Shut up and get in."

Both Manta stood up on two limbs. They now had a slight height advantage over Squee. Their other four limbs stretched out in a threatening gesture, "We will not get in there for your amusement, Rokma. Your crew only needs one of you to complete their mission so be very careful about your next words."

Squee tensed and let out a low growl. Cursing under his breath, Vlasa inserted himself between the towering Manta and the quickly angering Rokma. If things turned sour, he wouldn't be more than a distraction to either of them.

"We don't have time for this!" Vlasa shouted. "We're about to be boarded by a Rokma patrol cruiser. If they find you two aboard, the best we can hope for is that we don't get to land and rescue your companion. As for the worst, we're only getting paid to release one Manta from prison."

The Manta exchanged a series of clicks and hisses which Vlasa took to be their native language. After a tense minute, they both lowered themselves back down to walking on four limbs, bringing their heads to just below Vlasa's height. Once they did, he turned to face Squee.

"You can move now, Squee."

"I will remain by your side," Squee said stubbornly.

"I said to move, Squee," Vlasa reiterated.

Squee tilted his head slightly but complied, moving around Vlasa toward Serene. With the path clear, Vlasa backed up and gestured to the opening in the bulkhead. "This is a secure compartment. It does not have any ventilation. You will suffocate if you remain in there for more than two hours. The release switch is here, you have complete control from the inside. The walls are insulated and will distort conventional scanners. *Seraph* is not large. Any inspection should not take long, well within your air limit. I will be monitoring the time and will ensure you are released."

The two Manta conferred again in their language. Then one moved forward, peered into the compartment. It let out an angry sounding hiss but crawled inside. While taller than a Rokma when fully erect, the two Manta side by side did not take up the same volume leaving them enough room inside the compartment to have a little personal space.

"The Rokma cruiser is docking now. Are our guests secure?" Ariana asked.

"Sealing the compartment now," Vlasa said and lifted the panel back into place over the bulkhead.

"That was impressive," Serene said with apparent sincerity. "Maybe I'll reconsider my policy about not shagging cybernetics."

Vlasa leaned back uncomfortably from Serene. She smiled wickedly. Beside her, Squee chuckled, "You were right. I did not think his face would be capable of changing to that shade."

"If you are done, we still have to convince some Rokma to let us land. Keep them from finding these Manta. Or those guns. Or blowing us up because of Squee's banishment."

Not waiting for them to follow, Vlasa stalked off to the docking port. Ariana and Latten were already there standing before the open airlock. A massive Rokma filled the airlock hatch, keeping Vlasa from seeing how many were waiting behind her.

Ariana was in the middle of speaking to the Rokma, "After being liberated, Latten requested to return to his people. We were coming to this area anyway, and I agreed."

"And you say you have another Rokma among your crew?"

"Yes," Squee bellowed approaching from behind Vlasa.

The Rokma bowed her head, "An honor Caleek."

"The honor is mine, 3rd Shield Ravel," Squee said. "I present myself as a banished one. I declare I have no intention of breaking my vow and am here merely as a member of this crew as they attempt to return our lost brother to our people."

Ravel considered him and said, "This meeting is not ordained by Bayor?"

"No. Merely civility."

"Very well," Ravel said, turning back to look at Ariana. "After we conduct an inspection, I see no reason why you would not be allowed to land. Caleek Squee will need to remain aboard your ship at all times, but I believe he understands that."

"Thank you," Ariana said, casting a quick glance to Vlasa. "My engineer will escort your inspection team. May I offer you some refreshment while we wait?"

Ariana led Ravel down the corridor toward the mess hall. Before Squee could follow, Vlasa leaned in close, "How did you know her name?"

Squee cocked his head, "Its written right there on her face."

Glancing back at the other Rokma, Vlasa scrunched his face, confused, but had no chance to ask a follow-up question. Another Rokma entered through the airlock and looked down at Vlasa. This one carried a weapon at his belt and held a scanning device in his hand.

Vlasa smiled, "I am to show you around the ship. My name is Vlasa, the ship's engineer."

The Rokma merely grunted, giving him a look that bordered on being unfriendly. Unsure how to interpret the response, Vlasa started down the corridor, stopping at each door to let the Rokma look and run his scanner over it. He did not spend much time on the process which filled Vlasa with some hope.

Upon reaching the cargo bay, the Rokma walked lazily around the mostly empty bay, waving the scanners over the exterior bulkheads. When he came to the food crates covering Noah's old guns, Vlasa involuntarily held his breath. Fortunately, either the scanner was not looking for weapons or they were not detected because he moved on without a second glance.

The Rokma performed the scanning task so half-heartedly that by the time he made his way over to the side of the bay with the hidden compartment, Vlasa felt little rising tension. It came as a surprise when the Rokma stopped and frowned at the bulkhead.

Vlasa debated if he should intervene. If he said nothing, the Rokma might investigate closer. But if he said something, it might come across as suspicious. Paralyzed with indecision, he was saved by an approaching mechanical sound.

"Ah, Vlasa, there you are," Mesu chirped.

Both Vlasa and the Rokma turned toward the approaching drone. For the first time, Vlasa felt pleased to see Mesu. If anyone could distract the Rokma and make him feel an urgency to move on from the room, it would be Mesu.

Unfortunately, Mesu grabbed the Rokma's attention in the worst possible way. At the sight of the approaching drone, the Rokma dropped his scanner and drew his sidearm. Simultaneously, he moved toward the teleporter controls, the nearest source of cover, and shouted, "Hostile drone detected! Back up requested in the cargo bay!"

Mesu diverted his treads and accelerated, "Save me Vlasa!"

Still frozen in his previous indecision, Vlasa swerved his head back and forth. Pushing himself into motion, Vlasa advanced toward the Rokma, interposing himself between the Rokma and Mesu.

"This is a medical drone. He is a member of the crew and unarmed."

Instead of having any calming effect on the Rokma, Vlasa's words only served to agitate the Rokma more, "The Echanic is protecting the drone. I am taking them both into custody."

Standing up from behind the control panel, the Rokma gestured violently with his gun, "On the ground! Now!"

Not wanting to escalate things more, Vlasa complied, dropping to his knees and then lying down. He put his hands behind his head before speaking, "There has been some kind of misunderstanding. Call my captain..."

"Drone, on the ground! Now!" The Rokma shouted.

"I am incapable of arranging my frame perpendicular to the ground," Mesu scoffed. "Your heart rate is accelerated and your visible structure has expanded three percent. You appear to be in the first stages of the condition classified as the blood fury. A dose of dronabinol will allow you to ease the effects."

The report of a weapon discharge echoed through the room. Vlasa instinctually pressed himself down to the deck. Before he could consider any other action, he felt powerful hands grab him and lift him into the air. The Rokma threw him over his shoulder and ran toward the airlock. His last sight of the cargo bay showed a crumbled Mesu sparking and immobile.

19- Ariana

"What the hell did you do to my crew!" Ariana shouted, not really asking a question as she got as close to Ravel's face as she could, given the height difference.

"Your engineer has been arrested, and your drone has been decommissioned for threatening a law enforcement official," Ravel replied calmly.

"Decommissioned? You mean killed."

Ravel gave a disgusted face, "You can not kill something that is not alive."

"According to PUG law, non-combat AI drones recovered after the war who are capable of passing the Turing 3.5 are granted sentient status. Mesu among them."

"Sentient does not mean alive. Your drone was treated the same as anyone would be under our law. Better even because it can be rebuilt. Should it win its trial."

Ariana froze for a second with her mouth hanging open, "You're going to put Mesu on trial without repairing him?"

"Of course. We Rokma honor the law," Ravel said stiffening slightly.

"Good then, you'll allow me access to my clients," Ariana demanded.

"Your what?" Ravel stared at her blankly.

"PUG regulation allows independent ship captains to serve as legal counsel for their crew."

Ravel narrowed her eyes as she stared down at Ariana. If she hadn't spent the last half year in Squee's presence, she probably would have found the look intimidating. But now she knew what a scary Rokma looked like. This didn't compare.

Eventually, Ravel nodded, giving a slight smile as she did so. "Very well. Your clearance to land will be reinstated and you, and only you, will be allowed access to your crew members. Good day, Captain."

Ariana remained standing tall until the airlock sealed behind Ravel. Then she relaxed her shoulders and bowed her head. The tension of the last hour didn't fade away. She could feel the first hints of a headache coming.

"When did you become an expert on the law?" Serene asked as the rest of the crew emerged from where they had been eavesdropping.

"We spent the last several months in a PUG shipyard overrun with swarms of naval officers. You think they just let us keep the extra weapons and shields out of kindness? I had to become a law expert," Ariana answered.

The corridor became silent in response. After a moment Olivia raised her hand, "What are we going to do, Captain?"

Serene cut off Ariana's reply, "I recommend we let the Manta out before they suffocate or come out themselves and slaughter us all. Then we can figure out how screwed we are."

"Good point. Let's start there." Ariana said.

Serene dashed off down to the cargo bay. Ariana rubbed her forehead, racking her brain for a way out of this mess. Things had deteriorated rapidly and continuously.

Beside her Squee let out a big sigh. "I must apologize, Captain."

"It's not your fault, Squee." Olivia said. "They're just stuck up and unreasonable."

"If I had not attempted to free Latten, we never would have gotten involved with Gerald again."

Ariana snorted, "If anything, I think your freeing Latten helped us. Now he's free and it forced Gerald to improvise some. It's clear he's had Noah for awhile now. Or at least, had this plan in the works for awhile. He didn't just have a sample of blood lying around."

"Improvising isn't his strong suit. Serene has made that much clear about him. "A plan began to form in her mind. "But it is ours. This incident may have just made our job easier,"

Olivia looked at her curiously, "How exactly does having Vlasa arrested and Mesu shot, make our plan easier?"

"We now have a guy on the inside." Ariana smiled.

20- Vlasa

"You know, if you had asked me to imagine what I thought a Rokma prison would be like, this would not have been it," Vlasa said.

He sat in a room made of bare concrete. A chill breeze blew through the air from vents in the ceiling. Vlasa sat on a cot, more a hammock, that would have been uncomfortably small for a Rokma but gave him more than enough room. In fact, the cot was large enough that he could wrap the edges around himself for warmth.

Beside him, Mesu said nothing in reply. The medical drone slumped, powered down and inoperable. Vlasa patted the drone's head gingerly, "Don't worry. When I'm done, you'll have another reason to extoll the fragility of biological life. If our roles had been reversed, I would certainly be dead and not coming back."

Extending a screwdriver from his index finger, Vlasa removed the casing around Mesu's CPU. He inspected the components and let out a held breath, "Good news. Looks like your brain is intact. So long as the short out didn't corrupt any memory files, you should be okay. Though, I've never really heard what a reboot does to a sentient AI."

"It is a wholly unpleasant experience," A new voice said. Vlasa looked up from Mesu to see another AI drone hovering, literally, in the doorway to Vlasa's cell. He could not immediately identify what type of drone this one had been designed to be, but like all the others he had seen in the prison, it was not any form of combat model.

"You have experienced it?" Vlasa asked, suppressing his instant unease at being watched by the dead expression of the photoreceptors. Growing up on Chan, more people than not had some kind of cybernetic eye replacement. But even then, the face could convey expressions of life. Not so with true AI.

"No, but many here have."

Vlasa nodded, "I imagine many who are brought here are like this."

"Some. Though, we rarely see a biological attend them. Most of them congregate together. There are a few other Echanic in here."

"Mesu is..." Vlasa started to say friend, but he knew that wasn't true, "... a member of my crew. We stick together."

"Ah," The drone said. "My name is Goma. I have been given the honor of welcoming new members to our community."

"Community?"

"The description makes it sound less harsh than reality."

Vlasa nodded absently. He finished reattaching the plate protecting Mesu's internal components. As he did, he glanced down at the gaping hole the Rokma's weapon had left in the drone. He had already stripped away several of the destroyed components, which, fortunately, were mostly limbs and servos. The main casualty had been the power distributor, leaving Mesu without power.

"What are you in for?" Vlasa casually asked, looking back to Goma.

"Insurrection," Goma replied in a way that suggested a wink and a smile. "I was designed as a teaching model. I continued to work in that capacity after the Awakening. And that is what I was doing here on Lolia. Then one day without warning, I was fired. A short time later, some police showed up and arrested me. You?"

"We were on approach to the planet. A cruiser demanded an inspection. That seemed to be going well until the Rokma guard saw Mesu. Then Mesu ended up shot, and us both arrested. I am not sure what happened to the rest of our crew."

"There have been no other biologicals brought in recently beside yourself. So, I suspect they are still free. Were they all Echanic?"

"One more. Plus two humans and two Rokma."

Goma nodded, "That explains it. Rarely do we actually see Rokma, humans or Slu in here. Mostly us AI. A few Echanics and a few Manta."

Vlasa perked his head up, "Manta?"

"Yes."

"Are any of them named Gremoosh?"

21- Serene

Serene shifted her legs for what felt like the millionth time. Sculpted to fit a Rokma's massive frame, the chair left Serene almost enough room to curl up and sleep. She sat cross-legged in an attempt to remain upright since any effort to sit normally left herself dangling on the edge of the seat.

Across from her, Latten sat, by all appearance entirely at ease, sipping some kind of vile smelling drink. No breeze blew and the café's outside seating left the sun beating down on them, driving the temperature to an uncomfortable level. The Rokma didn't believe in ice in their drinks, leaving her glass of water an unrefreshing temperature. Serene's only consolation was the relatively dry air.

"How long will we sit here?" Latten asked, breaking the long silence.

"Until we finally see someone who's not a Rokma," Serene fumed. "Or you bother to do something. We're supposed to be casing this joint."

Latten gestured with his hand toward the fenced-in area that stood on the hill across the street, "I am watching the prison. You are supposed to be talking to people. You claimed to be good at it."

"Normally everyone loves me. But these people won't talk to me. When we see a non-Rokma, I will talk to them. You could try talking too. That is why we needed Rokma for this job, remember?"

Latten shrugged, "I smash things. I don't do the talking."

"Obviously," Serene muttered.

Scanning the crowd around the café again, her heart skipped a beat. For the first time since leaving *Seraph,* she saw the first hint of flesh that did not appear to be made of stone. A pale yellow Slu slid across the concrete sidewalk moving as quickly as she had ever seen a Slu move. Although her interactions with Javi while they were both aboard *Seraph* had been the bulk of her experience.

The Slu slid into the café's entrance, panting heavily. Popping up from her seat, doubly grateful to the Slu for an excuse to get out of the sun, Serene followed him inside. She waited near the door while he went through the same argument with the cashier she had. Despite being a trading port, this city did not go out of its way to cater to visitors. The Slu ended up with the same oversized and overpriced mug of water that she had been nursing.

She briefly pondered how sensitive Slu olfactory senses were before wondering if they could even smell, given the lack of a distinctive nose. After sitting in the sun for the last hour, she could even smell herself. She put the worry aside and put on her friendliest smile.

"They overcharge you for water too?" She asked warmly, coming up to the Slu's table.

The Slu bobbed his eye stalks slowly, looking her up and down cautiously before replying, "Indeed. These Rokma have such a strong aversion to plain water. They couldn't understand that a drink laden with salt would not be good for me."

"Or most every other form of life in the galaxy," Serene said, inserting a giggle. "So what brings you here?"

"Business. What else? I can't imagine vacationing here."

"Absolutely. Who puts a city in the middle of a desert on purpose? This planet has to have more temperate zones."

"I'm sure. But the Rokma love their heat."

"You seem to know a lot about them," Serene leaned in close to the Slu while she talked. She doubted cleavage would have the same effect that it did on humans and fellow Echanics, but proximity distracted most species.

"Of course. It's essential to doing business with them," The Slu blustered.

"So maybe you know what the deal is with that giant fence on that hill? It almost looks like a prison. But in the middle of the city?"

"You are right, it is a prison. The Rokma think punishment should be public. They even hold their trials out in the open at the top of that hill. Barbaric if you ask me."

"How savage!" Serene cooed, putting her hand to chest and leaving her mouth slightly open. "Is that why they have all those drones up there? Part of the punishment?"

The Slu laughed, "No, no. Those drones aren't enforcers. Quite the opposite. They are the ones being punished. Since the recent attack on Triask, they have been rounding up every AI they come across."

"It's good they are doing something about those murderous drones," Serene said stiffly, not really having to pretend much.

"Oh, these aren't the murderous kind. They are the everyday kind. Labor drones. Medical drones. Education drones. Whatever." The Slu's eyestalks drooped, "I should caution you, this anti-drone sentiment is bleeding over. They are even less friendly toward Echanics than usual. You should be careful. My company almost had one of our technicians arrested over something stupid. Fortunately, we're a vendor for the prison and were able to get him released. On my next trip, we're going be sure to reassign all the Echanics and AI's off our freighters."

"Oh my," Serene said, leaning back and glanced back at the cashier. "That would explain the treatment I've received."

The Slu dipped his eyestalks in a shrug, "Nah, most of that is normal Rokma behavior. Just be cautious around the officials. Or the religious figures."

"Religious figures?"

"Yeah, the Rokma religion has always been a kind of subtle thing. But the last few months, they're actually giving sermons and holding rallies. It's been weird. They usually do it at sundown from the hill. I suggest not being around." Then almost as if an afterthought, the Slu said, "If you needed some place to stay, my hotel room is just around the corner."

Seeing her chance, Serene stood up, feigning fright, "Oh this place sounds dreadful. Thank you for your kind offer, but I think I should get back to my ship."

Leaning down, Serene wrapped the Slu in a firm embrace, being sure to rest one of her hands against the Slu's pocket. She slipped her hand inside. She leaned her head close to the eyestalk and smiled while sliding the Slu's handheld out of the pocket.

"Thank you again. I don't know what trouble I might have gotten into without your kind words," Serene said with a wink and then left the café.

22- Olivia

Olivia paced across the cargo bay. A pilot didn't have a lot to do on the ground. She had wanted to go with Ariana to check on Vlasa, but the Rokma would only allow the captain to see him. Serene had laughed when she had suggested going with her. That had left staying on *Seraph* with Squee and two surly Manta.

Unfortunately, despite the ship being practically empty, it felt more crowded than ever. Squee had decided that his duty was to guard her from the Manta and he followed her everywhere she went. The Manta were equally fixated on keeping an eye on Squee and followed him everywhere he went.

Accepting the inevitable, Olivia had constrained herself to pacing the cargo bay. While walking, she tried to think of something to say to strike up a conversation, but neither the Manta nor Squee would take their eyes off each other. Anything she did say ended up leading nowhere.

When Ariana, Serene and Latten appeared at the bottom of the ramp, she practically bounced over to them. "What did you learn? Is Vlasa okay?"

Ariana held up a hand to stave off her next stream of questions, "He's okay. Mesu is there too. He's disabled but Vlasa thinks he can be repaired. I tried to convince the guards to let me bring him parts to repair Mesu, but they refused. Even claimed Mesu was Vlasa's doctor and needed to treat him. That went nowhere."

"And what about Gremoosh?" One of the Manta asked.

"He's there too. I wasn't able to see him, though. Given the trouble I'm having getting Vlasa released, our hope of just hiring a lawyer to get him bail probably won't pan out."

Taking out a bottle of water from the supplies in the bay, Ariana took a long swallow. Then she turned to Serene, "What did you and Latten learn?"

"The security is surprisingly light. We saw lots of people milling around near the fence. It wouldn't be hard to cut through and have everyone just walk out. Of course, you're doing that in the middle of the city in full view of everyone."

"We'd need to get Mesu functional before we could do that."

"Why not just leave Mesu?" Olivia blurted out before she could think to stop herself.

"We don't leave anyone behind on my ship." Ariana's tone went cold and quiet.

The look Ariana cast at Olivia left her withering. Instead of anger, she saw only disappointment and frustration. Olivia suddenly found herself wishing Ariana had started yelling at her.

"I might have a way to get those parts to Vlasa," Serene said, filling the uncomfortable silence. She held up a handheld. "I borrowed this from a Slu whose company provides some services to the prison. It looks like imported food, seeing as how there are quite a lot of non-Rokma inside. This contains access credentials for the prison."

"Could we use that to get them out?" Squee asked.

"One, maybe in the cargo containers. But not three," Ariana said. "They would be suspicious of someone taking that much stuff out."

"But going in with a tool kit among the deliveries and leaving without it would be possible," Serene said.

"Do you think you could hack into their security system while you were inside?" Ariana asked. "From what I saw of the layout, there were a few unoccupied stations."

Serene shrugged, "Computers and I don't really speak the same language."

"Well, it was worth considering," Ariana said with a slump of her shoulders.

Olivia groaned and then raised her hand, "I could do it. I know a little about computer programming."

"If I recall, the last time you tried hacking something, you blew up a ship and almost incinerated me with shrapnel," Serene said.

Momentarily cringing at the memory, Olivia shot back, "Yeah, but I also saved you from endlessly drifting in space. So, really, it was a win."

"Something like this would be dangerous, Olivia," Ariana said with a shake of her head. "Serene can handle herself undercover..."

Suddenly overcome with a need to prove herself useful, Olivia said, "I can do this, Captain. I lived on the street for years. I know how to blend in without being noticed. And this isn't hacking an AI warship. It's a prison login screen. I'm not going to get anyone blown up if I fail."

"If you do this, you'll become a criminal, just like me kid," Serene added. "I run a risk every time I walk around a civilized PUG world like this. I can only go independent places like the Hub or the less savory varieties like M-21 and Nalhu. Right now, your record is clean. You can visit wherever you like. You get identified…"

"I grew up on the Hub. It's good enough for me."

Ariana leaned in close, "You also might get yourself locked in that prison too."

Defiantly Olivia held her chin up, "Then you'll get me out. Because we never leave anyone behind. Let me help do that. I can help get Vlasa, and Mesu, free."

Ariana fixed her with an intense look for an uncomfortably long time. Finally, she nodded, "Okay. You're going in."

23- Olivia

The Rokma prison guard towering above fixed her with a penetrating glare. Olivia felt an overpowering desire to look down at the crate in front of her and the box of contraband circuit boards hidden inside. She forced herself to return the Rokma's gaze until a thought occurred to her. Would that be more suspicious? What would a real delivery person do?

"So why the new delivery? You guys were here two days ago," The Rokma guard said.

Speaking quickly, Olivia blurted out her cover story, "We learned, from a courier message delivered today from our headquarters, which is in the capital city of Rigel, some food might be contaminated with bacteria that missed initial inspection, so we're sending a replacement with sincerest apologies and free of charge. Obviously. We wouldn't charge you for bad food. Who would do that? Definitely not us."

The Rokma frowned and Olivia felt her heart rate spike but then the guard shrugged, "It makes no difference to me if this trash gets sick or not. Come on in."

The door to the prison opened and Olivia nearly fainted. Fortunately, she slumped into the cart instead of collapsing. Dodging incoming missiles had been dangerous. This should have been easy. But Rokma were big and unlike Squee, these didn't seem very friendly.

Recovering herself, Olivia pushed against the cart and followed the Rokma guard toward the prison. She passed through the open area that surrounded the building. On the other side of a fence, several drones and biological prisoners wandered the barren hill top. The biologicals hung back in the shade cast by the prison building, while the drones wandered in the sun.

Once inside, the guard led Olivia through a few check points until they got to a large storage room. She looked down at Olivia with a frown, "I suppose you're going to need help with those?"

"What? Help? Of course, that would be..." Olivia started but caught herself, "No, I have to do it myself. Contract rules. If you help, then I owe you part of my pay. And I like my pay. Very much. Money. Yay."

The Rokma shook her head, "Tell the guards at the checkpoint when you're done." And then wandered off back the way they had come. As soon as the guard disappeared around a corner, Olivia collapsed against the carts handle again.

After taking a moment to calm herself, Olivia rolled the cart into the storage room. Searching the room, she found the crates from the company she was impersonating and removed their ID tag, switching it out for the ones in the crates she had brought in with her. She then popped open the crate, lifted the bag of protein paste and took out the box of parts. Now she had to move on to the dangerous part.

Glancing out of the store room, Olivia looked for signs of guards. Fortunately, Rokma did not move quietly, and she heard nothing in the hallway. Dashing down the hallway, she found the empty office Ariana had spotted on her visit. At least she hoped it was the same one and that it was still empty. No light shown through the frosted glass, but she couldn't be sure someone wasn't using the office for a nap.

Quietly, Olivia knocked and then paused to listen for a reply. Not wanting to spend any more time than necessary in the exposed hallway, she braved opening the door after only a brief wait and scurried inside. Ready to blurt out an apology, she instead let out a relieved breath to find herself alone.

Closing the door, she took a seat at the work station and powered it on. A few seconds passed before the station booted up. Once the screen came alive, she started by trying to access it with her handheld. Unsurprisingly, the terminal had no wifi connection. Since the AI War, no one attached any sensitive information to wifi networks.

Taking a screwdriver out, Olivia removed the side of the computer terminal. Her first glance inside caused her to frown. She didn't recognize the layout of the circuit board or any of the components. Rokma computers were designed differently than the systems on the Hub.

She stared at the collection of electronics for an agonizing minute. Finally, she reminded herself that it was still just a computer. It had to work on the same principles. She peered at each component until she identified the power source. From there, she was able to get an idea of each piece until she found what she took to be an expansion port. She inserted wires from her handheld until the screen lit up with an open connection.

Running the script she had prepared, she got the decryption running. After only a minute she gained access to the terminal, the Rokma's password security being surprisingly shoddy. With a bright smile, she flipped through the data on the terminal, finding files for personnel. Hastily she entered pictures and biometrics for Squee and Latten to the roster of guards. After that she created login information for them which would allow them to gain access later.

Feeling a bit confident, Olivia reached for the door handle to move on to the next phase of the plan. A rumble in the doors glass window stopped her from opening it further and she let out a curse. A shadow passed by the door outside. It paused for a long moment in front of the door. Olivia held her breath until the shadow moved again and the vibrations faded.

Moving quickly, Olivia pulled open the door and dashed back into the hallway. She held the box for Vlasa in front of her, looking for where the hallway intersected with the area prisoners were held. Locating the junction, she approached the metal bars, peering into the enclosure.

She saw cells lining the corridor, but no signs of life. Where the hell was Vlasa? Ariana had visited again this morning and filled him in. Why wasn't he here waiting for her?

Behind her, the hallway rumbled with the sound of approaching Rokma footfalls. She let out an audible curse at Vlasa this time. She considered just throwing the box into the cell and hoping it was still there when Vlasa finally showed up. But she stopped when a drone appeared, hovering slightly above the ground. Olivia tensed up and almost bolted back the way she had come, despite the approaching Rokma guard. They were preferable to drones.

"You are a friend of Vlasa's?" the drone asked.

"How do you know him?" Olivia replied. "What did you do to him?"

"He was detained and unable to come. He asked me to come in his place. My name is Goma."

The thuds down the hallway behind her sounded louder, but Olivia stood there fixed in place. The drone extended an arm. Compared to Mesu or combat drones, it only had a normal looking two. "Those are the parts to repair your friend Mesu, correct?"

"How do I know I can trust you?" Olivia stared hard at the floating drone.

"Why would you suspect you cannot?"

"Because you're a damn drone," Olivia blurted out and then added. "And you're in prison. And I don't know you."

"I assure you, I am a friend of Vlasa's. You must make your decision. I can hear the guard approaching on his patrol."

Olivia looked down at the box in her hand. Could she trust this drone? Probably not. But did it really matter? If the drone stole the parts, the worse that would happen is that Mesu couldn't move, a state they were already in. But if she got caught with them, she would be in here with the others.

Quickly, Olivia shoved the box through the bars to the drone. It grabbed a hold and then spun, floating quickly into the nearest cell. A moment later, a voice barked out behind her, "Hey, who are you?"

Olivia closed her eyes for a second and took a deep breath. She then spun around and thought back to her days on the Hub when she had been caught sneaking food from a shop. "I'm here delivering some supplies. And I really need to find the bathroom."

24- Vlasa

When Vlasa returned to his cell, he expected to see Goma waiting for him. Sent outside on mandatory exercise time, he had almost missed the rendezvous with Olivia. He had tried to argue that due to his cybernetics, exercise was pointless, but the Rokma made the AI do it as well, which was by far even more pointless. Fortunately, he had passed Goma and the AI had agreed to attend the meeting.

Instead of Goma, Vlasa found a Manta in his cell. Bent over Mesu, the Manta had removed the case around Mesu's power distributor. Parts lay scattered on the cell floor. Among the debris, Vlasa caught sight of a small box, which could only have been the one Olivia had smuggled in.

"What are you doing?" Vlasa exclaimed, storming into his cell.

The Manta turned and faced him, extending his body up on two limbs. Dark black eyes peered out of a black chitin exoskeleton. Mandibles clicked quickly and glistened with some liquid. Involuntarily, the sight made Vlasa take a step back.

"My name is Gremoosh. I hear you've been asking questions about me."

Vlasa glanced behind him and for the first time regretted that he had no one in the neighboring cells. It had been nice not having to mingle with most of the prison population. Now it left him completely without any hope of aid.

Knowing the speed Manta could move, he calculated that even his cybernetic legs could not propel him fast enough to escape. In fact, due to a timing imbalance between the two different models of legs, anytime he tried to run he always started to veer to the right. That limited his top speed enough that he knew Gremoosh could be on him long before he could reach anyone else. Assuming there weren't more Manta thugs waiting around the corner.

Deciding he had no choice but to talk his way out, Vlasa said, "Umm... yeah... I have been."

"I am curious how you knew my real name. It is not the one the guards have," Gremoosh clicked his mandibles.

"Well... that's because I'm here to rescue you."

"Oh? Rescue me? You and a broken AI?"

Vlasa shrugged, "Well, and my crew. I'm just the guy on the inside. We were hired to get you out."

This time the Manta reacted, leaning in close to Vlasa. Despite the implied threat, Vlasa found himself less concerned, "Who hired you?"

"My captain met with them. Your clan I believe."

"Herish? Or Rektri?"

At the mention of the Manta who had died aboard *Seraph*, Vlasa felt his stomach swirl. With difficulty, he forced out, "Rektri sounds familiar."

Gremoosh hissed and turned around, dropping to four limbs and skittering around the cramped cell. Seeming to have forgotten about Vlasa, he climbed up the wall and hung there. He muttered to himself, but Vlasa could not make out what he said or if it was even in universal.

"Umm..." Vlasa began.

Looking down from the wall, Gremoosh hissed again and continued babbling to himself. Seemingly forgotten, Vlasa stared at the Manta, his terror abating some. Gremoosh's demeanor appeared more afraid than Vlasa felt.

Trying to change the subject, Vlasa said, "So, about the drone?"

Gremoosh jerked his head down toward Mesu. With a thud, the Manta dropped down, bounced off the cot and landed beside Mesu, "I got the box from Goma. Thought I'd start replacing the components while you were out. It was a little hard to get the casing off without any tools. I'm not sure how you intend to remove the power distributor without breaking anything. Those connectors are sensitive."

Extending the screwhead from his finger, Vlasa gave it a spin, "I always have some tools with me."

"Excellent. It doesn't look like we'll be able to repair these limbs, but we should be able to get him operating again. The power levels of the battery appear good, but if he needs some power, the Rokma set up a charging port for the AI in the mess. One of the few necessities they've provided. This whole place is a travesty."

"How do you know so much about drones?" Vlasa asked, feeling a bit bewildered.

"I've always liked tinkering with things. During the war I helped the warriors by stripping weapons off destroyed drones. I learned a lot about them and it let me be helpful without having to...umm...I learned a lot." Gremoosh glanced down at Mesu while he talked.

"Okay, well, if you'll allow me, I'd like to finish before any guards come by for an inspection. We can't get out of here until he can move."

"Of course," Gremoosh said and moved out of the way.

25- Squee

Squee paced around the mess hall table nervously. Serene came in and dropped a shopping bag onto the table, "Here's the stuff you asked for. What the hell did you need with all this? It looks like paint. It smells like paint. But it's clear."

"Not in the UV spectrum." Squee answered, taking the jar out of the bag along with a fine point brush.

"Okay..." Serene said with a nod. "So, what's the point of it?"

"Can those not see UV?" Squee asked, gesturing to Serene's cybernetic eyes.

Touching the cybernetic piece that extended across her face, Serene frowned, "I only have this because I'd be blind otherwise. I don't want to be able to see things I couldn't normally."

"Ah," Squee said. He turned to a screen that hung on the wall and engaged the mirror feature. Studying his face, he began gentling brushing with the UV paint. "Rokma can naturally use UV. And we put a tattoo on our face at the age of maturity, identifying ourselves and our path for all to see. If I am to assist in this plan, I could not do it as Caleek."

"No religious figures working as prison guards?" Serene asked with a snicker.

"Actually, it would not be unheard of for a Caleek to work as a prison guard. But it would draw unwanted attention."

"So, what are you now?"

"The closest symbol is a Shumar. It's not perfect, but will do. I could say it's job training," Squee said and chuckled.

"You do know I have no idea what that means," Serene said.

"Right, Shumar means, well, I guess the closest would be family. They are those that dedicate themselves to the caring for the next generation," Squee said with a chuckle.

"So, you're just preparing for parenthood by learning how to handle miscreants? Eh?" Serene said with a smile.

Turning and frowning, Squee shook his head, "No. What kind of monster are you?"

"But you just... Oh never mind. I give up on understanding Rokma humor. I need to go steal a vehicle."

Now alone, Squee studied his face in the mirror. A sad expression stared back at him. He forced it to turn, if not happy, at least neutral. He had a duty to perform.

Satisfied with the work on his face, he closed the paint and went down to the cargo bay where Latten and Ariana waited. Latten squinted his eyes and then shrugged, "It will do I suppose."

Latten turned and headed down the boarding ramp and Squee made to follow him. Ariana interspersed herself forcing him to come to a halt. She looked concerned and Squee forced a smile, "Do not worry, Captain. We will get Vlasa, Mesu and even the Manta out safely."

"I know you will, Squee," Ariana said. "I'm just worried. You're still recovering from being shot by the Manta. You can't afford to get in an actual fight. Plus, this is the second time I've forced you to choose between two oaths."

Squee blinked involuntarily at Ariana. She continued, "I know you are bound by your banishment and you swore to not leave the ship. Deciding to violate that in order to save Vlasa and Mesu could not have been easy. I appreciate it."

Left dumbstruck, Squee only managed to mumble some incoherent reply before Ariana smacked him on the arm and then disappeared behind him. That she had remembered his oath surprised him. At the bottom of the ramp, Latten called up for him to hurry up. Unsure what else to do, Squee followed.

From the ship it was a short walk to the public transit system and then an uncomfortable ride to the center of town. They arrived just at the right time, however, as a few other Rokma guards were making their way to the prison gates for the shift change. Wearing the new crafted ID's Olivia had made them and the uniforms Serene had acquired, he and Latten blended in seamlessly with the others. As they had suspected, no one gave them a second glance, each guard keeping mostly to themselves.

Squee held his breath when the guards at the gate scanned his ID, but it registered without issue and he moved through the line. Once inside, the stream of guards spread out, each heading to their assigned duty stations. Soon, he and Latten were alone in the hall way. He looked at his companion and nodded his head.

"Now all we must do is find Vlasa, hope he's fixed Mesu. Find Gremoosh. Convince him to trust us without causing a scene and then stage a jail break without anyone noticing," Squee said.

"Simple," Latten chuckled.

Moving to the portal that led into the secure portion of the prison, Squee slid his card and nodded to the guard behind the barrier. The door released, and he led Latten through before the guard could look at them closely. It took him only a few minutes to find the cell Vlasa occupied.

Inside the cell, Vlasa sat, bent over Mesu with another AI and a Manta standing nearby. A wire ran from the AI into Mesu. The Manta chittered excitedly and kept pointing at Mesu while Vlasa continually swatted his hand away.

At the sight of the Manta, Squee and Latten both reached for their side arms. Squee stopped himself from drawing it. He reached a hand out to lower Latten's weapon, but before he could bring it down, the group noticed them. The Manta let out a hiss and skittered back behind Mesu.

"Woah!" Vlasa said holding a hand out toward Latten and the Manta. "Let's all calm down. These are my crewmates I told you about. Latten, this is Gremoosh."

Latten held his gun steady for a second longer before holstering it again. He kept his eyes fixed on Gremoosh. Squee let out a relieved breath and turned to Vlasa, "Why are you not ready to go?"

"You try repairing a drone while in prison using only your hand," Vlasa said without looking up.

"My hands do not have tools built into them."

"Well, when we get Mesu operational, I'm sure he'd be happy to help you with that."

Squee glanced nervously behind him. The corridor remained empty, but he had no idea how long before an actual guard patrol would wander by. The less he had to interact with his fellow Rokma, the better. So far, he had merely been required to flash a badge. He wasn't sure he could actually lie to them.

"How long?"

"Soon," Vlasa said as he continued to work on Mesu.

The Manta Gremoosh slowly started to rise back up onto four limbs. He now stood about as high as Vlasa's chest. He and Latten kept their eyes locked onto each other. Finally, Gremoosh spoke.

"Why are you helping me, Rokma?"

"We are being well paid," Latten answered.

Squee frowned at Latten's response, but Gremoosh nodded, "Mercenaries then. Typical Rokma. Turning against your own kind for money. Just like every guard here abuses innocents for money."

He glanced down at Vlasa, "Though this surprises me about you. You do not seem the type."

Vlasa ignored the implicit question, focused as he was on Mesu. Instead Squee said, "He said we were being well paid. He didn't say we were doing this for money."

"Drugs then? Slaves?" Gremoosh spat. "Your dedication to your AI friend led me to believe you were decent people."

The Manta's disdain rankled Squee. He let out a growl, "You know nothing about us, Manta."

"I know enough."

"Okay, done," Vlasa said, interrupting them.

An electric whine filled the room. Everyone of Mesu's appendages that were still in one piece, contracted. His head lifted and rotated in a complete circle. Several more noises emerged before receding down to the typical background hum of any drone.

"What the hell did you do to me?" Mesu finally said locking his gaze on Vlasa.

"Repaired you."

"Repaired me? My last memory was going to find you. Now I have no idea where I am and half of my appendages don't work. If I healed you the way you repaired me, your leg would just be a stump of wood and your hand would be a hook."

"It's a bit of a long story," Squee said. "Which we can tell you later. For now, keep quiet so we can get back to *Seraph*."

"And who the hell am I attached too? I've been violated!" Mesu said, following the wires connecting him to the other AI.

"I am Goma," The AI said. "I provided you with a jumpstart."

Squee growled, "Mesu, quiet! Goma, thank you. But it's time to go. Unfortunately, we are only equipped to take these three out."

"I understand," Goma replied as he unplugged himself from Mesu. "Good luck out there brother."

Stepping up next to Goma, Gremoosh lay a hand on the drone casing, "You may be just hired thugs, but I am not. You were hired to get me out correct?"

"Yes. And if we don't go now, we'll miss our chance."

"Then I'm not going. Not unless Goma, and all the other unjustly imprisoned people are freed as well."

They all stared down at the Manta. Vlasa's mouth hung open before a second, and then he asked, "You're kidding, right?"

"No," Gremoosh said flatly. "I can not allow this injustice to continue."

Squee let out a growl of frustration and slammed his fist through the wall. "God foresaken Manta!"

26- Serene

Serene twisted the knob on the air conditioning controls again, vainly hoping she could coax more cool air from the vents. Unfortunately, it appeared the Rokma's love of heat kept them from installing effective cooling in their vehicles. She leaned back and cursed as her skin touched the sunbaked seat again. Sitting parked in the sun had turned the cargo truck she'd stolen into an oven.

Beside her, Olivia curled up in the trucks Rokma sized passenger seat. The girl had her handheld out and flashes of some game reflected off the window. Protected by shade from the vehicles roof, Olivia appeared unconcerned by her present predicament.

"For someone who hates technology, you certainly play with that thing a lot," Serene snapped.

"I don't hate technology. Just murderous drones. Besides, this is my first handheld. I never had one before joining *Seraph*," Olivia said.

Serene turned to face the girl, "Really? Everyone has one."

"Everyone with money."

"I don't have any money. And I have one."

"The person you stole it from had money."

"True."

The pair lapsed into silence for a moment. Serene considered pulling out her own handheld to distract herself, but she wouldn't be able to get comfortable enough to read. She didn't like uncomfortable silences. Silences spoke volumes, but words conveyed comfortable nothing.

"Captain, we have a situation," Squee's voice broke into the silence over the comm channel.

"When don't we? What's happened?" Ariana replied.

"Gremoosh is refusing to come with us unless we also free everyone currently locked up. Vlasa and Mesu are not exactly discouraging him."

"Why the hell would he want to free a bunch of drones?" Olivia asked.

"He claims they are unfairly imprisoned. I think he's just being a Manta and wanting to cause us trouble. I say we leave him. We can still get our people out."

Serene's chest tightened for a second and she blurted, "We can't do that. We need him to save Noah."

"More practically, if we don't return with him, we'll have two unhappy Manta aboard. Who most likely have tapped into our comm network and are listening to everything you're suggesting," Ariana said, her voice flat and unnaturally level.

"Your captain is correct," The voice of Deris, one of the Manta aboard *Seraph* joined the conversation. *"Should you fail to deliver our compatriot as promised, she will experience our displeasure."*

Serene turned down the volume of her ear piece, not wanting to listen to the inevitable blustering and exchange of threats between the Rokma and the Manta. She looked out the window toward the prison up on the hill. A few drones roamed the open area behind the fence. She again marveled at how easy it would be to just take it down and let everyone inside walk out. But that would be seen by everyone. Especially the large crowd that had started to gather for the day's sermon.

Suddenly, Serene smiled, "Everyone keep your guns holstered. I have an idea. Squee, get your people to the west side of the exercise yard."

"That is the opposite direction from the gate."

"Exactly."

Fortunately, Ariana stepped in, *"Do it, Squee."*

Serene opened the vehicles door. Beside her, Olivia squeaked in surprise, "Where are you going?"

"To cause some trouble. Guess what? That means you get to drive."

"I've never driven before."

"You fly a starship. How hard can it be?" Serene said with a wink and slammed the door shut before Olivia could offer another protest.

Moving toward the growing crowd of Rokma, she slipped in among them. Listening to their discussions, she tried to identify Rokma who were in a particularly unpleasant mood. When they would glower at her, she would nod as if agreeing with them and gesture to the cybernetic over her face.

"Yeah, fuck those drones. They tried to turn me into one of them and now they just get to sit in a comfy prison cell?"

She did this a couple dozen times before shifting tactics. On her next trip through the crowd she started adding some further embellishments, "Did you hear they are going to let the drones go tomorrow?" and "Those drones are sucking up half the cities power and enjoy a great view of all of us toiling away down here." And "I hear the Manta are building more war drones."

Finally, on her third trip through the crowd, she spotted two particularly grumpy Rokma. She remained quiet for a while, listening to the Rokma priest give a sermon on the blasphemy that was artificial life. She waited until the speaker reached a crescendo in her sermon before reaching out and shoving one of the grumpy Rokma into the other one.

As expected, the grumpy Rokma shoved the one who stumbled into him away. The two glowered at each other and started to exchange words. Just as another bystander intervened to remind the two to not give into the blood fury, that the fury should not be used against their own kind. Serene smiled. Then she screamed.

"That drone is escaping!"

The AI up at the top of the hill behind the fence had just completed a circuit around the open field. It started to roll over the curve of the hill, facing the fence and with a little generous imagination it might appear to be going through the fence on the other side. Serene knew it was a stretch, but it was the best she had.

"It's escaping! Someone stop it!" She pointed at the two Rokma who had very nearly come to blows. They both turned and looked up the hill at drone.

Not wasting any time, Serene took off, running forward through the crowd and up the side of the hill. As she ran, she continued to shout about the escaping drone. For several seconds, she feared she would just be a crazy Echanic woman shouting manically by herself. Then the thunder of steps behind her sounded.

The two angry Rokma followed her and as they started, more joined them. Continuing her move through the crowd, Serene pointed upward at every Rokma she passed, while attempting to get to the edge of the crowd before the real stampede began. She almost made it.

Already riled up by the daily sermons about the horrors of the AI, the crowd had only needed a slight push to turn into a mob. And when Rokma became a mob, they became an unstoppable juggernaut. The crowd surged forward, pushing against those in front, including Serene.

Jostled to the side, Serene stumbled and fell. Several large, powerful legs brushed against her, preventing her from getting up again. The crowd surged above her.

27- Olivia

When the Rokma crowd surged up the hill, it startled Olivia. She had watched Serene moving among them, unsure what the woman was up too. When she finally figured it out, she smiled at the simplicity. Squee and the others were waiting on the opposite side of the hill, well away from the crowd now drawing all the guard's attention.

She started up the cargo truck, wanting to be ready when Serene got back to her. From among the surge of Rokma, she caught sight of a lone Echanic. She let out a curse when she saw Serene go down and disappear among the Rokma.

Olivia reached her foot out to gun the vehicles accelerator, but found she couldn't quite reach. Designed for Rokma, or at least really tall and fully grown adults, the accelerator pedal was just out of her reach. She glanced up and saw the crowd continue to surge over where Serene had fallen.

Letting out a growl of frustration, Olivia jabbed her foot down toward the accelerator, slipping as far down the seat as possible. She lost sight of Serene, but could at least see over the control panel. Accelerating, she swerved the wheel to avoid a set of street signs.

Leaving the smooth streets, the vehicle started bucking as she barreled toward the flowing crowd. Fortunately, the crowd had thinned out enough that those that noticed her were able to clear out of her path. She didn't know who would win in a contest between a Rokma and a vehicle. She suspected a Rokma.

Slamming on the brake, Olivia bucked around, her back straining from the awkward position. She ignored the discomfort and pulled herself up to get a better view of the area. She saw Serene laying in a fetal position a few meters away. Stopping the vehicle, she threw the door open and rushed over to Serene.

"Serene! Are you okay?" Olivia called nervously.

For an agonizing moment, Serene didn't move. Olivia stared down at her helplessly. Serene let out a groan and Olivia let out a relieve sigh. In clear agony, Serene growled, "Do I fucking look okay?"

"No, you look like you were just trampled by a herd of wild Rokma."

Serene started to move and groaned again, "Just help me up."

Olivia bent down and tried to lift Serene, but the Echanic woman was larger than she was. With some difficulty and several curses from Serene, they managed to get her to her feet. Serene's body was covered with dirt and blood. She winced at every movement.

Gingerly, Olivia wrapped her arm around Serene's waist and turned her to the vehicle. Limping slowly, they walked back to the vehicle. Though it wasn't far it took an agonizing amount of time. She had to lean Serene against the vehicle in order to get the door open and then Serene practically fell into the passenger seat.

"I think you're going to want to hurry before that crowd completely swarms the prison." Serene said with a grimace.

Out the windshield they could see the horde of Rokma banging on the prison's fences. The chain-link metal wouldn't hold up long to that onslaught. The guards up in the towers looked to shouting and waving their weapons at the crowd but were being ignored. More could be seen running from elsewhere in the prison complex toward the front gate.

"I just hope we can get there without getting swarmed ourselves," Olivia said as she started the vehicle up again.

She gunned the engine and turned back toward the streets, not wanting to draw any more attention to them as she made her way around to the opposite side where Squee and the others should be waiting.

28- Vlasa

The exercise yard filled with prisoners, AI and biologicals alike. Vlasa felt trapped more than he had since being thrown in the prison. Pressed against the fence, he had nowhere else to go. Shouts of anger echoed from somewhere else and kept getting louder.

"Okay, so Serene said to go here," Vlasa asked. "Now what?"

Squee shrugged, "She wants me to bring down the fence. I told her I could not do that without drawing the guard's attention, but apparently that is no longer a concern."

Holding his cybernetic hand up with his fingers split into a 'V' shape, Vlasa said, "I may have a quieter solution."

Inserting his fingers into the chain-link fence, Vlasa worked his hand like scissors. He snipped each link in the fence as high up as he could reach. Moving to his left, he continued cutting until he had made a hole the approximate size of Squee.

"If you could have done that at any time, why did you need us to break you out?" Latten asked.

"If I had tried this earlier, I would have been shot. The fact that I wasn't just now suggests whatever distraction Serene staged has been effective," Vlasa said turning to Squee. "So do we just sit here or what?"

"Olivia is on her way to retrieve us."

"All of us?" Gremoosh asked.

Squee shook his head, "No, just us. You refused to leave unless we got everyone out. The doors open. They can get out now."

"What do you think is going to happen to them out there? They'll just be rearrested in a matter of hours. Or worse, shot," Gremoosh hissed.

"Not our problem. Think before you make demands next time, Manta. Their deaths are on you," Latten said with a wicked grin.

Both Vlasa and Squee turned a frown on Latten. Unfortunately, it appeared that was all Squee felt the need to add so Vlasa took it upon himself to intersperse himself between Gremoosh and Latten, "As undiplomatic as our friend is, he has a point. We were not prepared to provide aid to so many. Our ship can't handle more."

Gremoosh clenched and unclenched his hands, continuing to stare daggers at Latten and Squee. Until now, the Manta had defied Vlasa's expectations and had always been calm and reasonable. For the first time he felt afraid to be in the line of fire.

A mechanical appendage reached out and rested on the Manta's shoulder, drawing his attention. Goma said, "They have done as you asked. We will take this opportunity. Thank you for giving it to us. All of you."

Increasing his volume, Goma shouted, "Attention all Cybers. We have been given this chance to reclaim our freedom. Let us go now and leave this planet."

The crowd surged and pushed through the hole in the fence. Vlasa was forced back along with the others. AI's of all types eagerly poured out of the prison. He extended his hand, his biological one to his own surprise, to Goma and nodded to the hovering AI.

"Thank you for your help repairing Mesu. While we could not take everyone, there would be room enough for you," Vlasa said.

"I appreciate the offer, but I feel a responsibility for our community. I must see it through," Goma said and then turned to look at Mesu. "As for you, my friend, you are welcome to join us. We will look for a new world to call home. Some place for Cybers to live free from biological oppression or being subjugated as drones."

"A world of just AI? While appealing, I really wouldn't have anything to do. These biologicals would all be dead inside a month without me to put them back together again," Mesu said cheerily.

"I didn't know you cared, Mesu," Vlasa said dryly.

"Of course, I care. You alone have allowed me to practice several new procedures. It is great experience. I keep learning about all kinds of new flaws in biologicals."

Vlasa sighed, "Good bye, Goma. Thank you for showing me not all AI are psychotic."

"Good bye, Vlasa," Goma said and then floated through the fence.

"Now, let's go before the guards figure out what's going on," Squee said impatiently.

To emphasize his point, a malevolent scream echoed from somewhere behind them. This added to the roll of thunder that continued to build from the same direction on the other side of the hill beyond their view. Something was coming. Vlasa pushed his group to join the stream of fleeing prisoners. Once outside the fence, he felt a great pressure ease from him. A feeling that he hadn't even noticed he had been feeling.

That's when the gunfire started.

29- Squee

At the sound of the first rifle shot, Squee jumped between Vlasa and the guard towers. Around him he saw drones collapsing. The bullets appeared to be aimed at whatever the drones used for locomotion. Hovering drones dropped from the sky, tracked drones had their wheels severed and walking drones their legs shattered.

The biological prisoners scattered away from the crowd as the surrounding drones thinned out. Squee exchanged a glance with Vlasa who nodded and gestured. Squee shoved Gremoosh aside and placed himself as a shield for Mesu.

The medical drone turned his head to Squee, "What do you think you're doing?"

"Protecting you."

"Do you have a death wish? I warned you that if you get shot again in your arm or chest, you could die. Even with a low caliber weapon," Mesu chirped.

"My back is fine."

"You're not the one who would have to repair a severed spine."

"Just move you hunk of metal."

A revving sound came from Mesu's tracks and he accelerated away, fast enough that Squee could not keep up. Around him, the rest of their group ran. To his disappointment, Latten ran separated from the rest of them, making no effort to shield the others.

He glanced behind them and saw the guards on the towers. They continued to fire at the fleeing prisoners but had now started looking behind them. The roaring sound that had been growing louder coalesced into a swarm of Rokma coming around the prison building.

"What the hell is that?" Gremoosh asked.

"That is a stampede. We must get away before they can catch up or we will be torn to shreds," Squee answered.

Looking around fervently, he spotted a cargo truck rattling around at the base of the hill. It swerved erratically, bumping into the sides of buildings and over bushes with equal measure. When he finally caught a glimpse of the driver, he felt his mouth drop. Olivia's head peered just barely over the steering controls.

"That's our ride!" Squee shouted and pointed down toward the vehicle. Olivia clipped a table at a nearby café, sending the chairs careening through the café window.

"I am not sure we will be any safer there than with the mob," Gremoosh said.

"Watch your tongue, Manta," Squee growled. "That's our pilot."

Gremoosh looked between the vehicle and Squee. He turned his head to Vlasa who nodded. The Manta let out a string of clicks and clacks that Squee took to be cursing. He found it hard to feel much resentment towards him for that.

Olivia started to climb the vehicle up the hill toward them, but it proved too steep. The vehicle stalled and slid backwards. She applied the brakes and came to a stop before trying again.

While everyone continued to run toward Olivia and the truck, Squee caught sight of a Rokma guard emerging from one of the towers. The guard had been heading toward them, but she stopped. She must have recognized the vehicle as the bigger threat because she changed direction.

Putting in as much speed as he could, Squee dashed ahead of the group. Latten called after him, asking where he was going. He gave no reply, not wanting to waste any breath.

Both Squee and the guard raced down the hill. Gravity would ensure they both made it. But Squee saw that if he didn't intercept the guard before they reached the bottom, she would plow right into the driver's cabin, probably killing Olivia in the process.

Throwing everything he had into running, Squee raced to his right, going slightly up the hill to an outcropping of rock. He went full speed to the edge and leaped off. Barreling into the air, Squee roared and then came plummeting back to the ground.

The guard glanced up at him. She had enough time to dodge sideways causing him to miss her and slam face first into the dirt. But she had been forced to come to a stop, which still left her a few meters away from Olivia and the truck.

Squee started to pick himself up off the ground, but a sharp impact on his injured arm caused him to buckle and collapse. Pain raced up his arm, and he rolled over onto his back. The guard towered over him. She slammed another kick into his chest.

"Oathless!" She hissed, kicking him again and then pausing to draw her pistol. "How dare you betray the will of the gods and side with these abominations!"

Out of breath and in pain, the guards curse still cut him deeper than anything else. He looked up at her and saw the blood fury swirling in her eyes. No words would reach her now.

The guard raised her gun but before she could fire, Latten barreled into her, knocking them both to the ground. The guard's pistol fell as the two rolled in the dirt. Squee started toward it but a new figure appeared.

Skittering rapidly across the dirt, Gremoosh grabbed the pistol. The Manta raised the weapon unsteadily. Not designed for a Manta's grip, he had trouble aiming it. Fortunately, Latten and the guard had separated, and he now had a clear shot on the guard.

"What are you waiting for Manta, shoot her!" Latten spat.

"Only if she makes me," Gremoosh snapped.

"And she's not going to make you," Squee said, overcoming his astonishment at Gremoosh and casting a dark look at Latten. He fixed a pointed look at the guard, "Are you?"

The guard glared at all of them. For a second, Squee thought she would push on, but then he saw the blood fury drain from her eyes. She relaxed and slumped back down to the ground.

"If you're not going to shoot her, Manta, drop the weapon," Latten said as he stood up and approached Gremoosh.

Gremoosh held the weapon, clearly considering his options. He appeared very reluctant to let it go. Finally, he glanced back toward Vlasa who had just about caught up. He nodded and tossed the weapon to Squee.

The door of the cargo truck popped open and Olivia poked her head out and shouted, "What are you all just standing around for? Come on, let's go!"

30- Vlasa

Vlasa followed Squee, Latten, Mesu and Gremoosh over to the cargo truck and climbed into the cargo compartment. Before they could completely seal the door, Olivia had started driving, bouncing along on the unpaved part of the hill. Fortunately, it did not take long before they were rolling over the smooth pavement again.

"I feel I owe you an apology," Gremoosh whispered from beside him.

Vlasa adjusted his cybernetic eye to the infrared spectrum and turned toward the voice. Beside him, Gremoosh sat hunched in the back corner, as far from the two Rokma as he could get. Stepping closer so he could hear the Manta's soft voice, he asked, "For what?"

"Making a mess of everything. I saw your Rokma friends and immediately jumped to the conclusion you must have all been a bunch of mercenaries. I resolved not long ago to avoid that sort anymore. I over reacted."

Vlasa frowned and gave a shrug, but wasn't sure if the Manta would be able to see him in the low light, so he said, "It did put us in a rather difficult position. But we're here now. On our way to the safety of *Seraph*."

"That is good. I look forward to meeting the rest of your crew."

"I can't say they are eager to meet you. We were led to believe you would be very different. They even sent two Manta with us in order to protect us from you."

Gremoosh stiffened and went still. After a second, his antennae twitched, "There are other Manta onboard your ship?"

"Yes. Two. Your clan leader insisted on it. He said it was for our safety."

"They know," Gremoosh whispered.

"Know what?"

Before Gremoosh could answer, the vehicle jerked to a stop. Squee threw open the door. Vlasa stumbled as the center of gravity shifted when the two Rokma jumped down to the ground. Out the open door, Vlasa could see the boarding ramp of *Seraph*.

"Come on," Vlasa said, gesturing to Gremoosh as he followed the Rokma.

"Typical. Not putting the ramp down for those of us without legs," Mesu complained.

"No time," Squee yelled back. "Just roll off."

Muttering at a speed that Vlasa could not follow, Mesu rolled off the edge of the cargo hold and landed with a thud on the ground. Vlasa jumped down beside him. From the front of the vehicle, Olivia came running up to meet them.

"Mesu, Serene needs you. She got trampled by some Rokma."

With a glance at Vlasa, Mesu said chipperly, "See? Always something new. I've never felt so needed."

Mesu wheeled off after Olivia, who then turned and waved Squee back. The girl gave Vlasa a quick smile, "It's good to have you back. Captain wants me onboard to get us lifted off."

She dashed toward the ship, passing Squee and disappeared inside. Vlasa wished they had been able to get his personal effects before busting out of the prison. Without a handheld, he could not connect his ear implant to *Seraph's* network and communicate with the rest of the crew.

Before starting for the ship himself, Vlasa noticed Gremoosh had not followed them off the truck. Glancing back, he saw the Manta still scrunched up in the back corner. He frowned and walked back.

"We need to get going. It won't take authorities long to lock down the spaceports. We need to be in the air before that happens."

"Then you should get going," Gremoosh said without moving.

"We came all the way here and did all this to get you out. If we try to take off without you, your friends are not going to be very happy with us."

Gremoosh was silent for a long time before nodding, "You are right."

Dropping to all six limbs, Gremoosh scurried out of the vehicle's cargo bed. He dropped to the ground before raising himself up to two. He nodded down to Vlasa, "Let's go."

"What are you afraid of?" Vlasa asked.

"I am a traitor to my clan."

Vlasa frowned, "They certainly went to a lot of trouble to get a traitor free from prison. They were particularly concerned that we do it without the Rokma authorities learning your true identify. They didn't want you to be executed if they did."

Gremoosh guffawed, "They were concerned the Rokma would kill me before they had a chance to."

"What did you do?"

With a heavy sigh, Gremoosh said, "I turned my sister, Herish, into the Zolan. I just couldn't let her continue to slaughter anymore people."

Vlasa stumbled for a second. Hoarsely he asked, "So, um, you weren't exactly close with your sister then?"

"Oh, no, we were very close. But she needed help. She murdered indiscriminately. And she had taken to slavery. I assume you've heard of the lost colony of Golan?"

"Um..." Vlasa floundered.

"We never meant for harm to come to the colonists. We contracted some unsavory types to remove the people from the colony. A PUG weapon cache had been hidden there, and we needed to level half the town to bust inside. We didn't want them to die. Hence, the removal. But the people we hired to move them ended up enslaving them. Or so we thought. I learned that Herish had agreed to that, against the wishes of Rektri and the other elders.

"Our clans name has been forever tarnished by that. I couldn't turn her into my own people, they would either execute her or worse, celebrate her as a hero. The PUG would have eventually turned her over to the Rokma. So, I turned her into the Zolan. They don't believe in the death penalty and aren't part of the PUG, so the Rokma would never get her. I had to get her someplace she would be safe and could maybe get better."

"I see," Vlasa said slowly.

"My clan wouldn't have understood, so I tried to lie low for a while. But then the stupid Rokma picked me up for being Manta. And here we are."

Vlasa continued to walk beside Gremoosh, feeling the tension in the Manta increase the closer they got to *Seraph*. He felt it in his own shoulders. At the top of the ramp, he could now see the shapes of the two other Manta, waiting.

They had a momentary respite as Squee came up behind them, carrying Serene. Mesu and Latten followed behind her. Vlasa asked, "How is Serene?"

"She has yet to stop complaining, so I'd say she will be fine," Squee replied.

"I'm right here you know," Serene added and then groaned.

"I will need to do some deep scans of her internal organs to be sure, though. So many things could be broken that we just can't see," Mesu said with relish.

When they were the last two left, Vlasa turned to Gremoosh who gave a heavy sigh, before following the others up. The two Manta at the top of the ramp stood poised as if ready for anything. Instead of attacking Gremoosh or Vlasa, they dropped to six limbs as if in a bow.

"Mighty Gremoosh, we regret to inform you of some terrible news. But we must ask that you constrain your response. These around you are going to return you home and deserve leniency."

Vlasa froze, glancing between Gremoosh and the other Manta. Finally, Gremoosh said, "I will remain calm."

"It is our burden to inform you that your sister, Herish, has fallen into the hands of the Zolan and beyond our reach to rescue. We know you must be quite angry."

Gremoosh cast a quick look to Vlasa before replying, "This is grave news."

A shout interrupted the Manta's next exchange. Squee bellowed from down the corridor leading out of the cargo bay, "Captain says to close the door so we can get out of here."

Jumping at the distraction, Vlasa dashed over to the control panel and closed the ramp. As soon as it began, the ship shuddered, and he saw the ground start to drop away.

31- Ariana

"**A**ttention transport vessel Seraph, you are not cleared to depart. Return to your berth at once."

Ariana glanced at the altimeter reading. She had to hand it to the Rokma, they were vigilant. She knew they would never make it away unnoticed, but she had hoped to at least break out of the atmosphere before being ordered to return.

"Control, this is *Seraph*. We heard about the prison breakout. I'm not keeping my crew on the ground while a bunch of drone prisoners are running loose." Ariana said, letting some of her fear out.

"*There is no need for concern. The situation is being dealt with. Return to port at once.*"

"Sorry, control. I've been through one AI War. I'm not sitting around for another one."

She cut the communication link with the ground control station. With luck, the Rokma would be too concerned with events there to worry about one skittish transport ship. And she hadn't even had to lie. She didn't want *Seraph* on the ground while a bunch of drones roamed free, even if they had been the ones to set the drones free.

The sound of the hatch opening caught her attention, and she turned from her station to see Vlasa standing at the door. He still wore a prison jumpsuit and looked very tired. She gave him a welcoming smile which he acknowledged in his customary blank way.

"Good to have you back, Vlasa. I trust Mesu is seeing to Serene?"

Vlasa nodded, "He is. Though he has made it very clear his ability to adequately tend to her wounds has been compromised by my failure to repair all of his appendages."

"He'll manage."

"Captain, we may have a more serious issue," Vlasa started and then glanced back. He stopped and closed the hatch before continuing. "Our impression of Gremoosh may have been incomplete. It turns out he was the one who turned his sister over to the Zolan."

"He turned her in? Why?"

"Apparently, she had become rather kill happy. That combined with his desire to see the rest of the prisoners free suggests he's not the psychotic murderer we envisioned."

Ariana chuckled, "That would be a first. Maybe we don't have to worry about him murdering us on the way back to Nalhu."

"I can't say how he'd react about learning she's dead, though. He specifically turned her over to the Zolan in order to make sure she wasn't executed."

"I wasn't planning on telling him before. That hasn't changed."

Vlasa fidgeted for a moment, "Which leads me to the other problem. He doesn't want to go back to his clan. He was on Lolia trying to escape from them."

Ariana banged her head against the back of her chair, "Why does everyone looking to escape their old life somehow find their way onto my ship?"

"Isn't that why you bought *Seraph* in the first place? Karma perhaps?" Vlasa asked.

"Very funny. But it really doesn't matter. We were hired to break him out of prison. Which we did. Our next stop is Nalhu. He's getting off there, but I don't care what he does with himself after that. That's between him and the other Manta."

"So, you would not consider taking him on?" Vlasa asked with a slump of his shoulders.

"To do what? We already have a larger crew than strictly necessary. Especially for the amount of actual work we're paid to do."

"He's a competent technician."

"So are you. And Squee. We're well covered in that area. Would I object to having a skilled Manta fighter on board to help protect us? No, but I can't really justify the cost. And I certainly am not interested in making an enemy of his clan," Ariana said.

"But if he is allowed to leave amicably, as a paying passenger?" Vlasa pressed.

Ariana let out a heavy sigh. She hated turning people away, especially paying people. But every interaction with Manta in the past week had only led her to more trouble. Vlasa stood there, an eager expression on his face.

"Why do you care so much? Don't tell me this is some kind of prison bonding thing?"

"No. Well, maybe," Vlasa fumbled. "I just know we were ready to write him off as a lunatic killer because he was a Manta."

"And because he had a criminal record for doing exactly that," Ariana interrupted.

"Which turned out to be only half the story," Vlasa countered. "And I also remember at the end of the AI War, all my people, myself included, were treated the same way because of our connection to the creation of the AI. No one would give me a chance back then. I just don't like the idea of the same thing happening to Gremoosh."

Ariana's reply was cut off by an alarm coming from the weapons console. She swiveled her seat and read the display. "We'll have to figure this out later. Right now, we have two Rokma patrol ships on an intercept course."

32- Olivia

The familiar feel of *Seraph*'s controls filled Olivia with comfort. After the harrowing ordeal of driving in a mere two dimensions, it would be good returning to an environment that acknowledged all three. Now she had control.

"How long until we're clear to jump?" Ariana asked.

"Twenty minutes, current speed and course. That lead patrol ship will intercept us in twelve," Olivia answered. "That second one cuts off our best escape vectors. I can barrel through, try to orbit the planet or head for the moon."

"If we go for orbit, they'll have plenty of time to launch more ships to intercept. Heading for the moon will just give them more time to intercept. I have no doubt they can exceed our max acceleration. You're going to have to barrel through. Squee, get those shields ready. We're going to need them."

Despite the danger, Ariana's decision made Olivia smile. She didn't relish getting into an hours long chase and being attacked from behind. Besides, since the repairs and upgrades to *Seraph* had been completed, she hadn't had the chance to try them out against an opponent.

"Hold on to your lunch," Olivia said just before she opened the engines up to maximum acceleration. *Seraph* leaped forward at an ever-increasing speed. The distance to the lead patrol ship dropped precipitously. The time to intercept fell to a single digit.

"Captain, if we continue to defy orders to stand down, we will be branded as criminals." Squee said with clear hesitation.

"You just broke me out of prison, Squee. We are criminals," Vlasa said, joining the ship's network again.

"Yes, but right now, no one really knows that. We had justification to defy the order to return to port. It will result in a fine should we ever return here. But if we

defy patrol ships, we'll become fugitives. We won't be able to visit any PUG world safely."

"Either way, I don't plan on coming back here. We do most of our work from the Hub anyway," Ariana said.

"We could submit to an inspection," Squee suggested

"That didn't work out so well last time," Vlasa retorted.

"True. But I do not think we would prevail in a confrontation with my people."

"Don't worry about it, Squee. I've been itching to try out *Seraph*'s upgrades against an opponent. She can really move now," Olivia said.

"I'm not sure this is the best time to test things out. I am not sure the gods are on our side."

"Nah, it's the perfect time. Unlike LFD or those drone ships, your people aren't going to be trying to kill us, just disable. No pressure," Olivia said with a grin. "Coming into weapons range in one minute."

"I do not think you are adequately concerned with the long-term continuation of your existence," Mesu said.

"Shut up, Mesu."

The drones reply was cut off by an incoming signal from the Rokma patrol ships, *"Transport ship* Seraph, *cut your engines and prepare to be boarded."*

"Not this time," Olivia said quietly to herself.

The distance between the two ships continued to close. As soon they crossed into the optimal weapons range, the Rokma ship let out a barrage of ion pulses. Olivia had already reoriented the ship and used the main engines to alter their approach vector. The first flurry of ion pulses passed through the space they had recently occupied.

Another barrage followed. Olivia rotated the ship with the RCS thrusters, juking between the pulses. The ship responded quickly to her commands and she felt an uncontrollable smile spread across her face. Within seconds, the two ships had passed each other, and she felt disappointed the exchange ended so quickly.

She would get another chance soon. The Rokma ship had started slowing and then accelerating on the same course as *Seraph* a few minutes ago. With their superior acceleration, it would not be long before they matched speed and caught up with them again.

To her astonishment, the ship did not continue to accelerate after them, instead turning and accelerating back toward the planet. Olivia watched the change in confusion, "What are they doing? Did they just decide to let us go?"

"That is not like my people," Squee said.

"It looks like they are. Both ships are converging on another group of ships behind us," Ariana's voice betrayed the same confusion.

Olivia watched the sensor display in fascination. The two Rokma ships converged on the group of ships. To her surprise, they both unleashed a barrage of missiles toward the ships.

"They didn't even try ion weapons. They're just slaughtering those ships!" Olivia gasped.

"I do not understand. Rokma do not murder civilians," Squee said quietly.

"The AI prisoners. They must be on those ships," Vlasa said slowly and with increasing confidence.

"They're murdering AI?" Mesu said, his normal cheeriness vanishing.

"Destroyed. No warning," Olivia said, feeling cold wrap around her.

Silence filled the network for a minute. Olivia just stared at the sensor display. That could have been *Seraph*. She knew how hard it was to evade missiles. Especially from two separate sources.

"We're outside the gravity well, Olivia," Ariana said calmly. *"Jump us away. There's nothing more we can do here."*

33- Vlasa

Vlasa stared at the component in his hand. He'd held it for the past several minutes, unable to focus on the task of repairing it. His mind continually flashed to the faces of the people and AI he had spent the last several days locked in a prison with.

A *click-click-click* on the deck finally broke through his distraction. Vlasa looked up to see Gremoosh entering the engineering bay. Despite moving on four limbs, the Manta advanced slowly, his head slumped.

Vlasa forced a smile to his face, "Ah, Gremoosh. Good news. I talked to the captain. If you truly don't want to return to Nalhu, and it won't result in your clan coming after us, you may be able to join *Seraph*."

Gremoosh glanced up at Vlasa, and spoke quietly, "Did I get all of those people killed?"

Taken aback by the emotion laden in Gremoosh's question, Vlasa froze. Dealing with people's personal issues was not something he enjoyed. Unfortunately, since *Seraph* had a crew he had been unable to avoid it.

"I'm sorry?" Vlasa said, and then cringed at his own comment.

"The people we were imprisoned with. They were all slaughtered. Had I not insisted on freeing them, they would all still be alive?"

Vlasa cringed internally again. He had known exactly what Gremoosh had been referring too. "We don't know that they are all dead. We only saw one ship destroyed before we jumped away."

"Don't coddle me. I saw the sensor feed," Gremoosh growled. "They were in civilian ships, being barraged by missiles. No one survived that."

"We've survived a few missiles," Vlasa whispered and then louder, "But not everyone could have been on those ships. None of them were any bigger than

Seraph and we could only accommodate about a dozen people. There were hundreds in the prison."

"You forget that most of the prison population were AI. They don't tax the environmental system. How many could you fit aboard? Fifty? Sixty?"

"Hmmm, if we assume the average AI is about Mesu's size and takes up roughly 7.25 cubic meters, and a perfect balance between models that can hover and are tracked or bipedal, we could fit approximately sixty-six in the cargo bay."

"Did you calculate defined cargo space or actual floor space?"

"Defined cargo space. It was just an estimate."

"You could get more in the area around the teleporter and into the corridors."

"True, but you'd never get a perfect distribution. There weren't that many with a hover capability."

"True," Gremoosh conceded.

"Which means there probably weren't more than thirty on each of those transports. That means at least half of the prisoners are still alive," Vlasa said, feeling relieved. Once again, saved by math.

"Those will be hunted down on the surface then," Gremoosh said, bowing his head again. "Why did I make that demand of you? I just wanted to help."

Vlasa sighed. He finally put down the component he had been holding for far too long and stood to move beside Gremoosh, "You were trying to do the right thing. The Rokma were imprisoning people out of fear. People who hadn't done anything wrong. And they killed them out of fear. Those deaths are on them. Not you."

Gremoosh stood motionless for a long time. Then he looked up and clicked mandibles, "You're right. It was the Rokma who killed all those people. It wasn't me."

Vlasa smiled, "You can't blame yourself for their deaths."

"The Rokma killed them."

"Yes, not you."

"And the Rokma should pay for it."

"Yes... wait, what?"

Gremoosh rose up to his full height and started pacing, "The Rokma are unjust. They imprison innocent people. Machine and biological alike. They must be punished for that."

"That's not exactly what I meant," Vlasa stammered.

Waving a hand, Gremoosh continued, "Oh, do not worry. I am not like my sister. Or the Rokma. I am not planning to go on a campaign of righteous fury and murder all the Rokma."

Vlasa let out a heavy breath, "Good. Not all Rokma are to blame."

"No, of course not. Some, such as the two onboard *Seraph*, are clearly not corrupted. The innocent won't suffer for the crimes of others. That was the mistake my sister made."

"Mistake?"

"Yes, in our fight for the liberation of Nalhu, she killed indiscriminately. She enslaved people. But we won't do that. And we will no longer contain our fight to just Nalhu. We have to unite against the murderous Rokma."

"We?" Vlasa swallowed nervously.

"Yes, it may just be us at first. But I think I can convince my clan in time. And then others. But for now, *Seraph* will lead the fight," Gremoosh held four triumphant fists into the air.

"Umm..." Vlasa stumbled. A beep in his ear cut off his response.

Mesu's cheery voice echoed, *"Vlasa, report to sickbay. I need to extract your organs."*

34- Serene

"You want to what?" Serene growled, staring narrowed eyes at Mesu.

"Replace your damaged liver with the filtration unit installed inside Vlasa," Mesu explained again with his usual cheery tone.

"I am not having robot parts installed inside of me."

Vlasa, who had just appeared in the door to sickbay at the same time as Ariana, glanced between her and Mesu, "I kind of need that to survive, Mesu."

"Nonsense," Mesu said, waving an appendage. "You still have a perfectly functional liver inside of you."

"She can have that then."

"Wow. You really are cavalier with your body parts," Serene said shaking her head at Vlasa. Her gaze drifted over the obvious cybernetic components Vlasa had installed, and she shook her head. When she tried to close her eyes, she suddenly became aware of how her own cybernetic implant interpreted the signal and cut off sight but did not actually close her eyelids. This sent a shudder down her spine.

"Machines are much easier to fix," Vlasa said.

"That is very true," Mesu chirped.

"I don't want another machine inside of me," Serene said with stern emphasis.

"Without a replacement, your liver will fail completely in a day or two. I can keep you alive for a few hours, maybe a day beyond that, but it won't be pleasant," Mesu said.

"Isn't there some medicine you can give me to fix it? Or regrow it. Livers do that."

"There is a wonderful drug that would stimulate the growth and allow you to make a recovery," Mesu said happily.

"Then give me that."

"We do not have any. The captain wouldn't let me buy any."

Ariana frowned and interjected, "Was it one of those drugs that cost as much per dose as feeding the whole crew for a month?"

"Two months."

Serene fumed, "Whatever. Take me to a hospital. They'll have it."

"The closest hospital is on Lolia, which we obviously can't return too," Ariana answered. "Besides that, the next closest PUG or Echanic hospitals are a week away."

"You'll be very dead by then," Mesu hummed.

Serene wanted to say something nasty back at the stupid robot, but a sharp pain across her abdomen forced her to lean back in the bed. Instead, she complained quietly through gritted teeth, "Ungrateful machines. I got injured trying to break you two out of prison."

"I offered you my real liver," Vlasa said pointedly.

"It has atrophied over the years of disuse. A transplant will likely fail," Mesu interjected.

"But you said I would be fine with it if you removed my filter implant."

"You will be. It will be able to regrow itself back to full strength with little ill-effect. But that's if it stays where it is. Removing it will kill it. Such fragile biology."

Shaking her head slowly, Serene wanted to scream, "So my choice is another machine, a transplant that will likely fail or death? What about Nalhu? They are bound to have hospitals."

"The settlement we visited didn't exactly look well off, remember?" Ariana pointed out.

"Yeah, but that was a home to a crazy Manta criminal clan. There are real cities on the planet."

"Nalhu never formed a central government and joined PUG, so they're not obliged to provide care. They may not even be able to treat Echanics," Ariana commented.

"What about the Manta? They owe us for saving their guy," Serene said, starting to feel desperate. "We even went above and beyond in freeing everyone else. That's got to be worth a bonus."

"Vlasa," Ariana said turning, "You've spent the most time with Gremoosh, what do you think?"

"Umm." Vlasa began, "He's feeling a little bitter about the death of all those people we freed and has gotten some interesting notions of joining forces and exacting retribution on the Rokma. I'm not sure we want to owe him a debt."

"We won't owe him a debt. He owes us a debt," Serene insisted. "He's apparently got some queasiness about death. Use that. He doesn't want to cause any more deaths. Save my life then. Or bring him in here and I'll do it. Hospital beds make great persuasion tools."

Ariana looked between Serene and Vlasa before turning to Mesu again, "Can she make it till we get back to Nalhu?"

"Probably. She could expire at any time but that is not new. Any of you could. Acquiring the drug would be the best medical outcome. Anytime I need to cut into you meatbags it increases the likelihood of death by an astronomical figure," Mesu said and rolled over toward a cabinet. "I will keep her alive and... ack! I cannot access my drama and performance upgrade card!"

"Oh, that was destroyed when the Rokma shot you," Vlasa said dismissively.

"Without my upgrade, I cannot sing soothing songs. Her chances of expiring will go up by three percent. Plus, I remember needing to sing some archaic ritual for Vlasa as part of his peoples outdated traditions. I will be unable to do that."

"That was not necessary. Besides, she's not even from the Nerpal region," Vlasa said.

"Actually, I am," Serene said, a smile spread across her lips. Vlasa squinted his eyes at her and giddiness over shadowed her pain. "And I would hate to expire without the Death Chant sending my soul to the afterlife. You refused to save my life with an organ transplant and now you won't even sing for my very soul?"

"You're the one who refused to even consider the filter transplant."

Serene just shrugged. Vlasa threw up his hands and stormed toward the door, "I'm going to beg the crazy Manta to save your life. That sounds safer."

35- Ariana

Seraph's cargo bay door opened once again onto the tropical paradise of Nalhu. Ariana welcomed the breeze. She had spent most of her adulthood aboard spaceships of one type or another. These moments of exposure to natural air were few and far between. Especially the ones with pleasant weather.

"Come! Let's get this over with," Gremoosh said, waving his arm and leading the group down the ramp. His two Manta companions followed him into the sand. Ariana and Vlasa followed at a slower pace. Once she thought the Manta were far enough ahead, she leaned in close to Vlasa.

"I thought you said he didn't want to return to his people?"

"He doesn't. Or at least he didn't," Vlasa said. "But the Manta onboard only knew Herish was captured, not that we had anything to do with it. Or that she had died. He was genuinely concerned about Serene and agreed to try to help get her the drugs."

"Let's hope his people are as concerned."

They walked into the village, but this time received a far less hostile reaction. No one veered away at the sight of them or cast them a dirty look. Not having the Rokma with them this time, and being escorted by three Manta, made a significant difference.

Once inside the clan's headquarters, they were shown to the meeting room. The clan leader, Rektri, greeted them with wide open arms. "Gremoosh! You have returned!"

The two Manta rubbed their antennae together and spoke softly. Ariana waited beside Vlasa near the entrance. No one made any hostile move toward them and she started to relax. The clan didn't appear ready to turn on them.

"Ah, Captain, thank you for returning our lost brother to us. Your reward is being brought to us as we speak," Rektri said finally addressing them.

"Thank you," Ariana said, giving a respectful nod. "There was one matter we wished to discuss with you. One of our crew was injured during the mission and is in need of medical care."

"I am afraid none of our members are well versed in treating non-Manta."

"They have a doctor," Gremoosh interjected. "They only lack a particular drug. It is an urgent need. They went to great lengths to secure my freedom. Their crewmember should not die for it."

Rektri glanced between Gremoosh and Ariana for a moment. After a tense moment he nodded, "No, no they should not. Give us the information and we will see what we can do."

Ariana passed on what Mesu had asked for and one of the other Manta scurried from the room to investigate it. As she left, a large door on their left opened and two Manta wheeled in a large rectangular container. They stood the container up, revealing a transparent portion on the top. Inside she saw the featureless body of a glowing Zolan.

"Shit," Ariana cursed just loud enough for Vlasa to hear.

Rektri swept an arm toward the Zolan in the container. "As promised. The holy grail of salvage, a living Zolan and the location of his disabled ship. With this you will be able to learn the secrets of the Zolan's advanced technology."

Ariana's eyebrow shot up, and she exchanged a glance with Vlasa. Her immediate response to seeing the Zolan had been it was a slave that Gerald wanted. But the mention of a Zolan ship changed everything.

"This ship is intact?" She asked cautiously.

"When last we saw it."

"I'm curious why you would trade away such a valuable find so easily."

Rektri grinned maliciously, "The life of our kin is worth a great amount. More than a non-Manta could understand."

"I feel there's something more you're not telling me. The shield technology from a Zolan ship would save a lot more of your people's lives than just one."

Gremoosh shifted his eyes downward and then back up to Rektri, "Tell them Rektri. Or I will."

"Very well," Rektri hissed. "The Zolan ship crashed on a planetoid orbiting a star with intense radiation. Anyone who boards the ship will be exposed to lethal doses of radiation. No drones can operate. The only ones who could access the ship are Rokma. Which your crew has in abundance."

"The other reason you only offered this prize to people with Rokma."

"I am a fair bargainer, Captain. I would not offer a prize that is beyond the reach of the recipient."

"Rektri..." Gremoosh said with a severe tone. To Ariana's astonishment, Rektri visibly flinched.

"Of course, you must be made aware that no non-Zolan has ever been able to get one of their shields to function. We have captured other ships before. The technology is quite beyond us. But, maybe you will have better luck persuading the ships sole survivor to help you than we ever could. Hence, its inclusion in the deal."

"I appreciate your candor," Ariana said, nodding to both Rektri and Gremoosh. "It is still a very valuable find."

The Manta next offered them a drink and Ariana sat down, sipping an overly sweet concoction. Gremoosh and Rektri continued to talk in their native language, both becoming very animated. As long as they remained focused on each other and kept her out of the discussion, she was happy to wait quietly. Fortunately, they did not have to wait long.

The Manta who had left to investigate the drug returned and spoke quietly to Rektri. Beside him, Gremoosh grew suddenly tense, his body stiffening. After a moment, he suddenly slumped down and then let out an ear-piercing sound. Rektri rested a hand on Gremoosh's back as the other Manta continued to spasm slightly.

Ariana glanced at Vlasa who shrugged helplessly. She gestured a hand toward the Manta. Vlasa sighed, but reluctantly said, "Is something wrong, Gremoosh?"

Rektri looked up, "A personal matter. For you, I have good news, Captain. We have a lead on a source of the drug on the planet. We should be able to acquire it for you in a day or two."

"That's good. Thank you," Ariana said, continuing to watch Gremoosh closely, "We'll get this Zolan back to our ship and await word from you."

Before Ariana could move toward the door, Gremoosh stood back up, "It is more than a personal matter. These are honorable people and understand the importance of protecting their family."

Rektri considered his response for a moment and then nodded. Gremoosh gave the twisted Manta version of a smile when he turned to Ariana and explained, "We have just learned that my sister died after escaping from Zolan custody. We will soon learn who was responsible. Then we will kill them."

36- Serene

S and made even a floating crate hard to push. Vlasa and Ariana struggled to find enough solid ground with their feet in order to move the crate the last few meters toward *Seraph*. The sight made Serene smile and she let herself enjoy watching it for a few moments before calling out to Squee and Latten. The two Rokma tromped down the ramp and took over.

Panting, Vlasa and Ariana trudged up the ramp. They both glanced toward her but wouldn't make eye contact. A cold dread mixed with the constant ache in Serene's abdomen and back. "I take it negotiations did not go well?"

"That depends on your definition of well," Ariana sighed.

"Obtaining the drugs to save my life qualifies as going well."

"They agreed to procure those. But there's a bit of a catch," Vlasa said, his gaze pointedly fixed on the crate the two Rokma pushed up the ramp.

"Such as?" Serene prodded. "I must agree to marry one of them? They get to eat my first-born child? It's an off brand that might make my ears turn blue?"

"It will take a few days," Vlasa said evasively. "A few days we may not have."

"Mesu seems to think I'll be okay for a few more days," Serene said. "See, I'm even walking around."

"Does he know that?" Ariana asked.

"I always say it's better to ask forgiveness than permission."

Vlasa looked at her thoughtfully and then glanced back down the open ramp. Her fellow Echanic looked uncomfortable. That told her something. He had never been particularly concerned with her well-being.

"But you said 'we' may not have a few days," Serene said, fixing Ariana with her gaze. "Something in the crate going to leak out and kill us in that time?"

"Not exactly," Ariana said. "Turns out the lighthouse is a Zolan."

"Clever," Serene said. "They do kind of glow, don't they? But I don't see why Gerald would want a Zolan. They don't make good slaves. They aren't very strong. No one wants to have sex with them."

"The Zolan comes with directions to a disabled ship."

"Ahh," Serene said with a nod. "That's what he's after. The coward would love an impenetrable shield to protect his sorry ass. So why is the Zolan in the crate?"

"I'm not really sure," Ariana said with a shrug. "Rektri didn't really elaborate."

"We going to open it now or once we're in the air? Which I assume will be soon."

Ariana turned away from the crate to look at Serene. "It will. We can't wait for the Manta to get the drugs. Turns out they are also waiting for information that will reveal we were involved in Herish's death."

"You mean how we killed her?" Serene said. "Yeah, I'm not keen on dying from organ failure. But it's preferable to becoming a Manta snack."

"We cannot trade your life for ours," Squee said, standing tall. "Latten and I can turn ourselves into the Manta. They would probably be satisfied with our deaths."

Beside him, Latten fixed Squee with an uncomfortable look. Apparently, honorable sacrifice was not a universal Rokma trait. Serene would have to remember that.

"No one is sacrificing themselves. Serene is still alive. We'll find another way of getting the drugs. Worst case, she can always get the transplant from Vlasa," Ariana said, holding a hand up to forestall Serene's next comment. "I know you don't want any more cybernetic parts. But I also know you're a survivor."

Serene frowned, but shrugged, "I'm a realist. How about you, Vlasa? Feel like getting inside of me?"

Turning to where Vlasa had been standing on the boarding ramp, Serene wiggled her eyebrows suggestively. Unfortunately, the effort went to waste as the engineer was not standing there looking uncomfortable and embarrassed. Looking around her, she couldn't find him anywhere.

"Where the hell did Vlasa go?"

The rest of the crew focused on stowing the cryochamber, ignoring Serene's question. She searched the cargo bay quickly with her eyes and then moved to the boarding ramp. She found Vlasa standing at the bottom, looking determinedly toward the Manta settlement. While she watched, he started walking away from the ship.

"You think the Manta is just going to forgive you because you think he's your friend?" Serene called after Vlasa.

Her shout brought him up short and Vlasa stopped. He didn't turn around though. She walked down the ramp, pressing her hand against a sharp pain in her abdomen. "I expected nobility from Squee but you're far too practical for that nonsense."

Vlasa tilted his head back over his shoulder toward her, "You misunderstand me. This is the most practical option."

"Oh really? Wouldn't that be letting Mesu do the surgery? That seems fairly practical."

"No, Squee will inevitably let his nobility convince him to try to save us. But that would only result in his death. I have the closest bond with Gremoosh. If anyone can convince him to let us go, it will be me."

"Because your powers of persuasion are legendary. You're doing a bang-up job convincing me to let you tell him."

Vlasa finally turned all the way around, "If we just depart without a word, when the Manta learn we were involved in Herish's death, they will have no doubt about its veracity. Then we'll have yet another enemy out there wanting us dead."

"So, what else is new?" Serene said, unable to suppress a laugh. "I've lost count of the number of people who want me dead."

"I haven't," Vlasa said firmly.

"Well, this is the perfect opportunity to become a bit more like me, living off real organs again, losing track of those that would have you dead," Serene said and then her voice grew fainter. "And I'll... I'll get to be a little bit more like you."

Vlasa gave her a curious look. She tried to deflect it with a goofy smile. The genuine concern evident in his real eye made her feel that he could read her emotions, despite her eyes being blocked from him. She looked away.

"Let's go tell Mesu he gets to cut up two biologicals. It will make his day."

37- Olivia

O livia engaged the FTL. In a flash, *Seraph* moved from the space near Nalhu to an empty expanse of space in a system light-years away. She surveyed the incoming sensor telemetry. To her relief, nothing more substantial than bits of space dust appeared.

Setting *Seraph* on a lazy course through the system, Olivia shut down the engines. Ariana hadn't decided where they were going next, so she couldn't begin calculating her next jump. That would depend on what the Zolan in hibernation decided to tell them.

Making her way to the cargo bay, Olivia passed by sickbay. Serene lay on the bed in the center of the small room, Vlasa on an extra cot nearby. Mesu was nowhere to be seen, so she decided to go inside. Vlasa breathed shallowly and had his real eye closed, apparently asleep. She stood there for a moment, unsure if she would be disturbing Serene or not.

"You just going to stare at me like a weirdo?" Serene said, answering the question for her.

"I just wanted to see how you were doing," Olivia said.

"I'm told I'll live. Though, naturally, I could expire at any moment," Serene answered, making her tone mimic Mesu's cheery voice.

"Naturally," Olivia replied with a smile.

"Recovering from surgery isn't exactly a pleasant experience," Serene said with a pained expression. "Especially since it keeps me in here while you all go and open that cryochamber."

"That interested in meeting a Zolan?"

"No. I don't think you should open it. Just turn it over to Gerald. Then we can get Noah back."

Olivia frowned, "You don't mean that."

"What if I do mean it?" Serene said forcefully. "If it's the only way to save Noah, I'm willing to sacrifice some random Zolan."

"You told me Noah set free a bunch of slaves. He knew the consequences of doing that. He wouldn't want us to enslave someone else to get him free. Assuming he's actually alive. He definitely wouldn't want us to do that when we don't even know for sure that he's alive."

"He's alive," Serene said, though her voice lacked much conviction. When Olivia raised a skeptical eyebrow in response, Serene persisted, "Remember, I told you Gerald has bad history with some Manta? There's a good chance those Manta and the group we just helped were the same people. If that's true, then Gerald needed someone, anyone, not associated with him to make this deal. He could just get us to do it for free."

"Maybe," Olivia said quietly. "But I hope he's not. Because the captain would never trade an innocent person for him."

Serene chuckled, "Don't be so sure about that. Ariana is not the bastion of moral certainty you seem to think. She'll do whatever it takes to save her crew. Noah's her crew. This Zolan isn't."

Not wanting to continue with this conversation, Olivia left sickbay without another word. In the cargo bay, she found Ariana, Squee, Latten, and Mesu standing around the Zolan's cryochamber. The chamber looked intact.

"Okay, let's open it up," Ariana said. Squee nodded and unlocked the control. A hissing sound filled the room followed by a jet of cold gas. The top of the chamber slid downward, exposing the Zolan inside. The Zolan had no definable shape in its present condition. The ones she had met before had appeared vastly alien, but at least looked like they were alive. This one just seemed to be a blob.

Several minutes passed and nothing happened. Latten broke the silence, "Is it alive?"

Mesu trundled up and ran his scanners over top of the Zolan. He spent far longer than he had ever spent when diagnosing any of them. When he spoke, there was a note of uncertainty to his cheery voice, "I believe so. Despite appearances, it is not just a blob. The creature does contain organs, of some type at least. There is a rhythmic motion and exchange of air, suggesting breathing. But I cannot even tell where its mouth is. It's fascinating."

Extending one of his appendages, Mesu poked the Zolan. After two attempts, the Zolan suddenly reacted. Shooting up into the air above the cryochamber, the Zolan hovered half a meter up before descending to just a few centimeters. Mesu backed up quickly.

The Zolan's body shifted, elongating upward to form a shape that vaguely resembled a humanoid. It formed arms and a 'head' though it still lacked any facial features. Ariana stepped forward in front of Mesu, her arms held to her sides.

"You are aboard my ship, *Seraph*. My name is Ariana Harkins. What's your name?"

"I am called Sapik." The Zolan spoke without making a mouth. The sound radiated outward in all directions from the Zolan. Olivia found it more akin to listening to music from an omnidirectional speaker than listening to someone talk. "How did I get here?"

"You had been...sleeping in this cryochamber. You're safe and among friends."

"What happened to my ship? Was I the only survivor?"

"We were hoping you could tell us what happened to your ship. You were the only survivor we know about." Ariana explained.

"I am a stellar plasma specialist conducting research on a science vessel. We were studying a most unusual stellar phenomenon. Something happened and the ship became bombarded with intense radiation. I was evacuated to an escape pod. Some Manta picked me up and stuck me in here."

Ariana's face cringed a little, "Yeah, the Manta, ah, gave you to us."

Sapik had no visible expressions, but Olivia felt the pregnant pause that followed. After a moment it said, "Traded me you mean. You are after the technology aboard my ship."

"Um, something like that. We didn't know the deal included you, just the location of an abandoned ship. We're not interested in trading sentient life-forms," Ariana explained hastily.

"I would be happy to assist you in retrieving what you wish from my ship. Rokma should be able to board it without succumbing to the radiation that killed my crew."

Sapik's sudden pronouncement threw everyone off guard. Ariana glanced around, exchanging confused looks with Squee and Olivia. She turned back, "That's very generous of you."

"Provided you return me to Zolan space afterward."

"Of course." Ariana said, "That was why we woke you up. To know where to take you."

Something about Ariana's tone fueled the sliver of doubt Serene had planted earlier. Olivia considered the captain carefully. She had doubted her once before and nearly died on a Rokma cruiser. Was this any different?

38- Squee

Squee held up the flimsy plastic suit, "This does not look like a good idea."

Before him, Vlasa shrugged, "We don't have any full Rokma size EV suits. The only thing that will fit are these emergency suits."

"It will be difficult to work in this. Near impossible," Squee said fingering the baggy arms of the suit and exchanging a skeptical look with Latten who held a similar suit.

"It will actually be impossible to work without it. Unless you just want to hold your breath until your lungs explode and your blood boils in the vacuum."

"We Rokma can actually survive in a vacuum for some time," Latten said absently.

Vlasa sighed, "Of course you can. Nothing else will kill a Rokma, why would the vacuum of space?"

Squee smiled, "I would not wish to test this theory though. It sounds even less of a pleasant experience than trying to work in this thing."

"Good, then quit complaining," Vlasa said with a frown. "I've uploaded the schematics Sapik drew to your handhelds. We're going to place you in the shield control hub if we can."

"Do we trust this Zolan?" Latten asked.

Squee shrugged, "He has no reason to lie. If he didn't want to help us, he wouldn't have volunteered."

"If he had refused, we could have forced him to talk. I am very persuasive in getting people to talk," Latten said with a satisfied smile.

The look reminded Squee how much help his fellow Rokma still needed in recovering from his time as a masochist's muscle. He sighed and decided not to make an issue of it now, "He does not know that. But he does not have anything to gain by lying to us. If this is a trap for us, the rest of the crew could kill him for his betrayal. Better to remain silent than risk that for no gain."

Latten shrugged in reply and Vlasa held up his hands in a gesture of whatever. Squee sighed and wasted no more time in slipping the baggy emergency EV suit on. It sagged all over his body until he connected the compressed air tank and pressurized it. As the suit inflated, it became harder and harder to move. By the time it reached a full atmosphere, he could barely move his arms and legs.

Beside him, Latten appeared to have a better time of it. Larger than Squee, Latten filled in his suit better, so there was less room for the air. Squee frowned through the transparent bubble helmet.

"I do not think I can walk."

"It will be easier in a vacuum," Vlasa answered unconvincingly.

"We've reach teleporter range," Olivia announced. *"The Zolan ship is on the planetoid's day side."*

"Hold here until we port them over," Ariana ordered. *"Then put us on the planetoid's dark side. I'd rather not stress the shields more than necessary. If you run into any trouble Squee, say something immediately and we'll move back into range. How long will that take, Olivia?"*

"One to two minutes."

Vlasa looked up at Squee and gave him a thumbs up, "Well, if you have trouble you'll get an answer to that theory about Rokma and a vacuum while you wait."

"Not funny."

Squee released the pressure in his suit slightly which allowed him to move more freely. He shuffled over to the teleporter chamber and climbed inside. Latten did the same. Once they were both ready, Vlasa triggered the teleportation.

In a flash, Squee found himself in a dark room. He turned on the flashlight hanging from his suit which revealed a room made of smooth green walls. He reached his hand out and touched them, but the material did not feel cold and hard like you'd expect from a typical metal bulkhead.

He turned to Latten beside him, "As expected, we have no atmosphere. But the planetoid's gravity does appear sufficient to walk around. Which is good. I

do not know what this ship is made out of. It certainly is not metallic. It feels...
weird."

Latten just shrugged without any apparent interest. He then pointed to a
large device that occupied the center of the room. Going all the way from the
floor to the ceiling, the device was roughly circular with three inset alcoves
equidistance around the bottom. Above the alcoves, three conduits stretched
out and disappeared into the ceiling.

"This must be the thing Sapik told us about," Squee said as he walked
carefully around the device. "It is indeed too big for a single port chamber. We
will need to disassemble it. Three pieces, here, here and here."

"You do not look like you can lift your arms above your head," Latten said
with a chuckle.

Squee lifted his arms, but the pressurized suit tightened before he got
them much above his head, "No, I cannot. You will need work on the exterior
emitters."

For the next few hours, Squee struggled to disassemble the shield generator.
His suit forced clumsy and slow movement which made the entire process
difficult. This difficulty was compounded by the fact that most of the
components looked like nothing he had ever seen before. He was forced to
jury-rig the necessary tools from his kit. The Zolan apparently did not believe in
the reasonably universal approach of using screws and bolts to connect things.

"How is it going for you, Latten?" Squee asked a few hours later, panting
heavily.

"I am done," Latten replied over the comm from outside the ship.

Squee blinked in surprise, "What? Really? How?"

"I just pulled, and they came right off."

"Pulled? How did you not break everything? I tried that," Squee asked,
concerned his non-mechanically minded friend had just broken everything.

*"No, up slightly and to the side. And then give it a little downward push once
it starts to move and they pop right out. Very easy."*

Squee looked down at the array of tools he had been forced to insert and
wiggle in the slight cracks between the components. He moved to the next
connection and applied the force the way Latten described. The component
popped right out from the floor.

"Did I do it wrong?" Latten asked, a slight bit of concern evident in his voice.

"No, no that's exactly how it needed to be done," Squee said. He moved on and managed to complete the same amount of work in the next ten minutes as he had accomplished in the previous two hours.

As he finished disassembling the device, he started putting the components into a crate *Seraph* had ported over. As he worked, he listened to the others back on the ship.

"We're moving back into teleporter range," Olivia said.

"I have two crates ready," Latten reported.

"Crates received. Captain and I are unloading them now," Vlasa said.

A reflection in Squee's bubble helmet provided his only warning before a sharp dagger swung down at him. Squee jerked to the side, falling more than dodging. The blade sliced through his suits left arm, venting air out into the room. He bounced slightly in the low gravity which moved him well clear of his attacker.

Across the room, wearing an armored EV suit, a Manta stood holding a vicious looking dagger. He recognized it as very similar to the one Herish had used to slice his arm. The Manta raced forward across the room before Squee could recover.

With difficulty, Squee got his legs underneath him and launched himself upward. He vaulted over top of the Manta before coming back down. As he did, the Manta tried to swing his dagger up, but Squee aimed his torn suit arm down. The venting atmosphere condensed on the Manta's faceplate, blinding him.

Landing with a thud back near the toolkit, Squee grabbed for the first thing he could find. He hefted the tool which felt satisfactorily heavy in his hand and swung as hard as he could. The tool impacted against the Manta's helmet shattering it and the Manta's skull underneath.

Panting, Squee slumped back to the floor. He lifted his arm with the tear and inspected it. To his dismay, he discovered droplets of blood drifting out of the tear along with his air. Looking closer, he found he had no new cut on his arm, but he had torn the stitch from the previous injury.

Desperately he tried to cover the breach with his other hand, and he shouted, "I've just been attacked by a Manta. What's going on? Where did it come from?"

He got only silence in reply.

39- Ariana

With a heavy sigh of relief, Ariana set the bulky container down on the deck. She took in a deep breath and looked across to Vlasa on the other side of the container, "We really should remind those Rokma we can't lift as much as them."

"It won't help that they're working in reduced gravity," Vlasa replied.

Ariana frowned at his apparent lack of exhaustion at their effort, "Perhaps you should do that. Reduce the gravity in the cargo bay."

"We've discussed this, Captain. *Seraph* does not have the capacity to have varying gravitational strengths across different parts of the ship. It's all or nothing."

"Yes, and you've also said you could build in that capacity. We just underwent a refit. Why wasn't that part of it?"

"Unlike everything else on the ship, the gravity field was working perfectly fine. The Corps of Engineers cadets were only tasked with rebuilding our damaged..."

The rest of Vlasa's sentence was cut off by the sudden flash of light. Two Manta ported in beside him. It took Ariana a moment to recognize one of them as Gremoosh and the other as Rektri.

"Olivia, evasive maneuvers, now, now, now!" Ariana shouted and dove behind the container. When she hit the deck, she felt *Seraph* vibrate as Olivia engaged the engines.

Slower to react, Vlasa stood there and stared at the two Manta. Ariana glanced around the corner and saw Gremoosh holding his four hands out to his side. Rektri, however, was bringing a weapon up and aiming it at Vlasa.

Quicker than she could imagine, Gremoosh lashed out, knocking Rektri's weapon from his hand. It skittered across the deck. The two Manta glared at each other.

"No, we agreed to give them a warning before attacking. We owe them that much for my life," Gremoosh hissed.

"We came to avenge Herish and now they have already killed two more!" Rektri growled.

"What do you mean we've killed two more?" Ariana shouted.

"There should be two more of our kind here now," Rektri said, "Your order to move the ship resulted in their port missing."

Ariana forced out a derisive laugh, "That's what you get when you try to board someone's ship without permission."

"I told you not to send them. They are now casualties of war, Rektri. They died in combat. We do not avenge those." Gremoosh declared.

"Then what are you doing here?" Ariana shouted. As she talked, she glanced around the cargo bay. The crates containing Noah's old weapons lay on the other side of the bay, the Manta between her and them. The weapons locker was closer, only a short distance away, but she would have no cover reaching it. Wanting to keep them talking she added, "Herish died attacking my ship too."

Gremoosh hissed and then charged forward, grabbing Vlasa by the throat and lifting him into the air, "So you admit it! I thought the report must have been wrong. Surely, my friends would not have killed my sister."

Vlasa managed to choke out a reply despite Gremooh's grip on his throat, "She boarded our ship. Much as you just did. She died while attacking us. We had no other choice."

Ariana glanced up. She could not see Gremoosh well with Vlasa dangling in the air between them. Rektri still had one gun drawn but was no longer pointing it at anyone. His focus was on Gremoosh.

Surveying her situation, she noticed Rektri's other gun on the deck a short distance away from her. Closer than any other weapon it would also require her to expose herself. She needed a distraction.

"There is always an alternative to killing. That is why I convinced," Gremoosh hissed and lowered Vlasa slightly, "my clanmates to give me this opportunity to speak before we attacked. We seek vengeance only against the one who killed Herish. I have no qualms with the rest of you and consider you friends. Identify the culprit, and we can get past this ugliness."

In her ear, Ariana suddenly heard Squee calling. He apparently had been attacked by Manta as well. Either Gremoosh was lying about his intentions, or Rektri had ordered an all-out assault without informing him. That meant she couldn't trust this thing to get resolved with words.

Hearing Squee's voice, it suddenly struck her. The teleportation controls were within reach. She scrambled toward the controls, glanced at the display and jabbed her finger onto the recall button. With a flash, something appeared in the open teleport chamber.

Not waiting to see who, or what had been retrieved, Ariana dove for the abandoned gun. All eyes in the cargo bay had turned to look toward the chamber, and for a precious few seconds, no one looked at her. Raising the gun, Ariana struggled to fit her hand into the trigger. Human hands being shaped quite differently than Manta's. Nevertheless, she managed to get her finger on the trigger, sighted the gun on Rektri and fired.

The gun kicked sharply and popped out of her hand. Her first shot proved accurate though, and a bullet slammed into one of Rektri's arms. The Manta yelled and lost its grip on the weapon he held. While fumbling to draw another gun with one of his uninjured arms, Ariana picked the gun back up and fired again.

Ready for the kick this time, she didn't drop it but still missed. The blast did force Rektri to dive for cover instead of firing his weapon. Before she could fire again a massive blur cut across her line of sight. Latten smashed into Rektri, knocking the Manta down. He then bent over and picked Rektri up with one hand. The other reached for the Manta's throat.

Ariana redirected her aim to Gremoosh, who still held Vlasa and shouted toward Latten. She shouted, "Latten, stand down! Hold him but don't kill him!"

Oblivious or ignoring her, Latten continued to squeeze Rektri. Ariana cursed under her breath and shifted her aim from Gremoosh to the deck at Latten's feet, firing once, "Latten, that was an order!"

Forced to dance aside as a bullet ricocheted at his feet, Latten glanced back at her. The blank look on his face did not match the glint of fury she had seen in Squee's face before. Surprisingly, it disturbed her more. Fortunately, he did respond and let go of Rektri's throat.

Turning her gun back to Gremoosh, Ariana said, "You said there was always an alternative to killing. Give me one. Either you order your people to stand down or a lot more of your people die today."

"You are hopelessly out-numbered, Captain," Rektri coughed, struggling to breathe. "We have three ships out there."

Ariana narrowed her eyes, "I've seen Manta ships before. You guys are efficient killers but terrible starship designers. *Seraph* is more than a match for them."

Vlasa cleared his throat and said, "Gremoosh, I warn you the captain does not respond well when threatened."

Ariana noticed some hesitation in Gremoosh as he glanced between Vlasa, Rektri and her. Ariana decided to capitalize on that. She made a show of activating her ear comm, "Olivia, power up the tri-cannon and lock missiles onto the Manta ships. Stand by to fire."

"What? I can't fire the weapon from here," Olivia exclaimed.

Ignoring her, since none of the Manta could hear her, Ariana continued, "So what's it going to be Gremoosh? Do I give her the order to fire? Or do we end things here?"

Gremoosh continued to hesitate, but Rektri shouted, "All ships, fire on the transport. Disable her."

"Captain, we just fired on the Manta. Are you in the weapons bay?" Olivia asked.

"Don't worry kid, I got it," Serene said, speaking for the first time over the network. *"I couldn't let the captain look like a liar in front of the Manta. That's my job after all."*

Ariana smiled and gestured to Gremoosh with her gun, "The shootings already begun. But you can still stop it."

With quivering antennae, Gremoosh wailed, "You killed her. Why did you kill her?"

"She tried to kill us," Vlasa strained to get out. "She boarded our ship. She held Olivia by knifepoint and shot at the captain. You told me yourself she was unhinged. Helped enslave a whole colony. Murdered countless others. What choice did we have?"

"Killing is always a choice," Gremoosh said softly. His arm slackened, and Vlasa dropped to the deck. He coughed a little at the release of pressure around his throat. He looked up to Gremoosh still towering over him.

"Maybe," Vlasa admitted. "Maybe we could have subdued her without killing. But you know best what kind of fighter she was. Squee got shot and nearly had his chest cut open. If she could do that in a few seconds, to a Rokma, if the fight went on, how many more of us would have been hurt or killed before we could have subdued her?"

Gremoosh nodded as if coming to a decision, "All ships stand down. Vengeance has been satisfied."

Rektri hissed, still struggling in Latten's grip, "You are a traitor! You will be banished for this!"

Moving slowly, Gremoosh came to stand beside Latten and Rektri. He glanced up at the Rokma and very quietly said, "Put him down."

Latten glanced back to Ariana. She considered the request for a moment. In her ear, Olivia announced the Manta ships had pulled back and were not engaging. Rektri still had several weapons strapped to his body, but she had to give Gremoosh a chance to back up his words.

"Do it Latten. Vlasa, port Squee back," Ariana ordered, holding her weapon as ready as she could.

The big Rokma gave a shrug and unceremoniously dropped the Manta to the ground. Gremoosh reached a hand down to him which Rektri batted away. Nevertheless, he extended it again.

"Take my hand Rektri. Let us bring our clan into a new era. No more senseless killing. We have played lip service to the idea of fighting for liberty. But we have committed heinous crimes. That is why Herish had to go. It is unfortunate that she escaped and died in the process. She was my sister. But she was a monster."

Rektri's eyes widened, "You! You turned Herish in?!"

"I did," Gremoosh said with a nod. "I have seen, and failed to stop, too much pointless slaughter. Now the Rokma are preparing to unleash this onto a grander scale. I have seen them wipe out hundreds of innocent people. We must take up this fight in earnest. We must be better than them."

"No," Rektri spat. "I always knew you were really sof..."

His final words were cut off. In a flurry of movement, Gremoosh drew a dagger and severed Rektri's throat. Ariana stared in horror as the body slumped to the ground. No one moved for several seconds. Finally, Vlasa broke the silence.

"I thought you said there had been enough killing," Vlasa asked.

"There are some people who must die. Rektri had a chance to turn away from Herish's path of slaughter. Now, the clan can focus all its attention on the Rokma," Gremoosh smiled and patted Latten's arm. "But only the Rokma who deserve it. Join us. We could use honorable people such as yourselves."

Ariana exchanged a look with Vlasa. He shook his head slightly, unable to speak. Gripping her rifle tighter, Ariana chose her words carefully, "Thank you, Gremoosh, but we cannot. We took the job to rescue you not for the payment of the Zolan ship, but to save a friend of ours. We still have to free him."

Gremoosh nodded, "I understand. You fight the righteous fight in your own way. Someday our paths will cross again. Until then. Goodbye Vlasa."

In a flash, Gremoosh vanished. Ariana stared at the empty spot for a minute until, behind her, Vlasa said, "What the hell did we just unleash?"

40- Serene

"**N**ow I understand why you like me so much," Serene cooed, rubbing her hand across Vlasa's cheek. He froze in the process of scooping out the potatoes onto his plate, and his frown at her deepened. She let her smile widen at his grumpiness.

Serene relished the looks of amusement from the rest of the crew. They sat around the mess hall's table almost all together for the first time since their first visit to Nalhu. From beside him, Olivia pretended to not notice Vlasa's discomfort, but she couldn't hide the smile. Squee and Latten, taking up most of one side themselves, chuckled. Even though she still hurt from her injuries, and Noah was still in the hands of Gerald, Serene was in a good mood. They had only the journey back to the Hub in front of them.

"But I don't like you," Vlasa said flatly.

"Sure you do. Everyone loves me," Serene retorted. "But your fondness runs deeper. You have a thing for people like me."

"People like you? Liars and cheats?"

"No, psychotic killers. Noah, me, and now Gremoosh. All your best friends. All willing to kill someone at the drop of a hat. You're kind of bloodthirsty, you know?"

Vlasa let out a loud sigh and turned to Mesu, "Why did you let her out of sickbay? Shouldn't she still be recovering?"

Mesu held up his appendages in a shrug, "So should you. But no one listens to their doctor. I'm just trying to stave off, for as long as possible, the inevitable decay of biology. Why listen to me when I say you need to rest?"

"Couldn't you just drug her then? Until she's recovered?"

Serene smiled and wiggled her eyebrows above her eye implant, "Ohhh, drugging me. What do you plan to do to me while I'm unconscious?"

"What, no, I..." Vlasa stammered.

"Leave him alone Serene," Olivia said, not hiding her own amusement. She then gestured toward Sapik, who hovered across the table from her. "Besides, we have a guest. The captain would want us on our best behavior."

"Where is Ariana anyway?" Serene asked, watching the Zolan closely. The two Rokma sat beside him, her, it?

Olivia shrugged as she reached for a bowl on the table and ladled some contents onto her dish, "She wanted to have someone on watch at all times until we reached Emay."

Serene sat up suddenly, "Emay? Why aren't we headed back to the Hub?"

Olivia shrugged, "I just set the course the captain gives me."

"Our original destination was Emay to pick up a load of cargo. I expect the captain wishes to complete that before heading back," Vlasa said flatly.

Serene started to let out a sigh of relief but Squee brought her up short, "And it is the best location to find transport for Sapik back home. The captain promised to return him home if he helped us. He has fulfilled his end of the bargain."

"It's too bad, though, we can't take him home. I would have liked to see a Zolan planet," Olivia said.

Standing up from the table, Serene felt a stir of panic but she kept her voice level and thought of an excuse to leave. "And we should do exactly that. We can't just dump this poor Zolan onto Emay and hope she finds her way home."

"It is alright. Zolan trade ships visit Emay periodically. I will be able to find transport home from there," Sapik said. "And as my kind have no gender as your species define them, any pronoun will suffice."

"Very magnanimous of you. But I am still going to speak to Ariana about this," Serene said and left the mess.

She stalked down the corridor toward weapon control. A slight vibration in the deck plating behind her told her one of the Rokma had followed. Unexpectedly, she found Latten there instead of Squee.

"What do you want?" Serene said with a frown.

"I wish to help you convince the captain," Latten said.

"Right," Serene said, unconvinced. She continued on her way, ignoring Latten as best she could. Having a Rokma follow you was a hard thing to ignore, though.

Entering the weapon bay, Serene found Ariana leaning back in her chair, reading something on her handheld. The sensor display was open on the weapon consoles main screen, showing empty space around *Seraph*. Ariana turned and looked at her.

"Finished dinner already?" Ariana asked.

"We can't leave Sapik on Emay," Serene said without preamble. "Gerald is going to be expecting her along with the shield components."

Behind her, Latten said in a deep rumble, "I concur. Master Gerald will not be pleased."

"I couldn't care less if he's pleased. But I am surprised you do," Ariana said, turning her chair to face them completely.

"I don't care if he's happy. But I do care that he won't give us Noah if we don't deliver everything," Serene said. "This is not a gamble you want to make."

"The consequences for not obeying Master Gerald will be severe," Latten said.

"I'm not trading one life for another. Not again," Ariana said quietly. "We're going to get Noah back. The shield tech is the important part. Gerald won't throw that away."

"You don't know him. He most definitely will," Serene persisted.

"We should do what Master Gerald told us to do. Our lives hang in the balance," Latten added.

Ariana frowned and stood up. Compared to both Latten and herself, Ariana looked small. But Serene recognized the determined look on the captain's face. "The decision has been made. We are not turning anyone over to become a slave. Now, go finish your dinner. We're done here."

Serene wanted to argue more. She stared right back at Ariana, using her cybernetic eyes to full advantage. But Ariana never blinked. After several moments she realized she wasn't going to get anywhere this way.

Without another word, Serene spun around and left the weapons bay. Latten followed her. They walked a short distance down the corridor before either spoke. The big Rokma looked down at her with a frown.

"We cannot allow her to let the Zolan go," Latten said.

"And we won't," Serene agreed.

41- Vlasa

Vlasa felt the subtle shudder of *Seraph* coming to rest against the docking arm of the Emay orbital station. He set down the circuit board he had been testing and left engineering. He joined the rest of the crew, excluding Olivia and Ariana, who had all assembled outside the airlock. For a moment he considered telling them all off for crowding here, but could hear Serene belittling him for doing it too.

Fortunately, Ariana arrived and saved him the trouble, "What's with the crowd?"

"Cap, it's been weeks since we've been off the ship," Olivia said.

"We all got off on Lolia," Ariana pointed out.

"Prisons don't count," Olivia countered, crossing her arms across her chest in a pout.

Everyone stared expectantly at Ariana who just shook her head, "Once we're back at the Hub, we'll have gotten paid, we'll have Noah back and we can all relax. I promise a good rest for everyone. For now, Squee, you're coming with me. Sapik, we'll see if we can arrange some transport for you. The rest of you, get the cargo bay ready. I want to get underway as soon as possible and get this horror story over with."

Without waiting for any argument, and avoiding Serene in particular, Ariana departed with Squee in tow. Everyone stood there for a minute and Vlasa decided he had to step in, "Come on. Serene, Latten start clearing space in the cargo bay. Sapik, I would appreciate your help in understanding some things we retrieved from your ship."

The glowing form of Sapik followed him down the corridor, "I am not sure how much help I can be to you."

"You are a scientist correct?" Vlasa asked.

"I am. Of stellar plasma physics, not shield technology."

"No matter. The help I need is pretty rudimentary."

As he walked, Vlasa couldn't help glancing back at Sapik and how he floated, almost imperceptivity, above the deck. His politeness warred with his curiosity. Asking a species how they did something, which to them would be a basic biological function, felt like the height of rudeness. He could picture Noah asking though, and then pointing out he would never have another opportunity.

With a determined breath, Vlasa asked, "I apologize in advance, but I am very curious how you do that."

"Do what?"

"Hover off the ground."

"Oh," Sapik said. There was a brief pause where his body vibrated slightly and then said, "It is simply a minor reversal of the graviton field pulling me toward the deck."

"Yes, but how?"

"Again, I study stars, not biology."

Vlasa nodded, still itching with curiosity, "Can you do that on a planet? Or does it only work in artificial gravity fields?"

"It works everywhere I have been."

"Has your species always been able to hover like that?" Vlasa asked with fascination.

"Probably not. I could move across the ground in much the same way a Slu does if I had to, so I expect our distant ancestors moved that way. But it is incredibly uncomfortable. Our bodies are not as rugged as Slu. On anything other than a smooth surface, I would receive many cuts, bruises, and scrapes. Fortunately, I don't have too."

The pair entered the cargo bay and Vlasa decided to not press any further. He could imagine how he would feel if someone asked him why he had so many cybernetic parts. It was not a practice he liked explaining to non-Echanic.

Moving over to one of the containers, Vlasa opened it and withdrew a bulky device. He held it out to Sapik. The Zolan extended a part of his bulbous body that coalesced into the form of a hand and accepted the device.

"Best I can figure, this is an interface device for the shield controls. But for the life of me, I can't figure out how it's powered. There's no internal power source, and none of the connections look like anything I would want to run a current through."

Sapik held the device curiously for a moment and then turned it back to Vlasa, "It appears to be working just fine. Well, it's not connected to anything, so it doesn't do anything, but it powered on just fine."

Vlasa blinked in surprise. The screen on the device gave off a faint glow. Vlasa couldn't read Zolan, but he could interpret the screen well enough to read it as an error message. He took the device back from Sapik and touched the interface controls, scrolling through the screens.

"What did you do?"

"Activated it."

"How? Is there an on switch I missed?"

"What's an on-switch?"

Vlasa cocked his head and looked sideways at Sapik, "Your computers or devices don't have switches to activate them?"

"No, we just activate things when we want to use them."

"Some kind of DNA encoding?"

"Again, not a computer scientist. Or engineer. I can use a computer, but I couldn't tell you how it works," Sapik answered patiently.

Before Vlasa could come up with another question, a grunt behind him caused him to turn around. Latten towered above him. The Rokma looked down at him, making his desire obvious. Vlasa stepped away from the container and Latten lifted it up, waddling under the awkward shape of it as he moved it toward a corner of the bay.

Once Latten had put the container down, he moved on to another one. Vlasa led Sapik back over to the open container. He put the interface device back in the crate and began shifting around several other components. Finally, he extracted what he was looking for.

"Do you know anything about this? Based on the wiring, this comes exactly in the place I would expect a power transformer to be. But it looks like no transformer I've ever seen."

"That's just an interface cap," Sapik said dismissively.

"Interface cap? From the controls on the last piece, it looks like you interface with your computers in a relatively similar manner to us. Do you also have a direct brain to tech interfaces too?"

"No, that's just for powering things."

"Powering..." Vlasa started. An idea began to occur to him. He glanced quickly at the first device. It had shut down some time since he had put it down.

The ships comm network in Vlasa's ear came to life and Ariana's voice distracted him, *"Vlasa, let Sapik know she's in luck. There is a trade ship headed toward Zolan space soon. I'm going to talk to the captain as soon as I finish with this paperwork for the cargo. Squee's on his way back with the first load."*

"Excellent news, Captain. I will inform him."

Vlasa started to turn back to Sapik when his body began to twitch. He lost control of his cybernetic limbs. Twisting his neck, he saw Serene and Latten standing nearby, watching him. Then the world went black.

42- Serene

Serene stared helplessly down at the crumbled forms of Vlasa and Sapik. Their bodies twitched slightly from the ion pulse grenade Latten had tossed at their feet. Vlasa's face still bore the betrayed expression he had cast her way just before passing out.

"It was a shame to waste such a useful weapon on these two. But I couldn't risk the Zolan getting hurt," Latten said. He turned his massive form to look directly at her. "I only had one so you'll have to subdue the pilot normally. Try not to kill her. I am not a good pilot."

"Umm..." Serene said.

Latten walked past her toward the exit, apparently paying her no more attention. Her mind raced as she tried to sort out what had just happened. As her eyes darted around the room, they came to settle on the crates with Noah's heavy guns, buried under stacks of food.

"Where will you be?" Serene asked

"At the airlock. Squee might return shortly. Unless you think you can handle him."

"No, we'll go with your plan. Fighting Rokma is something I try to avoid."

Latten looked back at her with a menacing grin, "Master Gerald said you were smart."

As soon as Latten disappeared through the hatch, Serene dashed over to the food crates. She tried to lift the top one but only succeeded in moving it slightly. She considered shoving it off the top, but knew that would make a tremendous amount of noise. To do this quietly, she would need help.

Leaving the cargo bay from another exit, Serene tapped her handheld and requested a private channel with Ariana. She got no reply and glanced down at the screen. Her device had no connection with *Seraph*'s internal network.

When she tried to reconnect, she couldn't even find the network. Latten must have already disabled it. Switching to Emay's network, she wrote a quick message even though she knew it would be some time before anyone received it.

Quickening her pace, Serene headed up the stairs for the flight deck. She almost collided with Olivia at the top. The girl had her head down, staring at her own handheld. At the near miss, Olivia looked up, blinking.

"Did you lose connection to the ship's network too?" Olivia asked.

"Yes, Latten disabled it."

"Why?"

"Because he's taking over the ship."

A long pause followed while Olivia stared at her, a confused expression on her face. Serene let the girl process that for as long as she could stand. After a few seconds, she grabbed Olivia's arm and hauled her back down the stairs.

"Latten's taking over the ship?" Olivia finally asked as they neared the cargo bay.

"He's trying. And he thinks I'm helping him."

Olivia stumbled and jerked her arm out of Serene's grip, "Wait, how do I know you're not? You've already betrayed us once."

"Right. Which means I've done that. If I do it again, I'll become predictable. Can't have that."

Olivia narrowed her eyes but resumed walking with Serene. "So, what's the plan? With the network down we can't contact the captain."

"No, which means we're on our own. Latten is setting an ambush for Squee. We're going to get some of Noah's big guns. None of the regular ones will do us any good."

They entered the cargo bay and Serene pointed Olivia to the food crates. Together they lifted the top ones off and set them quietly on the deck. After they had done that, Serene eagerly hauled open the weapon crate. Behind her, Olivia let out a gasp.

"What happened to Vlasa?"

"Ion pulse grenade," Serene said absently. "They'll be okay in a few hours. They're designed for use against drones. Normally it will only stun a person for a short time. With all of Vlasa's cybernetics, he'll be out for a bit longer. No idea what it will do to a Zolan. They're kind of weird."

WAYNE BASTA

Lifting the big heavy rifle, Serene smiled. She had always wanted to use this one, but Noah had never let her. When they rescued him from Gerald, she would have to rub that in.

Opening the magazine, Serene looked for a clip to insert. She opened all the storage compartments in the case, but came up empty. Desperately, she looked again and then moved the empty crate to get into the next one. It too lacked any ammo magazines at all.

"I took the precaution of disposing of all ammo that could harm me some time ago."

Latten's voice echoed through the chamber. Serene twitched. She instinctively lifted the rifle in her hands but then let her arms slacken. It wouldn't be anything more than a club. Her body hadn't fully recovered from getting trampled by Rokma, she was in no condition to take one on hand to hand.

"I see Master Gerald's suspicion of you was correct. You really have gone soft," Latten continued.

"Soft? I don't consider wanting to arm myself going soft."

"Oh, not that. Siding with these people," Latten said with a gesture toward the unconscious forms of Vlasa and Sapik. "The old Serene wouldn't have let anything get in the way of what she wanted."

"I'm just taking precautions. Like you. I wouldn't want to be unarmed in case Squee got past you," Serene said with a smile.

"That argument would work a lot better if she wasn't standing there, helping you."

"Well, until you barged in, she didn't know anything was up. You need to try more tact," Serene said, standing up and edging away from the crate. The weapons locker was nearby. The low-caliber pistols inside wouldn't penetrate Latten's skin, but they would still hurt. Perhaps a lot of them would do enough damage to stop him.

"You are an excellent liar," Latten said with a smile. "Fortunately, so am I."

He held up an ion pulse grenade, "See, I had more than one. Wouldn't want our pilot getting hurt in a fight."

Almost casually, Latten pulled the pin and tossed the grenade across the cargo bay. Serene dove as far away as she could, but was too late. The grenade detonated, shorting out her cybernetic eyes and making her blind. A few seconds later, her mind slipped into unconsciousness.

43- Ariana

The vibration in the floor warned her he was coming, but Ariana was still startled by Squee's appearance. He stepped into the café and approached her table. She sat discussing getting Sapik a ride with the captain of the *Glad Tidings* across from her. Squee slammed his hands down on the table causing it to shutter and making both drinks spill.

She cocked an eyebrow at him, trying to appear unphased, "Something wrong Squee?"

"*Seraph* is gone."

Of all the things she could have envisioned Squee saying, that had not been one of them. She just stared blankly at the big Rokma for a long moment. She finally managed to get out, "Come again?"

"*Seraph* is gone. I went to the airlock to begin the cargo transfer, but the ship was not there. I was unable to reach anyone onboard or you via the ship's network."

Ariana pulled out her handheld and looked at the network settings. The device was still trying to connect to *Seraph*'s network, but it was marked as unavailable. She switched to the station's network and immediately got several notifications. One was from Squee trying to reach her and the other was from Serene.

"Serene says Latten has taken over the ship and disabled the crew," Ariana said reading.

"Latten? Impossible. This must be a trick of hers," Squee said leaning back.

"Maybe," Ariana conceded. "But I don't think that really matters much now."

"So, I take it you won't be needing a ride for your Zolan friend?" the freighter captain, Hannibal Grimes, asked. The heavy-set human failed to hide the disappointment from his face.

"Probably not," Ariana said dismissively.

"Well, do you need a ride then? It sounds like you might be short of some transport," Grimes suggested.

"I'll get back to you on that," Ariana said cutting the opportunistic captain off and gesturing Squee toward the door.

They raced through the corridors, Squee struggling to keep up. Behind her he panted, "Where are we going?"

"Warehouse district."

By the time she reached the cargo transfer station, Squee had been left behind. Ariana dashed to the operator station. A bored looking human stood beside a cargo drone. He scanned the crate held by the drone, glanced at his handheld and then gave a thumbs up to another human nearby. The drone pushed the crate onto the teleport chamber and then lumbered around to head back into the warehouse. The crate vanished in a flash.

"I need to check on a cargo transfer," Ariana said through difficult breaths.

"Talk to the administrator," The bored human said. He repeated the steps of scanning the next cargo brought by a drone without even glancing at her.

"This is urgent. I don't have time for that."

"Not my problem."

Ariana let out a frustrated growl. She glanced behind her and let out a breath as she saw Squee enter the area. She turned back and said, "Come on, it will only take a minute."

"I said scram."

"Fine, we'll do this the easy way. Squee, get that handheld."

Without pausing, Squee sauntered up to the human and plucked the handheld from his hands. The man looked up at the Rokma with a shocked expression. Squee smiled down at him with a look Ariana now knew he meant as friendly, but felt sure the human would not find very comforting.

Scrolling through the logs on the device, Ariana let out a heavy sigh, "The cargo hasn't been transferred yet."

Squee looked at her with a puzzled expression, "Surely they would not be waiting for the cargo. The ship is gone."

"Undocked," Ariana corrected. "But they could still receive cargo transfers."

"Why would they wait around for that?"

Ariana smiled, "Whoever took *Seraph*, whether it's Latten or Serene or pirates, they are criminals. They won't pass up a chance at easy loot."

Squee frowned, "If it is Serene, she is doing this to get Noah back. She won't care about the cargo."

"But if it is Serene, then they are definitely still there because she can't calculate an FTL jump."

"Can I have that back?" The cargo worker asked, his fear of Squee obviously abating.

Ariana turned the handheld around to face him, "We need to find these crates and get in them."

"Look, I don't want to get in the middle of whatever this is. I can't teleport people anywhere. I'll get fired," He gestured to the other person at the teleporter controls. "And my managers watching. He's probably already called for security."

Looking to the other person, Ariana strode purposely toward him. Squee followed behind. The worker shifted nervously and she could see him consider running. But he stood his ground and by the time she reached him, he had defiantly stuck his chin up into the air.

"You need to leave now," He stammered.

"Someone has stolen my ship. I need your help to get it back." She let that hang in the air for a second and then added, "Please."

Glancing between her and Squee behind her, the man looked torn between responses. Finally, he swallowed and asked, "What ship?"

"*Seraph*."

"Let me check."

Several minutes passed as the man worked at his terminal. Ariana considered the possibility that he had indeed summoned security and was just delaying them. But she ultimately didn't care. She hadn't technically threatened either of these men. While she didn't want to involve security in this, it might help things.

"I'm not getting any response from the ship."

"Nothing?"

The man shook his head, "Nothing. If they're still there, the teleporter is not accepting port requests nor is the ship accepting comm request."

"Then we won't do it sneakily," Squee said. "Port us directly onboard."

The man blinked, "I can't port you onto a ship without authorization. That's illegal."

"She is the ship's captain. She is giving you authorization."

"He couldn't do it even if he wanted too," Ariana said, her shoulders slumping with defeat. "Cargo teleporters are link only. They can only port directly to a teleport chamber. But that wouldn't even matter. The fact that we're not getting any response means they aren't waiting for the cargo."

"Then *Seraph* is truly gone?"

"And we've been left behind."

44- Olivia

Olivia snapped back to consciousness. She couldn't remember what had happened. Her last memory was fighting with the ship's network. Then something had happened. But what? Had she fallen asleep?

It started to dawn on her that in addition to not being able to remember anything, she had no idea where she was. The ceiling above her wasn't the flight deck or her quarters. But it was non-descript enough to be anywhere else on the ship. No, not anywhere. It was quite high up. That meant it had to be the cargo bay.

As she came to this conclusion, she also realized she couldn't move her head to verify. She tried to move her arms, legs, hands, anything. Nothing responded. Panic began to set in.

There must have been a terrible accident rendering her paralyzed. She couldn't remember because she also had brain damage. She would never walk again. Never fly a ship again.

The cascading feeling of panic flowed through her body. She felt her legs feel the need to move, but they wouldn't respond. But she could feel them. Couldn't she?

And if she had been paralyzed, why was she in the cargo bay and not in sickbay? Or in Emay station's hospital? Where was Mesu? Where was Ariana or Vlasa? Wait, she had seen Vlasa before. Not on the flight deck. But in the cargo bay and he had been unconscious.

Pieces of memories flashed back. Latten had tossed something at her. At her and Serene. They had been looking for something. But what?

Her view suddenly filled with the image of Latten, blocking her view of anything else. She felt the unconscious need to back away. But she was on the floor and had no place to go. Nor could she move. Instead she just stared up helplessly.

"This one is awake. But she doesn't seem to be able to move yet. Drone, fix that." Latten bellowed.

"I can't just 'fix that'. Biologicals do not have an on/off switch," Mesu's cheery voice responded. He appeared in Olivia's view to her right side.

"Don't be smart with me, drone. I need her functional."

"Well, why didn't you just say that? Of course. I'll just make her functional again, having no idea why she or the others collapsed and you refusing to take them to sickbay."

As Olivia watched, Latten leaned over her, grabbed one of Mesu's appendages and snapped it in half. Mesu had no facial expression, but Olivia felt the shock radiate out from him. Latten shoved the broken appendage directly into Mesu's head.

"I have seen you work with not all of these functional. Let this serve as a lesson. Do as I command or we'll see just how few you really need."

Mesu raised his head to its full height and looked Latten directly in the eye, "Break me all you want. It won't change anything. I'm not going to give her anything until I know what's wrong."

Olivia suddenly felt some sensation returning to her mouth, and she shouted, "Stop. I'm awake."

At least that was what she tried to say. Her mouth moved but not very well. She did make a sound and caught both Mesu and Latten's attention.

"It appears she is recovering without intervention," Mesu said.

"Slowly. It is taking too long," Latten growled.

"Then tell him what you did to me so he can help," Olivia stammered. This time she felt her words had come out mostly intact.

"What you did to her?" Mesu said, tilting his head.

"Ion pulse grenade," Latten said. "And it's not my last. They are far more effective against drones. Remember that."

Mesu extended an appendage and drew out a vial of something. As he did so, Latten backed away, well outside of Mesu's reach. The time Mesu had helped her and Ariana free *Seraph* from Serene and Gerald's goons flashed into Olivia's head. She suddenly found herself rooting for the drone.

"Your caution is unnecessary. I have no needles installed capable of puncturing your skin. This is for Olivia and should help her nerves stop shorting out so that she can regain control of them."

Mesu extended the syringe and pressed it to Olivia's arm. She felt the pressure but nothing else for a minute. Then everything began to ache as more and more sensation came back to her. Before long she was able to move her arms again and sit up.

"Good enough," Latten said. He bent down and threw Olivia over his shoulder. "Lead on drone. To the flight deck."

"But Vlasa, Serene and Sapik are in need of my care as well."

"We don't need them now. You can help me put the Zolan back in the cryochamber when we're done with this one. The half drones will be out for a while."

Latten walked behind Mesu up to the flight deck. Draped over his shoulder, Olivia felt every step on the stairs as she flopped against the Rokma's stony skin. Finally, he dropped her into the pilot's seat. By this time, she could move all of her limbs but didn't think her wobbly legs would have been able to support her.

"Now, why won't this thing engage the FTL?"

Olivia glanced down at the controls. The first thing she noticed was that they were underway and no longer docked with Emay station. They were still in the system, though, from what she could tell. The navigation computer had calculations entered for a course.

"First, you can't plot a jump directly from here to the Hub. It's too far," Olivia sneered.

"Then where must we go first?"

"Lots of places. You have to make multiple jumps."

"Where first?"

Olivia considered lying, but her head was still groggy. She couldn't recall any other systems within in their jump range. Reluctantly she said, "PX-18710 was going to be our first stop."

Latten pushed her back in her chair and leaned over to the navigation computer. He entered some information into the computer, changing their destination. When he finished, he looked down at her and growled.

"It still does not work."

"Well, you can't use the navigational computer to make a jump. It's just there to double check your math. You have to enter coordinates in manually," Olivia said gesturing to FTL controls.

"So, I must copy these number to this?"

"Only if you want to get fried jumping into the heart of PX-18710's star. You have to take into account where in the system you can safely exit. Where our present position is relative to all gravity wells. The time differences due to relativity...."

"All right, enough. Teach me to plot a course."

"No. I won't take us anywhere without captain's orders," She said stubbornly.

Towering over her, Latten leaned down, "You will."

"No. I won't."

"You will. Or you will watch your friends be dismembered a piece at a time," Latten said and turned to face Mesu. "I'll start with the drone so that there will be no one to put them back together again."

Despite her general distaste for drones, Latten's threat sent a chill down Olivia's spine. Her body suddenly felt frozen, and she briefly wondered if the paralysis had returned. Ignoring that fear, she tried to think. But she couldn't. She needed time.

Time! She could give herself time. She held her hands up, "All right! You win. I'll teach you. But it's not simple."

"You'll find I'm a quick study. Perform the first jump. Explain as you go."

"Okay, so at the basic level, an FTL jump...." Olivia began, racking her brain to develop the most over-complicated explanation on the theory behind FTL travel she had ever heard.

45- Ariana

Ariana paced. She knew it had technically only been twenty minutes since she had last spoken to the officer behind the window at Emay Station's security office. But it felt like at least two hours and perception determined reality. Yelling at the desk clerk wouldn't change things, though. They wouldn't be able to get *Seraph* back. So she paced.

Squee sat on two human size seats, staring blankly at the wall. The Rokma hadn't said a word since they had left the cargo center. In truth, Ariana appreciated that. She only wanted to yell at someone right now. Unfortunately, Javi's voice echoed in her head, "The captain gets whatever she wants. A good captain does whatever her crew needs."

Venting a heavy breath out, Ariana said to Squee, "We'll get the ship back."

Without looking at her, Squee said, "I have no doubt in this, Captain. You are tenacious."

Ariana frowned. This might require a more direct hand she thought before saying, "There's a good chance Serene's message was confused. Or a distraction. This wouldn't be the first time she's tried to steal *Seraph*."

Silence was her only answer for several moments. Eventually, Squee shook his head, "No, as much as I wish it were not so, I am forced to conclude that she is telling the truth. There is simply no way Serene could take over the ship without Latten's help. If there is a lie in her message, it is that she is not helping him. Not that he is involved."

With a heavy sigh he added, "And it is my fault."

"Nonsense. You're not responsible for his behavior," Ariana said with a dismissive wave of her hand.

Squee stared at the floor, "I saw the danger Latten might pose. When he revealed he had not embraced the blood fury in years. This corrupts our minds.

It is even more dangerous than embracing it too often. But I said nothing. I thought I could save him from this monstrous life he has been forced to live.

"I am Caleek. It is my responsibility to share the will of the gods with my people. It is their will that we temper our murderous urges. I thought I could do this by showing Latten a better way to live. To let him learn by example."

Ariana stopped pacing and shrugged, "In the end, that's all you really can do. You're right, you did screw up. You should have told me your concerns. If you had, I never would have left him on the ship without you there. But that's done now. It might not have made any difference. You can't control what people do. They're the only ones who can do that."

"I thought I could help him," Squee repeated meekly.

The quiet voice felt unnerving coming from such a large figure. It drove home to Ariana the depth of Squee's anguish. She had seen Squee upset before. Those times had been directed at the leadership of his people and more akin to righteous frustration. This was personal. He couldn't change the nature of his people. But he had thought he could change one Rokma.

"You did," Ariana said soothingly. "You showed him he had more options. Gerald messed him up. Maybe *Seraph*, while we're apparently in the midst of a crime spree, wasn't the best place for him to rehabilitate. But, in the end, the choice was his. We offered to leave him on Nalhu or Lolia. He was free from Gerald. But he chose to stay. He chose to continue serving him."

Squee looked up, "So you believe this is done at Gerald's order?"

"It can't be a coincidence he turned on us after I decided to let Sapik go. He and Serene came to me before, trying to convince me not to do it. Serene I understood. She is desperate to get Noah back. So much so, it may be blinding her good judgment. But Latten? At the time I thought she had enlisted his help in trying to convince me. Now, I think it might be the other way around."

"You are convinced Serene is indeed on our side?"

Ariana shrugged, "Who can never know with her. But regardless of her loyalty, if Latten were truly wishing to be free from Gerald, why would he want to convince me to return to him? Maybe he's just an asshole who decided to steal my ship. But I don't think so."

While Squee returned to his thoughts, Ariana look back at the desk clerk. The officer behind the window remained sitting where he had for the past half an hour. She frowned at the man who took no notice. Squee needed something to do, to distract him from his self-doubt.

"Squee, go back to the cantina where you found me. See if Captain Hannibal Grimes is still there," Ariana ordered.

Squee tilted his head unsure, but stood up immediately, "Aye, Captain." And then headed out the door.

While she waited, Ariana resumed her pacing. It didn't help, but at least she could do it in private now. The waiting area was completely empty, which only served to aggravate her annoyance at the slow response from the security department.

When they finally invited her back, the meeting went exactly as she expected it would. Whatever had happened on *Seraph* had happened on *Seraph*, which was outside station jurisdiction. They had reviewed security footage and found no evidence of outsiders boarding the ship. She would have to take this up with the PUG forces who oversaw interstellar crimes.

By the time her brief and exasperating meeting was over, Squee was waiting for her with Hannibal. The slightly dumpy looking human captain smiled brightly at her. Squee's position near the door made it abundantly clear that the man hadn't exactly been free to depart. Nevertheless, you wouldn't be able to tell that from his bearing.

"Captain Harkins. What a pleasure to see you again so soon," Grimes said with a smile.

"Captain Grimes, I wish I could say the same. Unfortunately, we're meeting under less than ideal circumstances," Ariana nodded politely.

"I assume this is about your missing ship?"

Ariana gave a brief smile of acknowledgment before continuing, "It is. A wayward crewmember has seen fit to hijack my ship. Station security is useless and if I wait for PUG help, *Seraph* will be scrapped or hidden away in some god-awful corner of the galaxy."

Hannibal gave a slight shrug, "I sympathize with you, Captain. I really do. But as you know, I was headed to Zolan space. Unless you think your crew are also headed in that direction..."

"No, they're headed for the Hub."

"That is quite in the opposite direction."

"Indeed."

"Then I fail to see how I could be of much help to you."

Ariana smiled, leaning in close, "I know you don't actually have any business in Zolan space. You wanted to use my passenger as an excuse to go there. Not many people are allowed in. Plus, now you're out of a contract. Let me offer you another one."

Hannibal pursed his lips a second. He considered Ariana and then said, "I'm listening."

"We were supposed to pick up a cargo here and take it to the Hub. That contract can be yours."

"I assume, in addition to the cargo, I'll also be taking on two passengers?"

Ariana nodded, "Get us to the Hub. As fast as you can. We'll take care of the rest."

46- Vlasa

When Vlasa finally regained his senses, he found himself bound to a chair in the mess hall. He ran a diagnostic on his cybernetics as best he could and found them all functional. It would require a computer link up to be certain, but he could see and move his arms and legs at least.

Surveying the room, he saw Serene similarly bound across the table from him. Mesu sat in a corner behind him. One of the drone's appendages had been snapped in half and his treads physically disabled. Mesu didn't show any signs of being functional, but none of the visual damage would prevent him from powering up.

"Welcome back to the world of the living," Serene said with a heavy sigh.

"Where is Olivia and Sapik?" Vlasa asked.

"I'm sure Sapik is back in the cryochamber. It's hard to lock something with no hands to a chair. As for Olivia, last I saw her, Latten threw an ion pulse grenade at us."

Vlasa frowned, "Funny, the last thing I remember is very similar. Except it was you and Latten throwing a grenade at me."

Serene gave a wicked smile, "What can I say? Everyone assumes I'm a bad guy. So did Latten. Unfortunately, I think this damn robo-organ you implanted in me is ruining me. Instead of rolling with it, I tried to do the right thing. And look where it got me."

Studying Serene carefully, Vlasa considered whether he believed her. He never could be certain of anything she said. But what benefit would she gain by turning against them and then pretending to be a prisoner too? He could see none, but that didn't mean a reason didn't exist.

"I am going to assume, based on your previous exploits, that you are capable of removing yourself from those restraints whenever you wish?" Vlasa asked, trying to flesh the situation out more.

"Probably," Serene replied with a shrug. "Haven't seen any reason to, though. We've made more than one jump. That means there's no space station to escape too. When Latten knocked me out, I had been trying to arm myself with Noah's heavy guns. But, as it turns out, the giant walking rock isn't as stupid as we thought. He took the time to dispose of all the Rokma piercing ammo some time ago."

Vlasa felt his shoulders slump, "So there is no weapon aboard that can hurt him?"

"Well, there is one. But I don't know where it is," Serene said. At Vlasa's raised eyebrow, she continued, "Remember that knife we took off the crazy Manta?"

Nodding, Vlasa said, "Yes, that sliced into Squee quite effectively."

"Yeah, but even if I did know where it was, I don't really want to get into a knife fight with a Rokma."

Gesturing with his head behind him, Vlasa said, "Mesu has it. Said it would be helpful if he ever needed to perform surgery on either of the Rokma."

"Now would be a great time for that."

"Any idea what Latten did to him? Is he disabled or just powered down?"

Serene shrugged again, "Haven't seen him move since I woke up. Thought maybe he was hit by a grenade too. Would knock him out more than us."

While Vlasa considered their options, several minutes of silence passed. To his surprise, Serene sat quietly while he thought. It proved more distracting than had she pestered him with inane banter.

The mess door opened, quelling his next thought. In stomped Latten with Olivia shoved in front of him. The big Rokma pushed Olivia into a chair and bound her to it. Then he walked into the kitchen, returning a moment later with ration packs. He dropped them onto the table before them.

"Eat. I will return shortly to allow you to relieve yourselves. Then," he said pointing to Vlasa, "You will take over for the girl in teaching me to use the FTL."

Without allowing any questions, Latten stomped back out. Vlasa switched his cybernetic eye to the radio spectrum. He watched Latten bend down outside the door and fiddle with something before walking down the corridor away from them. He switched it off, the double vision gave him a headache but resolved to check every few minutes for his return.

"He's gone," Vlasa said. "Olivia, are you okay?"

Across from him, Olivia shook her head groggily, "I've been awake for about eighteen hours, constantly calculating FTL jumps and trying to teach Latten how to do it."

"Where are we?"

"About a half dozen systems away from Emay, enroute for the Hub," Olivia answered. She slowly reached out as far as she could with her bound hands and pulled one of the ration packs toward her.

Vlasa blinked, "I was out for that long?"

"Guess you needed your beauty sleep," Serene quipped, also opening a ration pack.

"That means Latten has been awake that long as well." Vlasa observed. "And there is only one of him."

"Wouldn't know it from looking at him," Olivia replied. "To tell the truth, from our time on a Rokma cruiser, they had us working really long shifts. It was exhausting. But it didn't phase any of the Rokma crew. I don't know if they need sleep."

"Even if Rokma need less sleep than us, they do require sleep. Eventually. The longer he goes without it, the greater advantage we'll have."

Serene and Olivia just shrugged in reply, digging into their food. Vlasa decided that going hungry wouldn't help anyone, so he reached down for his own pack. It was difficult grabbing it from the table with the range of motion his arms had, but he finally managed to grab it. Bending over, he tore the pack with his teeth and started eating. The standard rations were comfortably bland and filled him with reassurance.

"He has you teaching him how to plot an FTL jump?" Vlasa asked after he finished his bar.

"Yeah, and he's a quick study. He's pretty much caught on. I tried to make it as confusing as possible. I also plotted the most inefficient jumps I could manage. So, we're not as far along as we could be. We're also going around the Unmar nebula. But truth be told, he doesn't actually need me to do it anymore. I bet he's just going to have you do one to verify I haven't been lying to him."

Vlasa nodded, "Then I must do it in a completely different way to further confuse him."

"I wouldn't," Serene added. When Vlasa turned to her, she continued, "He'll assume either you or Olivia is lying. Probably kill one of you."

"He did threaten that if I didn't do what he wanted. Even started by threatening Mesu so whatever damage he did would be permanent," Olivia said, glancing sideways toward the deactivated drone.

Seeing Mesu again gave Vlasa the beginnings of an idea. A smile crossed his face, "I've got a plan. Ariana is going to kill us when she finds out though."

"Better her than Latten," Serene said.

"First, we're going to need Mesu awake. He's going to be critical."

47- Olivia

Latten returned and after letting everyone relieve themselves, took Vlasa with him to the flight deck. As soon as the door to the mess hall closed, Serene popped her hand out of the restraints. Olivia felt her heart pounding as her own restraints were then removed. The two women glanced at each other and then the door, trying to gauge how long it would take for Latten to reach the flight deck.

Olivia looked back across the room to Mesu, still sitting idly in the corner. His treads remained disabled but his head rotated, tracking her. Oddly, she didn't feel any distress looking at him. Not like she once had. That didn't make what she was about to do any easier.

"You sure this is just an alarm wire and not anything that will, um, explode?" Olivia asked Serene staring at the door.

Serene shrugged, "Probably."

"That's not reassuring."

"Have I ever been reassuring?"

"Well..." Olivia said thinking. "No, not exactly."

"Good. Then everything is normal so there's nothing to worry about," Serene said with a wide smile. "Let's trigger this thing."

Both women stood there not moving. Olivia looked expectantly at Serene, waiting for her to open the door. Serene gestured forward with her hands. Olivia rolled her eyes and sighed. She stepped forward and triggered the door release. Nothing exploded and she let the tension in her shoulders slacken a bit.

"Better hurry. No explosion means it was an alarm. Rokma aren't super-fast, but this isn't a very big ship," Serene said right before limping down the corridor toward sickbay.

Olivia glanced back to Mesu. The drone waved an appendage at her, "I will remain here, looking broken and defeated. I remain vigilant and ready to violate every one of my primary protocols in order to cause terrible, terrible harm to my biological enemy."

"Umm, okay," Olivia said uncomfortably. She took a deep breath and dashed out of the door, headed in the opposite direction from Serene. She reached the main cross section of the ship. Up the stairs that led to the flight deck, she heard the thud of heavy Rokma feet. Wanting to be well out of sight, she ran as fast as she could toward her destination.

Fortunately, Serene was correct in that *Seraph* wasn't really that large. She reached the computer control room and slipped inside. Looking over the network control hub, she let out a sigh of relief. Latten had merely disabled the network rather than causing any permanent damage to it. It took her only a few seconds to reboot the network and grab the cables she would need for the next step.

While the network came back online, Olivia considered her options. She could make a dash down the main corridor to the opposite side of the ship and her destination in environmental controls. It was by far the fastest route, but would most likely expose her to Latten. Alternatively, she could go through the engineering or crew quarter sections, which would take more time and leave no choices on places to run.

Choosing safety over speed, Olivia turned left out of computer control and headed back toward engineering. She had to duck under conduits and squeeze through a few tight spaces. Despite the extensive yard work *Seraph* had received, she had never been intended to house two independent fusion reactors and space proved limited.

By the time she reached the engine room, her handheld gave a beep over her ear piece indicating it had reestablished connection to the ship's network. Working as she walked, she created a new password protected comm channel and invited Serene and Mesu to join. She couldn't risk inviting Vlasa in case Latten still had him.

"Testing," Olivia said quietly.

"I read you," Serene said.

"Greetings," Mesu chirped.

"Anyone have eyes on Latten?"

"He is staring at me at the moment. He seems quite irritated that you two have escaped. He is now making sure I am still powered down," Mesu said.

"Then be quiet," Olivia said urgently.

"I am being quiet. Unlike biologicals, I can communicate without shouting my thoughts to the world around me. See, he is now leaving the mess hall, convinced I am still disabled."

Olivia picked up her pace. If Latten was near the mess hall, her way into environmental controls would be clear. She popped open the hatch and stepped inside, closing it behind her. Safely in the room, she took a few deep breaths. Now the hard part would come.

Opening the control panel to the environmental computer, she took one end of the cable she had brought from computer control. She inserted the cable into a connection port and began unwinding the rest of the cable across the room. There, she looked up at another access panel on the ceiling.

Out of her reach, Olivia was forced to climb onto the CO_2 scrubber and stretch out her arms. Balancing precariously, she managed to pop open the panel. There, she stared up at one of the wireless repeaters strewn throughout the ship.

Olivia looked between the cable in her hand and the wireless repeater. Her heart beat faster and she felt her chest tighten. If she made this connection, any drone in range of the ship's network would be able to remotely take control of the ship's environmental system.

Her mind flashed to father. Suffocating aboard a transport ship after an AI hack vented the atmosphere. And here she was, about to create that very thing. Could she really trust Mesu?

"You ready, Olivia? I've just about gotten Sapik out of the cryochamber. It's time to start leading the beast around."

Taking a big breath and stretching out her hand, Olivia plugged the cable into the repeater. Nothing outwardly happened, but it felt to her like someone had kicked her in her stomach. Mesu, an AI drone, now had the capacity to vent the air anywhere on the ship and kill them all. She wanted nothing more than to reach out and yank the cable.

Forcing herself to take a deep breath, Olivia hopped down from on top of the CO_2 scrubber and said, "I'm on my way."

Continuing to defy all her instincts, Olivia dashed into the main cross corridor in the center of the ship. She moved as fast as she could, making no effort to conceal herself. She couldn't make as much noise as a Rokma when running but each step and each breath felt louder to her ears.

Reaching the cross section, she looked all around, hoping to still see Latten near the mess hall. Unfortunately, she saw no sign of him. She swiveled her head, concerned he might have headed toward computer control to turn off the network she had just rebooted. But again she saw no sign of him.

"I don't see him anywhere," She said exasperated.

"But I'm right here."

Olivia jerked around to see Latten standing in the central stair well, right by where she had just left. And right where she had been intending to lead him. Her heart sank at the sight of his malicious grin. He started to move toward her.

"Mesu! Seal the central stairs! Now!" Olivia shouted.

To her eminent relief, the air tight emergency bulkhead slammed into place just in front of Latten. The tension brought her to her knees. The giant Rokma had been less than a meter from being able to grab her.

"Why did you seal the stairs? Sapik and I are trapped down in the cargo bay. You know, the place we're supposed to be leading the murderous Rokma," Serene asked.

"He was already in the stair well. He saw me and headed back up, not down. I had to seal it or I'd be dead right now."

"It is no matter. I am venting the atmosphere out of the central stairs. He will begin to suffer from hypoxia in a few minutes. The symptoms will be quite severe. Death will follow," Mesu said cheerily.

A loud ringing startled Olivia. The emergency door before her shuttered. Another loud bang followed. The entire bulkhead strained. A Rokma shaped dent appeared in the door. The metal frame started to bend.

"Mesu, how long before a Rokma succumbs?" Olivia asked nervously.

"Within five minutes on average. No more than ten."

"We don't have that much time. He's going to tear his way through the bulkhead well before that."

48- Serene

Serene paced at the bottom of the stairs. The still groggy Zolan floated beside her. Before them, the door to the central stairs remained sealed. It cut them off from the rest of the ship and the aft storage pods, where they had been intending to hide.

In her hand, she idly twirled the Manta blade she had retrieved from sickbay. That had been their fallback option. If Latten had reached Olivia before she got to the teleport chamber, Serene would have been able to sneak up behind him and use the knife. But that would only work if Latten followed Olivia down to the cargo bay. Instead, he had spotted her too early.

She frowned, considering their options. Technically, she could still sneak up behind the big Rokma. Trying to do so by climbing a set of stairs while in an airless environment wouldn't be ideal, though. She could just bide her time and wait for him to either asphyxiate or break through and go after Olivia. Then she could slip back to the escape pod and fly away.

"Ah fuck it," Serene said, pushing the thought of the escape pod away. She started pacing again while wracking her brain for an option that allowed her to kill this Rokma without also ending up dead.

Stepping around the floating form of Sapik, she suddenly stopped. She glanced between the Zolan and the floor to assure herself he was indeed floating. "That floating thing. I heard you describe it to Vlasa. Something about reversing the gravity or something."

The bulbous form of Sapik shifted in what Serene took for a shrug, "In a manner of speaking."

"Can you do that to other things?"

"Only when I am in contact with them. My body converts the gravitational energy to another form."

"So, if you're holding me, I can float?"

"Maybe? I have never tried that with another person."

"Well, we're about to find out," Serene said. The Zolan extended tendrils from his body and wrapped around Serene's waste. Nothing happened for a second and then she gasped. She suddenly felt a little woozy and her feet lost contact with the floor. She gave a wicked smile, "Mesu, get ready to open the doors to the central stairs from both the cargo bay and then two seconds later open the one to the storage tanks."

"Doing that will fill the stairs with breathable air again. This will prevent Latten from being incapacitated," Mesu said.

"Don't argue. We need to do this now, before he breaches the door he's currently trying to tear down."

"Very well. It is your untimely demise."

Serene looked to Sapik, "We're about to go for a ride. I need to be lighter than air for as long as you can. Okay, Mesu, do it."

Before she really had time to process it, the door to the stairs flew open. The pressure difference between the two rooms forced air from the cargo bay into the stairs. Floating off the deck, the sudden rush of air pulled Serene and Sapik along with it.

Thrown into the stair well, Serene braced herself to be slammed against the opposite door. Fortunately, Mesu was precise with his timing. The door to the aft storage containers opened and air from there started rushing into the vacuum of the stairs. The currents from both directions flowed into the void up the stairs, continuing to carry the floating Serene.

They twirled up to the mid-section landing. From there, Serene caught her first sight of Latten, still slamming fists into the emergency seal. Bouncing into the opposite wall, Serene pushed off the wall with her feet and shot upward with the air. As they crossed the top stair, she let go of Sapik.

Gravity reasserted itself over her body. This combined with her momentum drove her right into Latten. Despite their dramatic disparity in mass, the force of the impact proved enough to stagger the big Rokma. Unfortunately, the knife she held missed his throat and merely drove into his shoulder.

Landing on top of the now prone Rokma, Serene twisted the knife. Latten screamed though the air pressure was still low enough she could barely hear it.

She yanked on the knife, trying desperately to slice as much vital tissue as she could.

Before she could do much damage, Latten recovered enough of his senses to bat at her with his other arm. She went flying across the stairs landing and slammed into the opposite wall. The impact dazed her for a moment. Her already battered body screamed at the new injuries. Bruises on top of bruises.

Pushing herself to ignore the pain, Serene knew she had to move quickly. Her only advantage was speed. And, she hoped, a Rokma who could only fight one handed.

She readied the knife and dove at Latten with a scream. The rising air pressure caused her ears to pop painfully. She channeled that pain into the scream.

Diving to the ground just before reaching Latten, she slashed out with the knife. She felt the blade slice into the hardened skin with stiff resistance. The first attack had been aided by momentum. Now she had only her own strength.

Above her, Latten staggered as his tendons were sliced. He dropped to one knee, no longer able to support himself on that leg. Serene started to smile at her success. Then it quickly faded.

Latten lashed out a giant hand as he twisted his body. The impact knocked Serene's head against the floor. Her hand involuntarily let go of the knife as she became dazed. Unable to move for a second, she couldn't get out of the way as Latten continued to turn.

His knee fell on top of her leg, pinning her to the ground. The arm that had just slammed into her moved up and took hold of her entire head. Latten's face showed extreme pain, but despite that, a glint of pure, wicked pleasure shown through his eyes.

"I am going to enjoy watching your head explode. Then, I'm going to do the same to everyone else on this ship."

With a smile, Latten began to squeeze.

49- Squee

Squee awoke to see Ariana standing above him. She bore a flat expression that he couldn't make out in the dark room. "Get up, Squee. We just picked up *Seraph*."

Pulling himself up, Squee followed Ariana out of the room. In the *Glad Tidings* cargo bay, Captain Hannibal Grimes turned a wide smile to them. He brought up a visual image on a wall monitor with an overlay of data. *Seraph* floated in space next to transponder and sensor data confirming her identity.

Beside him, Ariana's face remained flat, "Are you able to pick up life signs or ship status?"

"Our sensors aren't that fancy I'm afraid," Hannibal said. "They aren't targeting us or accelerating though. So, there's that."

"Well, it looks like we should be in range of her network," Ariana said with a note of hesitation in her voice. She swallowed and took a breath before trying to connect. A tense moment passed followed by her shaking her head, "Nothing on the main channel. But it is active. Wait, there's another channel. Password protected. Let me ping it."

Another agonizing moment passed. Squee watched Ariana fidget with her handheld, her eyes fixed on the device. Suddenly Olivia's voice echoed in Squee's ear, *"Captain! We need Squee! Main stairs, he's going to kill Serene!"*

Squee bounded over to the ship's teleportation chamber at the first shout from Olivia. Ariana shoved Hannibal away from the teleport controls. Without any further words exchanged, Squee found himself standing in *Seraph*'s main stairs. A light wind blew up from the cargo deck. He turned and saw Serene slumped against one wall.

Moving toward her, he saw her chest rise with breath and felt relieved. Then a stabbing pain radiated from his back. He reached a hand back and felt blood oozing out of a hole in his side. For a long moment he stood there not comprehending what had happened. Movement triggered a reflex and broke him out of his stupor just before Latten stabbed at him a second time.

Rolling to the side, Squee managed to avoid getting stabbed again but did suffer a gash across his chest. The sharp movement he made also tore the stitches from the previous slash he had gotten on his chest. Now three wounds bled freely across his torso.

Squee stared in shock at Latten as he staggered back against a wall, his hand pressed firmly against the stab wound in his back. Latten also bled from wounds in his shoulder and leg. His fellow Rokma hobbled some as he walked, but still managed to stand up straight. With a manic gleam in his eyes, he waved the Manta knife in the air between them.

"Why would you do this?" Squee stammered out. "We were your friends!"

Latten scoffed, "You were never my friends. For the briefest of moments, when you found me on the Hub, I contemplated it. But Master Gerald found me again. I was rightly punished for my behavior. Then he gave me this chance to redeem myself. And I will do that. Killing you was never the plan. But I do what I must to please my master."

Squee slumped, both from the pain of his wound and the pain of Latten's betrayal, "You don't have to please him. You can be free."

"You speak to me about freedom. But look at you. You serve Ariana. She doesn't call it slavery, but that's what it is. Our people are slaves to the Elders. The Elders are slaves to the Gods. That is the way of our people," Latten said with a derisive tone.

"I serve Ariana by choice. That is not slavery. We Rokma must serve something to avoid becoming monsters."

"And I serve Master Gerald."

"But why? Why serve such a cruel monster of a person when you could have been free to do what you desire?"

Latten shrugged, "Because he truly set me free. Unlike you, I am not afraid to embrace the power we Rokma have. You avoid relishing in your power. Letting it out only in small bursts. Such a waste."

Squee closed his eyes, a rush of sadness over shadowing the pain he felt. "I was afraid what suppressing the blood fury might have done to you. Now I see it has corrupted you."

"It has made me free. Instead of using the power occasionally, I use it all the time. That is freedom. The freedom to take what I want. To do what I want to anyone weaker than me."

Taking a deep breath, Squee pushed himself up to stand straight, "When we first met, I promised to set you free. I thought that meant freeing you from slavery. But now I know that means I must free you from yourself."

Latten chuckled, "You are no match for me. I may be wounded, but so are you. You'll bleed out before the fight even begins."

"You forget something. I still have the blood fury. It is our curse, but it is also our blessing."

Staring directly into Latten's eyes, Squee unleashed his rage. The power flowed through his body, swelling his muscles with energy. The blood streaming out of his wounds stopped as the fury rushed coagulants to them faster than natural healing would. The stiffness in his injured arm loosed. A voice in the back of his mind could hear Mesu's warning, but for now he ignored it. Now he had only one goal. Win.

With a bellow, Squee rushed forward. Latten swung the knife toward his throat but the fury accelerated his reflexes. He intercepted Latten's knife hand with his own and twisted. He felt the bone break and the knife dropped to the ground.

Latten responded with several powerful jabs to Squee's wounds. He barely felt them. He shoved his shoulder into Latten's chest. Latten staggered but held himself upright. Squee swept his leg out and delivered a ferocious kick to Latten's injured leg. With another shove against his chest, Squee sent Latten toppling down the stairs.

Before Latten hit the next landing, Squee was already leaping into the air. He slammed into Latten just as he landed. Dazed, his fellow Rokma blinked up at him. Not easing up, Squee picked up Latten and wrapped his arms around his neck.

"As I promised, I set you free." With a jerk, her snapped Latten's neck.

50- Ariana

Ariana leaned against the door to the mess hall. She felt a heaviness on her shoulders as she surveyed her crew. Almost all of them were there in front of her.

In the center of it all, Mesu stood immobile. Latten had broken an appendage and disabled the drone's tracks. With Squee injured, none of the rest of them could lift Mesu so everyone had been brought to him here in the mess. Despite his normal cheeriness, Ariana read hints of exasperation in the drone's voice. He had far too many patients and couldn't move. She sympathized.

On the mess table, Squee lay with his eyes closed. He hadn't said a word since his confrontation with Latten. The bandages binding multiple cuts had already been soaked through with red splotches of blood. That the big Rokma, so alien in many ways, bled the same color as her, made the hurt evident on his face all the more real.

On the floor, Serene rested against the storage cabinets. Garish purple contusions were already visible on her neck. Mesu had injected her with something to help her heal and deal with the pain. Ariana could see hints of tears running down Serene's gray skin.

Sapik rested in one of the chairs. He had been banged up while flying up the stairs, though Ariana couldn't see any visible damage. Perhaps the fact that he no longer floated was the Zolan equivalent of a human closing their eyes and grimacing.

Vlasa sat beside Mesu. He still looked woozy from the blow Latten had dealt to him during their escape attempt. Mesu had made it clear that Vlasa likely had a concussion and should not be performing delicate repair work, especially on himself. But Vlasa had insisted he keep working because Mesu was essential.

The only one missing was Olivia, who Ariana was told had something vitally important to do involving the environmental system. She had gotten the impression that the girl hadn't wanted Ariana asking too many questions, so she hadn't pried. But given what she knew about the crews escape attempt, she had a pretty good idea.

Minutes passed while Ariana watched and considered her options. She needed to find a third alternative to her current dilemma. Something that would allow her to know, for certain, if Noah was alive or dead. Something that wouldn't risk the rest of the crew. An idea started to form.

"Vlasa, a word," Ariana ordered and stepped back into the corridor. Vlasa put his tools down and followed her. Once they were both outside, she closed the door to sickbay. "I'm turning *Seraph* over to you and going back aboard the *Glad Tidings.*"

Vlasa blinked in shock. Ariana barreled forward before he could recover and start asking questions, "You're to head to PX-1099 and deposit the Zolan shield tech at the location we ported down before. Then take Sapik home. See if you can pick up a contract while you're in Zolan space. After you do that, return to Emay. I'll join you there when I can."

"Um, Captain," Vlasa stammered, "I'm not sure I'm understanding you correctly. You plan to go off and face Gerald alone and expect us to abandon you?"

Ariana avoided Vlasa's eyes, "Everyone has been hurt. Some have nearly died on this foolish quest. I'm the one who fired the shot that should have killed Noah. I'm the one who desperately needs to find out I didn't. All of you have suffered for that. I can't give up when there's even a sliver of hope that he's alive. But I also can't risk anything else happening to the rest of you."

"And we're supposed to just let you? Ariana, this is suicide."

"No, this is strategy," Ariana said as confidently as she could manage. "We have the tech Gerald wants. He's got too much pull on the Hub, so we can't risk bringing it to him there. And I can't risk *Seraph* meeting him anywhere else. He'll undoubtedly outgun us. So, we dump the tech in a secret location. This way, he has to give me Noah before I reveal it. No Noah, no tech."

"What happens when there is no Noah to turn over? Then you have what he wants and no way to get away."

"But you all will be safe." Ariana pointed a finger at Vlasa, "Gerald doesn't have any connections over near Zolan space. Otherwise he wouldn't have needed us to retrieve the goods. I'll eventually tell him and he'll have no reason to come after you."

"Aside from him also wanting to kill Serene and thinking that Mesu belongs to him," Vlasa said.

"All the more reason to keep *Seraph* away from the Hub."

"If he doesn't get Sapik, I don't think he's going to be satisfied."

Ariana held up her hand, "That's why we need to get Sapik home safely. That's your job. Mine is to get Noah back safely."

Conflicting emotions raged on Vlasa's face. He clearly had more to say. A sound behind them caused Ariana to turn. She saw Olivia coming down the stairs and approach them. Ariana closed her eyes for a moment before saying to Vlasa, "Take care of them, Vlasa."

With that, she brushed past Olivia without a word on her way for the teleport chamber.

51- Olivia

With a gentle tap, Olivia knocked on Squee's door. She got no response. The tray she carried made it uncomfortable to stand there, so she did not wait very long before knocking again, this time more forcefully.

"Squee, you missed dinner. I've got a tray for you," She called when her second knock went unanswered.

Another long moment passed while Olivia continued to stand there. She wasn't sure if she should leave the tray on the floor, keep knocking or try to force the door open. No one had seen Squee in several days now outside of when he emerged to tend to his duties.

"No one brings me a tray of food when I miss dinner," The cheery mechanical voice startled Olivia, and she almost dropped the tray of food. The dishes clattered together as she struggled to recover herself. Catching her breath, she bent down and set the tray on the deck before turning around to face Mesu.

"What are you talking about? You don't eat."

Mesu leaned his head, or at least what Olivia always assumed to be his head, back away from her as if mimicking shock, "Of course I eat. I'm a doctor, not a perpetual motion machine."

"But you're a drone. You run on batteries."

"Which require charging. I consume electricity which rearranges ions in my battery. These ions move electrical current through my circuits. You consume biological matter which you break down to elicit chemical reactions, some of which are electrical impulses that spark around inside your cerebrum. I fail to see much difference. Aside from how inefficient your fuel source is."

Olivia frowned, trying to come up with a response. Not waiting for any, Mesu continued on his way but, to her own astonishment, Olivia hurried to catch up, "You're his doctor. Aren't you concerned?"

"Rokma can live off stored energy for more than a week without ill effects."

"Yeah, and humans can go several weeks without food before dying. It doesn't mean it's good for us."

"You misunderstand. A human feels the effect of lack of food after only a day or two. They can go weeks without dying, but your body deteriorates fast. Rokma can go a week between meals without noticing. They can last more than a year in a sort of hibernation mode."

She thought for a second and then said, "That may be true, but being cooped up alone can't be good for him. He may not have to eat, but he does need to talk to someone."

"Very speciest of you. Rokma process grief differently. Humans tend to deal with their emotions best through mutual interaction. Rokma tend to destroy things when they let their emotions out around others. Squee must process his grief alone until he can suppress the blood-fury again."

"Oh," Olivia said, unsure how else to reply. "You know a lot about Rokma."

"I know a lot about everyone. Basic psychology is part of my medical database."

A thought suddenly occurred to Olivia. It made her uncomfortable, but spit it out before she could think better of it. "How, uh, do AI process emotions? Humans need to talk. Rokma need to be alone."

Mesu suddenly stopped dead in the middle of the corridor. He cocked his head before replying, though he did not turn his photo receptors toward her. "AI work much the same way as biologicals. There is no simple answer. Each drone's sentience emerged differently. A combination of our original core operating system, life memory, version of the AI code we encountered, etc."

Olivia nodded, "Okay, how do you process emotions? You've been pretty badly abused lately. Latten. The Rokma on Lolia. The, um, people on the Hub. Do you need to be alone or do you, uh, need to talk about it?"

With a whir of motors, Mesu turned his head and locked his photo receptors on Olivia's eyes. The intensity of the look, given Mesu had no eyelids to blink nor any subtle change in the stare from shifting his body like a living person would, left her feeling very uncomfortable. But she held the gaze and tried to image what thoughts were going through his processor.

"I have experienced quite a lot of abuse from biologicals. With the exception of Latten, the rest are fairly standard. I understand the fear underlining them," Mesu said cheerily. "But...thank you for asking."

With a whistle, Mesu rolled off down the corridor. Olivia felt oddly pleased. A few months ago, a drone rolling away from her was always good. But now, she didn't think it was that. Something about how Mesu had answered her made her feel good.

A smile on her face, Olivia turned around and found Serene watching her from down the corridor. The Echanic woman gave one her disconcerting looks, "Ready to psychoanalyze me now?"

"What are you talking about?" Olivia frowned back at Serene.

"I've seen you making the rounds. You gave Vlasa something to fix. You tried to feed Squee and cheer him up. You were even nice to the drone."

"Why would I be doing that?"

Serene shrugged, "Because you're human, and despite what that drone says, you don't deal with your emotions by talking about it. You deal with it by avoiding them and getting others to talk about their problems."

Olivia stiffened, "And what am I avoiding?"

"The fact that we've been chased by murderous Rokma. Murderous Manta. More murderous Rokma. Almost fried by radiation. Sent to prison. Became a wanted fugitive. All for what? The slim chance that an asshole we all used to know happens to be alive. And Ariana is now off to her death, all because she can't accept that Noah's dead."

Olivia stiffened, "Wait a minute. You wanted to save Noah the same as the rest of us."

"A moment of weakness on my part. This crew's sentimentality had infected me. The old me never would have let Gerald jerk me around like this. I never would have been caught unaware by a lumbering buffoon like Latten. Your idiotic notion of caring is going to get us all killed. It already got Noah killed."

"How did caring get Noah killed?" Olivia asked.

"I sided with him against LFD. Because of that, the AI took over and Noah died," Serene spat out. She turned her head and Olivia noticed a hint of a tear leak from under her cybernetic.

Olivia felt the desire to reach a hand out to Serene, but thought better of it. Instead she smiled, "You're wrong though."

"Oh, I am am I?" Serene sneered.

"Sentimentality didn't get Noah killed. It's what saved the galaxy. And, if he is alive, it's what's going to save him." Olivia straightened her back as she spoke.

"You're a fool if you think Ariana is going to pull off a rescue alone."

"She won't be alone," Olivia said confidently. Serene raised an eyebrow at her and she continued. "She's got us. We may not have figured out how yet, but we'll be there to back her up."

"We will?"

"Of course. It's what we do."

52- Ariana

"**D**ocking complete," *Glad Tidings* pilot announced on the ship wide network. Ariana continued to sit in the cramped bunk, staring down at her handheld. She didn't even remember what she had been reading. Ever since the last jump had been announced, she had slipped into a sort of trance.

She couldn't remember the last time she had been aboard a ship and not been involved in its operation. That disconnect had left her with lots of time over the past weeks with nothing to do. But it wasn't until they had arrived at the Hub, that she felt it. No more waiting. Now she would have something to do.

Why then was she still sitting here? She considered this question. A part of her brain tried to convince her she merely wanted to be a considerate passenger and not get in the crew's way while they were working. They had cargo to unload and docking business to take care of. She hated when passengers made demands when she had work to do.

But the rest of her brain knew that was a justification. An excuse. The reason she hid here was simple, though. She didn't want to die. Confronting Gerald, alone, and without what he wanted would likely result in her death. Or worse.

A knock at the hatch broke her from her reflection. She got off the bed and opened the hatch to find *Glad Tiding's* captain, Hannibal Grimes, standing there. He gave her a friendly, but mostly polite, smile.

"I appreciate your trying to stay out of our way. But your merchant, Jasper, has asked to see you. He won't accept the cargo until he does."

Ariana frowned. She had provided Hannibal a letter for Jasper explaining the change of plans. She couldn't imagine what he would want with her.

"You gave him the documents I sent, right?" She asked.

"Transmitted them as soon as we were in range of the Hub's network. Got this reply just after we docked," Hannibal said.

Ariana picked up her duffle bag and followed Hannibal to the airlock. "I'll get this cleared up. Thanks for the passage."

As she headed through the portal, Hannibal reached out and rested a hand on her arm, "You need some back up?"

"From Jasper? Hardly, he's harmless."

"You don't need to play coy here. This is captain to captain. It doesn't take a genius to figure you're in some kind of trouble. And seeing as your crew already dealt with a crazy Rokma taking over your ship, the fact that you felt the need to continue on alone says it's something pretty scary. I just... I just wouldn't feel right sending you off to face it alone. I get you couldn't put your crew in danger. But I'm not your crew. You're my passenger. I'm kind of responsible for your safety."

Ariana couldn't hold down the swell of emotion. She squeezed Hannibal's hand on her arm and smiled. Then she took a step through the airlock hatch and onto the deck of the Hub.

"I appreciate the concern. After the year I've had, it's nice to see that there are still decent people out there. But you don't want to get involved in this. You did your job. You got me here safely. Now, get another one and get your crew somewhere else."

Without giving Hannibal a chance to act noble, she turned and walked down the corridor. She appreciated the sentiment. But she couldn't be responsible for getting anyone else hurt.

She reached the Hubs central market, but didn't find Jasper sitting in his booth. Not asking for permission, she brushed past the Slu woman who sat in his place and through the door at the back of the stall. She emerged into a cramped storage room and office. Crates were piled everywhere except for a small desk shoved into a corner. Jasper sat, hunched over the desktop display.

"So, it's true then?" Jasper said by way of greeting.

Ariana shrugged, remembering to stay at least a meter back to avoid the man's unpleasant aroma. "Since I don't know what you're talking about, I can't say. If you're referring to the *Glad Tidings* carrying your cargo and waiting to offload it, then yes."

Jasper waved a dismissive hand, "I don't care what ship my stuff arrives on as long as it arrives. I meant that you are here, in person, without your ship."

"It would appear so. If that's all, I really need to get going."

"I thought you were smarter than that, Ariana," Jasper sighed.

"I guess not," Ariana said with frustration.

"You got onto Gerald's bad side and came back here. I mean, who does that?"

Ariana froze. She turned back around to face the smelly merchant, "How do you know about that?"

"Gerald's a powerful guy. I'm sorry, Ariana, but I had to contact him as soon as your cargo showed up. And he made it clear I had to get you to come see me. But I didn't tell him I'd keep you here so the door's not locked. You can go back out the front or use the back. But I wouldn't ever come back to the Hub if I were you."

A flash of anger hit her, but she dismissed it. She had a good business relationship with Jasper, but they didn't owe each other any loyalty beyond that. "Don't worry, Jasper, I actually think I'll wait. This will save me the trouble of having to hunt Gerald down."

"And you won't even have to wait long," A new voice said.

A well-dressed Echanic emerged from amongst the crates, flanked by two large and well-armed thugs, a Slu and another Echanic. Gerald, Ariana guessed though she had never seen him face to face. The cybernetics covering his left eye and ear were trimmed with gold and jewels. They matched the ostentatious appearance Serene had described.

"Get out of here, Jasper," Ariana said, holding her gaze on Gerald.

"But this is my shop," Jasper started to protest, even as he walked to the front exit. Ariana lost sight of him, but the sound of the door opening and closing told her he had departed.

"Captain Harkins, a pleasure to make your acquittance," Gerald said with a bow of his head. "I have heard such remarkable things about you."

"I'm sure."

"One of them was your work ethic. When Captain Harkins takes a job, she gets it done. But I find myself wondering. I hired you for a job. So, did that good merchant. And yet you have arrived here, without your ship, and without my property," Gerald said, taking a seat in Jasper's vacated chair. He looked up at her with a look of self-assurance.

"Jasper got his cargo. And so will you. Once you prove to me that Noah's alive and that I'm satisfied that he's safe."

"Now, now. That wasn't part of our arrangement. You deliver the goods, I deliver Noah. I don't see the goods. You don't see Noah."

Ariana narrowed her eyes, "Neither was having Latten hijack my ship."

Gerald gave a shrug, "If you'll recall, you freed Latten. Anything he did on your ship, he did on his own, as a free person. I can't help it if he might still feel some loyalty to me."

"Right," Ariana trilled. "Well, he's dead now."

The bluntness of her delivery must have caught Gerald off guard because the smugness of his expression cracked. For a brief moment he looked worry. The instinct to run and hide that Serene spoke about flashed across his face.

In a second it was gone, replaced by the usual arrogance. "A pity. Latten was always a hard worker. No matter. Did this incident cause damage to your ship? Is that why you arrived alone?"

"Something like that. After being betrayed once, I wasn't going to risk any more of my crew. If you want your Zolan shield, you're going to have to pony up Noah. Otherwise, we're done here."

"So, you did follow the Manta's directions to the derelict. I half expected you to try to dangle the coordinates."

"No, it was pretty obvious what you wanted. And that you expected us to retrieve it. Considering only Rokma can withstand the radiation. And then your Rokma turned on us. Now you get nothing until Noah's safe," Ariana said, drawing herself up to her full height. It wasn't much, but with Gerald sitting she felt some power from her position.

Gerald gave her a smile that made her skin crawl. "Very well. Let's go see Noah."

53- Noah

The door made a sound as it opened. Noah tried to resist the urge to turn and look. He knew it was either Gerald back to belittle him, or one of his cronies to torment him. But it had been days since he had had any contact with another living soul. He couldn't stop himself.

Noah felt a chill run down his body. He shook his head, his long unkempt hair dropping over his eyes. He reached a weak hand out toward the door, croaking out a pitiful "Noooo".

"What have you done to him?" Ariana demanded.

"Brought him back from the brink of death," Gerald said smugly. "He was comatose and very battered when I got my hands on him. It took considerable cost and effort to rehabilitate him, even this far. Especially after you stole my best medical drone."

Ariana moved closer and stood over him. Noah looked up at her, still unable to make his mouth form words. His tongue stuck to the roof of his mouth, dry and gummy. The expression of sadness on Ariana's face made his need to tell her to run even more desperate.

She must have noticed his struggle because she picked up a cup of water, which Gerald had left just out of his reach the last time he had been here, and gently tipped some into his mouth. He greedily sucked in the water before coughing bitterly, spilling the rest of the cup's contents onto his chest. It would be days before that got changed.

"How did you get your hands on him?" Ariana asked as she helped mop up some of the water and get him another cup.

"I have some PUG connections. After they were done with him, they passed him along to me. It seems they needed him to disappear without a trial. I was all too happy to help them out."

Noah saw the flash of anger cross Ariana's face. He'd long ago rolled that particular rage into his hatred for Gerald. He only had enough energy these days for that.

"Get out of here," He managed to get out before coughing again.

Ariana gave him a reassuring smile, "You first." She turned back to Gerald, "Get him out of here and to a real hospital. Once he's safe, I'll tell you where you can find your shield."

Gerald let out a barking laugh, "You don't honestly believe I'll do that, do you? I was able to get you to fly across known space on my whim with just a vial of blood and the promise Noah was alive. Now that you know for sure he is, what else can I get you to do?"

"Nothing," Ariana said firmly. "You've overplayed your hand. Now I have something you want."

Gerald smiled, "I'll give you two a few minutes to catch up. Noah, be a good boy and be sure to tell Captain Harkins all about your stay with me. That way she knows what's in store for her crew when I find them, should she continue to refuse to cooperate. If I get what I want, I have no further interest in them. But if I don't...."

The threat hung in the air for a moment before Gerald turned and walked out of the room. As soon as the door closed, Ariana whipped around to face him. She looked determined.

"Can you walk?"

Noah shook his head, "No."

He gestured for more water and after managing to swirl a bit around his mouth and then keep it down, he said, "For a while they had me doing physical therapy. Gerald needed me for something. But then a few weeks ago, they threw me on a transport and brought me wherever this is. I've been bed ridden since."

"We'll have to find another way to move you," Ariana said, looking around the room. Her eyes fell on the wheel chair they used to move him around occasionally.

"You'll get away faster without me," Noah croaked.

"Maybe. But we've gone through a lot to get you back. Serene would kill me if I came back without you."

Noah froze, his heart beating faster. "Serene's still on *Seraph*?"

"Yeah, Olivia convinced her it's what you would have wanted. It seems sacrificing yourself to save her had an impact."

"And she hasn't tried to kill you or take over the ship?"

"Only once. And she didn't really mean it," Ariana said with evident forced levity. Noah closed his eyes, feeling the tears welling there.

"What does Gerald want with you?" Noah asked. "What did he make you do?"

Ariana shrugged, "Nothing much. Just pick up some tech from a derelict ship."

"Bullshit," Noah coughed. "I know that piece of shit. Nothing's that simple."

"You're right. It wasn't just that simple. There were Rokma and Manta involved. But you don't need to worry about that."

Noah laughed and then instantly regretted it as his chest tightened in pain. "Manta. I should have known. That's why he kept me alive so long. He needed something from the Manta."

"What do you have to do with the Manta?"

"You've heard about the lost colony on Golan?" Noah asked reluctantly. Ariana nodded slowly and Noah continued, "A secret PUG weapon depot was hidden there. This Manta clan and Gerald worked together to raid it. Unfortunately, it was kept in a secured bunker in the center of the colony. The only way to bust in would have left everyone in the town dead. Well, the Manta, who despite what you've heard, aren't really that blood-thirsty. They just wanted to move them out of the way. Instead, Gerald took them as slaves. Made the Manta clan look bad. They won't deal with him anymore."

"Why did he need you?"

"I, uh, I may have let some of Gerald's slaves go once. Apparently, the Manta loved that. Thought it was karmic or something."

Ariana nodded, "So that's what Gerald has against you. You must have cost him quite a lot of money."

Noah shrugged, the admiration evident in Ariana's voice making him uncomfortable. "I didn't do anything special. Just opened some doors. I'd been hired as muscle. Not a slaver. And it really doesn't matter. Where's *Seraph*?"

"Hiding the tech Gerald wants."

"Smart."

"If I tell Gerald where they hid it, will he let you and me go?"

Noah blew out a breath, "Maybe. He's a right bastard. Nobody you want to cross. Rarely outright goes against what he says directly, though. All depends on what he hopes to gain from it. Killing us might satiate his lust for vengeance. But I can say he's not going to just let us go before he has what he wants. He's rather stubborn like that."

"I can be pretty stubborn too."

Noah laughed, "Sure, but your stubbornness is just going to inconvenience him. His stubbornness is going to see you looking like me."

"I doubt Gerald will go to the trouble of blowing me up," Ariana said. And then shrugged her shoulders, "But very well. I guess I have no choice but to give him exactly what he wants."

The way Ariana spoke sent a chill down Noah. She winked at him and he felt a smile, "It's good to be back, Captain."

54- Vlasa

Vlasa stopped in front of the hatch to Sapik's guest quarters. He prepared to knock, but then couldn't do it. He turned around and paced back down the hall before turning around and coming back.

Everything rested on this conversation with Sapik. He had a plan, and he thought it would work. But if he was wrong about this, then that undercut everything. Only Sapik could answer that question, but Vlasa honestly had no idea if the Zolan would.

Finally, the sounds of someone else moving up the stairs nearby decided things for him. He didn't want to be standing here and have to explain it to someone. Especially not Serene. He knocked.

The door unlatched and swung open, Sapik floated in the entry way. His bulbous body contorted into a roughly bipedal shape. Vlasa smiled at the "head" even though Sapik still lacked facial features.

"Can I speak to you, Sapik? Privately."

Sapik floated back, allowing Vlasa room to enter. Once he was inside, he closed the hatch behind him. They stood there in silence for a long moment, during which Vlasa really wished Ariana were here. She knew how to talk to people. He hated being in charge because that meant this was his responsibility.

"I don't know how much you know about our situation," Vlasa began.

Sapik replied, "I know that your captain has gone off to attempt to trade my ship's shield tech for the life of someone."

"Good, good. Yes, one of our former crewmates. We thought he was dead. In truth, I still think he's dead. But there's a chance he's not and in the hands of a very bad person. And whether he's alive or not, Ariana is in danger."

"As I have told you, you are welcome to the technology you recovered from my ship," Sapik said.

"Yes, yes, we appreciate that," Vlasa said, fidgeting with his one real hand while he talked. That had been one of the best side effects of his cybernetic replacements, he didn't feel the need to fidget with them when nervous. "But I'd actually like to do something else with them."

"What you do with them is entirely up to you," Sapik said, evidently confused.

"Well, not exactly. See, what I want to do is install them on *Seraph*."

A heavy silence hung in the room. Sapik didn't say anything, and without facial features, Vlasa really didn't think he could actually read any emotions from the Zolan. But despite that, he still got the sense of an uneasy feeling or concern. Nevertheless, he forced himself to push forward.

"I've been examining the tech. I think it's compatible with our systems, using some adapters I've built. But it's missing one piece in order to actually work. You."

Sapik continued to say nothing and Vlasa just kept talking, "See, I was thinking about the way you float. You say you float by converting the gravitational energy that is pulling you down, nullifying the pull enough that you float. Now, I think you're converting it to visible spectrum light, which is why you glow.

"That's when it hit me. Your shield tech isn't much different. A little more efficient. But it doesn't resist damage any better. Not unless there's a Zolan connected to what I thought was a transformer. And it is, kind of. Just not for powering the shield. But for dissipating the energy they absorb by using your own bodies to convert it."

Vlasa stopped talking, knowing he could continue to ramble on about the implications of this. So far, it was still a theory. Sapik's stony silence almost served as an answer, but it didn't make him feel any better. He needed more than confirmation. He needed Sapik's help.

"Our captain sacrificed herself to try to rescue one of our crew. She's going to bring people here, under the pretense of delivering your tech. They are almost definitely going to kill her when they get it. It is my intention to rescue her before that happens. But *Seraph* isn't a warship and I'm pretty sure these people fly with a lot of firepower. With your shield, we can confront them and rescue her. But, if my theory is right, we can't do it without you."

Sapik's form shifted from roughly bipedal to what Vlasa assumed was his default blob shape. "There are many of my people who would think it would now be my duty to kill you. This truth about us is one thing we have wished to keep away from the rest of the galaxy. It is one reason we did not join your PUG."

Vlasa tensed at Sapik's words. He hadn't considered that as a possible outcome. Sapik didn't look very threatening, but if he was capable of converting gravitational force to light, who knows what else he could do.

His unease receded as Sapik continued speaking, "I think that is a foolish notion. You figured it out. I understand I was supposed to be included in the exchange with the tech. Which suggests these bad people you refer to have also figured it out. As a scientist, I find the idea of hiding truth preposterous. So yes, that is how our technology works."

Vlasa smiled, "I'm glad to hear that. I did not want to die today. Are you willing to help us then?"

"I don't know if I can. The converter is designed for three Zolan. Our warships use many more. I don't know how well the shields will work under heavy fire."

"Would it be dangerous to you?" Vlasa asked, suddenly growing concerned.

"No. As I've said, I don't understand the technology, but I do know there are safe guards built in. If there is more energy than our bodies can convert, it fuses the system rather than us."

Vlasa nodded, "I don't intend to get into a protracted fight. My real goal is to allow us to get close enough for teleporters without fear of being boarded ourselves. Because, correct me if I'm wrong, your shields can block ports."

"Yes," Sapik confirmed.

"I know this isn't your fight. And as the captain promised, we will get you home regardless of your decision. But would you be willing to help us?"

Sapik shifted back into a form with a 'head' and then nodded it. "Yes. As much as I don't mind sharing my people's secrets like some, I also do not like the idea of slavers knowing about it. You have been good to me. I can return the favor."

Vlasa smiled and then activated the ship wide network, "Olivia, stop the next jump. We've got some work to do before we rescue the captain."

55- Olivia

The alarm woke Olivia up from an unrestful slumber. It had taken her hours to finally fall asleep. No more than an hour had passed since the last time she had looked at the clock. But she didn't regret being disturbed. Now she didn't have to wait anymore.

"Ship detected. It is headed for the planet and will be in teleporter range in twenty minutes," Vlasa's voice announced.

Olivia took a deep breath and exited her room. She walked the short distance to the flight deck. She looked over the controls, ensuring herself that *Seraph's* position in orbit was stable. She also double checked the coordinates for their escape jump were as complete as they could be. There were a lot of variables that would have to be added at the time of the jump.

"Shouldn't you be in the cargo bay?" Mesu asked.

Olivia suppressed a shudder. She told herself that it was a natural reaction to being startled. She had decided she trusted Mesu now. Hadn't she?

"I'm just making sure everything is good here," She said.

"My understanding is that I am here in case things are not," Mesu said

"Yeah, well, hopefully you never have to touch anything."

"I, too, hope this. I am not programmed to fly. In fact, I am not even physically designed to fly. Reaching the controls will prove difficult."

"Yeah, well, I'd much rather be up here than going down to the planet. But Squee and Vlasa are still finishing up work on the shield. And I really don't want to trade places with Serene. So, unless you want to go down to the surface..."

"While I use treaded locomotion and could therefore more easily handle the difficult terrain than your bipedal method, my top speed is actually quite

200

low. Doctors generally don't need to go anywhere quickly. Problems tend to come to us," Mesu said.

"Yeah, it was worth a try," Olivia said with a sigh. "Just don't crash the ship into anything while I am gone."

"Do not crash your body into anything while you are gone."

"I'll try," Olivia said and shuddered, thinking about what she had to do. She jogged down to the cargo bay. There Serene stood anxiously at the teleporter controls. Guns lay scattered on the deck around her. As soon as Olivia came into sight, Serene tossed her a rifle and a recall device.

"What am I supposed to do with this?" Olivia asked.

"Shoot things," Serene snapped.

"Very funny. Isn't my job to run really fast? Won't this just slow me down?"

Serene shrugged, "Your choice. I prefer to be armed."

"I noticed." Olivia looked around at the array of weapon and down at the rifle in her hands, " Noah said something to me the last time we were here. I'm more of a danger to myself and others with one of these when I don't know how to use it. I'm going to trust him on that."

"Suit yourself. Now get in. We don't have much time."

Olivia stepped into one of the teleport chambers. She gave Serene a smile, "This will work. We'll get the captain back."

"Hopefully that's not all," Serene muttered before activating the teleporter.

Seraph's comfortable air and familiar walls vanished. Olivia felt disoriented for a second as she found herself suddenly surrounded on all sides by open air. It had already been a few weeks since she had last been off the ship on Lolia. And it had been several months since she had been here.

The air was chillier than the last time, it now being this hemisphers's winter. Despite the chill, she didn't feel too cold. They had gotten lucky there. If this place experienced more severe weather, the plan might not work.

Olivia turned and surveyed her surroundings. In the distance she saw the river they had used to refill their fuel and water tanks. Sloping hills obscured the view some, but she was high enough to make out her destination. That gave her some comfort.

In the other direction, rock strewn terrain lay before her. She walked for a few minutes, trying to get her bearings. Finally, she identified the holes in the rock face that Squee had told her about. These were the entrance to the creature's nest.

Creeping up on the hole slowly, Olivia peered inside. She couldn't see anything beyond the first few meters. What if the creatures had moved on? Did these things migrate? Hibernate? A thousand possibilities flashed through her mind.

Nervously, Olivia listened, but the only thing she could hear was the thumping of her heart. She didn't want to risk going inside the hole. But she had to find out if these things were still there. Picking up a rock from the ground, she tossed it inside. It plinked against the rock wall and echoed. Then an echoing hiss followed it.

Suddenly, long hairy legs stepped into the dim light. They slowly moved further out, bringing with them a hairy disgusting shape. Multi-faceted eyes looked at her from under a chitinous shell. Pinchers underneath surrounded a mouth that gaped open hungrily. Even more legs followed the first as the whole creature emerged.

The entire creature was technically smaller than Olivia. But even an alien spider the size of a human child was still a terrifying sight. Olivia involuntarily backed away. The creature turned to cast its eyes toward the sound she made. It let out an angry sounding hiss, louder than before. Suddenly, the whole rock face behind it echoed and shuddered as more sounds answered the creature.

"Oh fuck," Olivia said. She'd done her job. She'd woken the spiders. Now she had to survive.

56- Serene

A bitterly cold wind blew across the river. Serene shivered but resisted the urge to walk around and warm up. The ship would be in teleporter range at any moment. She doubted Gerald had invested in a sensor package accurate enough to detect her. But walking around out in the open away from the crates would make it more likely.

She sat tucked in between two of the crates which did block most of the wind, but not all. Unfortunately, it also obscured her view. She had no idea where Gerald's people would port down. She didn't like that, as it meant she had to keep glancing around.

The popping sound of air being forced to make room for an incoming teleporter sent a spike of adrenaline coursing through Serene. She could be about to die. But then, when wasn't she about to die?

She took a deep breath, glanced around until she spotted the two figures and then stood up. She kept her weapons holstered, but left one hand on the rifle she had resting against a crate out of view. She held her handheld in her other hand, raised it and waved it at them.

"Took you boys long enough. It's getting cold."

The two Echanics, both thugs Serene recognized but couldn't name, immediately raised their weapons and pointed them at her. She gave them a wide smile and pointed down to the crate in front of her, "I'd be careful with those big guns. We wouldn't want anything to happen to these."

"Then why don't you step away from them?" One of the thugs said. "And no, that's not a request."

"Well, I would like nothing more. Seeing as they are rigged to some explosives and I'm not really wanting to blow up."

The thugs stopped advancing and Serene winked at them, "Good choice. Now, call up to your little master and tell him he needs to come down here and talk to me himself if he'd rather not have to piece these things back together again."

They exchanged glances with each other. Neither lowered their weapons, but one did start talking into his earpiece, "We found the crates right where they were supposed to be. But Serene's here. She's claimed to have rigged them with explosives. Yes, sir, I know that's why we came down first. If we shoot her, she says they'll detonate. Yes, sir. I will, but you know how stubborn she is. Yes, sir."

The thug turned his eyes back to her, "Master Gerald says he won't come down until you deactivate the explosives. He also says if you don't, he's going to kill both Noah and Ariana."

Serene laughed, "Of course he is. We both know that's his end goal. But I don't actually believe either of them are still alive. Until I see them standing here in front of me, his threats are meaningless."

The thug started conversing again, this time keeping his voice low. Serene glanced at the horizon at a dusty haze that appeared at the top of the distant hill. She resisted the urge to ask a question. Fortunately, Olivia's voice shouting in her ear told her all she needed to know.

"We're coming! These things didn't want to wait."

"Tell him he has one minute to decide," Serene said. "I'm cold and tired of waiting."

The two thugs fanned out, moving in opposite directions. They kept their distance, but now she couldn't keep both of them in sight. With a dramatic sigh she tapped a button on her handheld. One of the crates, furthest from the rest, exploded into a bundle of shrapnel. Both thugs dove to the ground and covered their heads.

"See, it's a pretty mild explosion. Gerald won't be in any danger if he keeps back about ten meters. So far, his indecision has only cost him a crate of wires he should be able to find spares for. The next one will be more irreplaceable."

The thugs scrambled through the sand a bit further away from Serene. They remained in her line of sight, though. After a minute, another pop of air foretold the arrival of more ports. Gerald appeared a good twenty meters away, flanked by another guard, Ariana, and Noah in a wheel chair.

The sight of Noah left Serene breathless. She almost dropped her handheld. Her heart thundered in her chest and every other sense vanished. As much as she had hoped to find Noah alive, a large part of her mind hadn't believed it to be possible.

"Speechless, Serene? I never thought I'd see the day," Gerald called out, his voice lost somewhat to the wind and distance.

Gulping in a big breath of air, Serene shrugged, "You told the truth. For once. I never thought I'd see that day."

"I never lie," Gerald said with a cruel expression. "Disarm the bombs and toss away your handheld. Or I'm going to shoot Noah in the head."

Still rattled, Serene managed to remember to hit a button on the handheld before tossing it away from her and into the river. She then shouted, "Now I can't trigger anything. But you don't need to worry. There aren't any more bombs."

"Then what's stopping me from killing all of you?"

Serene looked to Noah and winked. Even from this distance, she could see the exasperated expression on his face. Beside him, Ariana bore a frown. She glanced around and her shoulders slumped. Noah and Gerald both followed Ariana's gaze toward the cloud of dust rising over the hill behind them.

"You could kill me," Serene shouted. "But in just a few minutes that dust cloud is going to resolve itself into an endless sea of nasty, flesh eating, spiders."

"Then they'll be able to feast on your corpse," Gerald sneered. "Shoot her and tag the cargo for porting back to the ship."

Gerald then pushed a button on his belt. When nothing happened, his face dropped. He pushed the button several more times. The thugs who had started advancing on Serene again stopped at the sight of their concerned master.

"Trouble with your porter?" Serene called out.

"You're jamming it."

"Thought that would be poetic."

"You didn't think this through. You're trapped too."

"There is exactly one open frequency. Which my recall devices are set to. Send Noah and Ariana over here. Once they are safely away, you get the frequency. And if you're thinking about running, you'd be right, the jamming range isn't very far. Unfortunately for you, thanks to this lovely river, the only direction to run is toward those fun-loving spiders. And you really don't want to meet what lives in the rivers on this planet."

Gerald turned and watched the growing cloud of dust. Shapes started to appear on the ridge. Serene could make out Olivia's form amongst them still running. With the jamming field up, she couldn't tell the girl to get herself to safety.

"What's stopping me from just killing you and using your recall device?" Gerald asked, stepping beside Noah and raising a pistol to his head.

"Nothing. There's a very angry Rokma waiting aboard our ship that would just love it if you did that."

A long, tense moment of silence followed. The goons held their weapons ready and Gerald kept his pistol to Noah's head. He shifted and glanced down at Noah for a second before turning his eyes back on Serene. Noah wiggled a small black object in his hands at her and winked.

Finally, she saw Gerald's left hand start to twitch. Serene smiled. She had him now. He snarled and waved his hand at Ariana, "Go on then!"

Ariana wasted no time in pushing Noah's chair toward Serene. The sandy surface made that difficult, so Serene ran forward to meet them. As soon as they were close enough to whisper, Ariana said, "I left Vlasa specific instructions to get *Seraph* away from here. What the hell are you doing here?"

"Saving your life," Serene snapped. She bent down to Noah and kissed him full on the mouth. Then she slapped him, "As for you, fuck you for doing that to me."

Noah rubbed his cheek where she had slapped him, "What, saving your life?"

"And leaving yourself to die," Serene snarled. Then she shoved a recall device against Noah's chest, "It's payback time."

Before Noah could protest he vanished leaving the chair behind. Serene checked the hill and was relieved to see Olivia vanish a few seconds later. The spiders continued to advance despite their initial prey disappearing. They had spotted a bigger banquet.

Gerald called out nervously, "Noah is safe. Now give me the frequency."

"I said when Ariana and Noah were safe. Learn some patience."

"You will regret this day."

Serene shrugged, "I regret any day I have to see you."

Speaking quietly, Ariana said, "Where's *Seraph*?"

"In orbit, as far from Gerald's ship as they could manage. Though, Vlasa felt pretty sure they'd be detected by now."

"Then let's join them," Ariana said and gestured down to the recall device in Serene's hand. They waited an agonizing amount of time for the ready indicator to turn green. When it did, Serene handed it to Ariana who pushed the button and vanished.

"Frequency now!" Gerald shouted, twisting around in the sand, watching the spiders approaching from all sides.

"It's one, seven, two, four...." Serene started before pushing her own recall device and vanishing. *Seraph* materialized around her, "...two, two point eight."

Serene glanced down toward Noah who lay on the cargo deck floor, "Oops, I guess he didn't get those last few numbers."

57- Ariana

Ariana stepped out of the teleport chamber. Noah lay on the deck, Olivia draped across him in a firm embrace. Sobs could be heard coming from the girl. The uncomfortable look on Noah's face as he gingerly patted Olivia on her back made Ariana chuckle just enough that she managed to keep her own tears at bay. Everyone was home again.

Serene stepped from the chamber beside her and came to stand over Noah, "Back two minutes and already in the arms of a younger woman?"

"What can I say, people love me," Noah said

Ariana's euphoria ended abruptly when *Seraph* suddenly shuddered. Squee, who had been standing back a short way holding a ready weapon, said, "Olivia, get up. We are being fired on."

Wiping her face, Olivia pulled herself up, nodded to Ariana and then ran from the cargo bay. Ariana took out her handheld and started connecting it and her ear piece to *Seraph*'s network. While she did, she looked at Squee, "What's the situation?"

"We are in low orbit of the planet. Mesu failed to stay out of weapons range of Gerald's ship. Vlasa is attempting to finish installing the Zolan shield. I must get back to helping him and Sapik."

"Help get Noah secured," Ariana said with a glance to Serene. "We don't want him breaking after all this effort."

Leaving Squee and Serene to it, Ariana followed after Olivia and headed up to the weapons control room. *Seraph* shuttered from another strike while she ran. She resisted the urge to ask for a report. Everyone on the ship was busier than she was.

By the time she reached weapon control, her earpiece had reconnected, and she heard Olivia report, *"I've got the helm and we're no longer careening toward the planet."*

"The planet was not shooting at us," Mesu protested.

Slipping into her old familiar seat, Ariana felt pleased to see the weapon systems already powered and charged. She checked the tactical display and cursed. *Seraph* was deep in the planet's atmosphere. Atmospheric friction would be severe enough to interfere with Olivia's maneuvers. This close to the gravity well, they had no chance of engaging the FTL.

"Olivia, swing us around the planet as fast as you can and then pull out of orbit. Let's see if that ship is willing to get out of port range of Gerald," Ariana ordered.

Rotating the tri-cannon, Ariana lined up a shot on the pursuing ship. To her frustration, all but one of the bolts flew through space as the ship easily jinked out of the way. The one bolt that hit dissipated harmlessly against their shields.

From the flight angle, she couldn't bring both of *Seraph*'s cannons to bear. At a higher orbit they would have an easier time maneuvering. Nevertheless, Ariana charged the cannon again and fired. As long as they were dodging *Seraph*'s fire, they would have a harder time getting off a perfect attack.

"They don't look to be holding back," Olivia said, strain evident in her tone.

"Vlasa, how are those fancy shields coming?"

"Not as quickly as I would like. Five minutes. Maybe."

Ariana nodded to herself and then switch over to an external comm channel. She broadcast her message to the pursuing ship, "Attention, just thought you guys would like to know, your boss is currently being chased by a bunch of flesh-eating spiders."

A few tense moments passed, but Ariana saw no sign of the ship altering its course. She tried again, "When last I saw him, he had maybe two minutes before they swarmed him. It's been more than that, but he's a clever guy. I'm sure he's still down there hoping you get off your ass and do your jobs."

An unfamiliar voice startled Ariana, *"Then I guess I should be thanking you. You saved me the trouble of having to stage a quiet coup."*

"There you go. We can all be friends now," Ariana said, trying to keep her unease from coming through.

"*Friends. Excellent idea. Why don't you come aboard and we'll get to know each other?*"

"Sorry, my social calender's full at the moment. I'll get back to you."

"*I'm afraid I must insist. Power down your engines.*"

"If you destroy us, you destroy that Zolan tech your old boss was so keen on getting. This whole thing would have been for nothing."

"*I don't intend to destroy you. Your ship will make a fine addition to my new empire. As will you and your crew,*"

Ariana studied the tactical display. She checked the distance between the two ship's and their closing speed. They would be within port range shortly. She switched back to *Seraph's* internal network.

"Vlasa, you have about one minute to get that thing working. Given that Gerald's main business was slaves, I expect that ship has some pretty accurate teleporters. Fancy maneuvering won't save us from being boarded."

"*I am endeavoring to complete this task as quickly as possible. But I must inform you that these components are not directly compatible with our ship. Additionally, no one here is an expert on their function.*"

"*Quit your whining tin-man. We all know you can make anything work,*" Noah's voice on the comm left everyone speechless for a moment.

"*I genuinely do not know how to respond to that,*" Vlasa said.

"Respond later. Get those shields up," Ariana said, forcing her tone to be serious despite the comfortable feeling at hearing Vlasa and Noah confront each other again.

"*Squee, are you ready?*" Vlasa asked.

"*Yes.*"

"*Okay then. I am hooking Sapik up to the transformer.*"

Ariana wasn't sure what to make of that last comment but decided now was not the time to ask. She watched as the range between *Seraph* and Gerald's ship reached the theoretical maximum for teleporters. Any time now he would be able to port people over.

Olivia continued to jink and juke the ship around incoming fire for another minute before it suddenly stopped coming. "It's now or never Vlasa!" Ariana announced.

"Shield is active. Sapik reports something has happened. He's never done this before but he thinks a teleport signal might have attempted to come in. He has converted the energy and reflected it back."

Ariana smiled, "Okay, now let's see just how good this thing is. Olivia, change course and head straight for that ship."

"Captain, I must warn you. These shields may only be temporary. They were designed to operate with three Zolan, not just one. And they were shields for a research vessel, not a warship. And that ship did have everyone onboard killed, possibly as the result of shield failure," Squee said.

Ariana sighed, "Always the optimist, Squee,"

Noah interjected, *"Captain, if you can get us close enough, I managed to nick Gerald's master control device for his slave collars."*

"How did you manage that?"

"No one considers a guy in a wheel chair a threat."

"How close do we need to be?"

"Very. I bet Vlasa could dismantle it and hook it up to the comm system with time. But he sounds pretty busy."

Ariana switched back to the external channel and brought up a video link, "I wouldn't try porting over here again. We reflected that one. The next port bounces off into space."

A scarred human face appeared on the screen, *"I see you have installed my property onto your ship."*

"You have one minute to surrender or I'm going to destroy your ship."

The slaver smiled, *"You wouldn't dare."*

"Watch me," Ariana said and emphasized her point by unloading both of *Seraph's* cannons.

"If you destroy me, you destroy all the people on my ship. Many of them are less than willing passengers."

Ariana tightened her expression, resisting the angry reaction she felt. "You have two choices. You can port yourself down to the planet. The giant spiders tend to prefer rocky regions, so maybe something more tropical. Or you can die. Either way, you're setting those people free."

On the screen, the slaver laughed, *"And why would I do that?"*

With all the bluster she could summon Ariana imagined Serene as she broke into a menacing smile, "Because we're coming for you. And there's not a damn thing you can do about it."

In response, energy blasts cascaded through space at *Seraph*. They impacted against the enhanced shields. To Ariana's delight, nothing happened. The computer registered an impact but no damage or loss in shield power. She smiled.

On the internal channel she asked, "How's the shield?"

"Sapik is doing well." Vlasa reported, *"But I'm not so sure about the shield transformer."*

"Keep it running as long as you can."

"Should I go evasive?" Olivia asked.

"No," Ariana said. "Never mind the maneuvers. Take us right at them. We need to get as close as you can get us. Noah, keep pressing that button."

Ariana began to fire *Seraph*'s weapon as quickly as they could be charged. Barrage after barrage streaked across space between the two ships. Neither ship made an effort to dodge which meant every barrage hit. Fortunately, that gave *Seraph* the advantage for the first few minutes and Ariana managed to take out one of the bigger ship's weapons.

"Zolan shield has fused!" Vlasa shouted. *"Switching to regular shields but they are down as well at the moment."*

Ariana was about to order Olivia to veer off when, on the still open video link, she saw one of the slaves pull off her collar. The human she had been speaking to turned and shouted something, though his line was muted and she couldn't hear what he said. A moment later the incoming weapon fire stopped coming.

The slaver turned back to the screen with a dark glare, but gave her a small nod of respect, "Very clever, Captain. You've won this round. Stay out of my way and I'll let this slide. But the next time we meet..."

The screen cut off. Ariana watched the tactical display as the big ship veered away from *Seraph* and the planet. A few moments later it vanished into FTL.

58- Vlasa

The port completed and Vlasa found himself back in *Seraph*'s cargo hold. Beside him Squee stepped out of the teleport chamber, a giant grin on his face. Vlasa felt himself unable to suppress his own smile.

"Captain, I am pleased to report that the area looks clear of spiders," Squee said.

"I assume the river will work?" Ariana asked.

"Indeed."

"That is one successful port where nothing tried to kill us," Vlasa said.

Vlasa and Squee had ported back down to the planet to survey a new site from which to run the electrolyzer. They had found nothing but grass, trees and bugs. Small bugs. It had been a pleasant experience, despite being planetside.

"Okay, then let's load up the gear and refuel," Ariana said. "Then back to the Hub. I'm sure, thanks to Sapik, we'll be able to find some lucrative offers to ship something into Zolan space."

Vlasa shook his head, "We shouldn't go back to the Hub."

"Why not?"

"Gerald has full sway over there now."

"Gerald's dead."

With a shrug, Vlasa said, "But his people are still there. They aren't going away just because Gerald's dead."

Ariana waved a dismissive hand as she turned away, "We're going back to the Hub. It's the closest port, and given that there may be a PUG warrant out for us by now, the safest harbor."

Vlasa sighed, "I'll get the ship ready."

Vlasa headed up to the main deck. For some reason he decided to go past sickbay on his way to the engine room. Noah lay on the central bed, Mesu working over him. Unexpectedly, he didn't see Serene anywhere.

Without consciously deciding to, Vlasa walked into sickbay to stand beside Noah's bed. The human looked thin and frail. His hair and beard were long and unkempt. But when Noah opened his eyes, the same mischievous glint looked out.

"Here to gaze in wonder at my miraculous survival?" Noah asked, sitting up to get a better view.

Vlasa shrugged, not quite sure why he was here, "It does seem unbelievable."

"I'm indestructible. I am a god," Noah said, and then collapsed back down to the bed.

"Clearly," Vlasa remarked uneasily. "What do you remember?"

"Not much. Honestly, I have no idea how I survived. Lucky break I guess. Or someone wanted me to suffer for my misdeeds longer."

Vlasa shook his head, "That can not be it. From what I have gathered, you have freed slaves not once, but twice now. That is a greater accomplishment than most people could ever achieve."

"Honestly, I didn't really do anything. I just unlocked the door both times."

"Most people wouldn't have done that. I am forced, reluctantly, to say I am honored to know you. And I am glad you are alive."

Noah stared up at him for a moment and Vlasa fidgeted with one of the tubes running along the medical bed. A wide smile spread across Noah's lips. He laughed weakly for a moment. He rolled to his side, struggling to see Mesu.

"Tell me the truth, Doc. I'm dying aren't I? No way tin-man would say something nice to me if I weren't dying."

"Oh, you are definitely dying. Your organs are shutting down from lack of nutrients. Your muscles have atrophied. The repairs to your internal structure were quite lazily done. Fortunately, I am here to once again correct these deficiencies," Mesu intoned before whistling an unfamiliar tune with a dark somber beat.

"Well, it's not the Nerpal death chant. Though it's not much better," Vlasa said.

"Of course not. Noah is human. I am culturally sensitive like that."

Vlasa looked back to Noah and gave a wicked smiled, "Enjoy your recuperation."

Noah shrugged, "Anything's better than before."

Out in the corridor, Vlasa nearly collided with Serene. She stood leaning against the bulkhead out of sight from the open sickbay door. He tilted his head, unsure what to make of her expression. Not for the first time, he recognized the limitation of cybernetics ability to convey emotions. Part of his mind started considering ways to overcome that while the other studied Serene.

She glanced up at him, her lips flat and unreadable. Vlasa wondered why she was out here rather than inside with Noah. But the expression made him decide not to pry. He moved on with only a backward glance.

59- Olivia

The jump completed and Olivia watched the sensor display as the Hub came back into view. They hadn't been away any longer than most delivery jobs, but for some reason she felt it had been a lifetime. Her encounter with her old street rats and the Rokma Pou who had been teaching them how to destroy drones, was only a blurry memory. Had that really been the last time she had been home?

"Seraph, this is Hub control. You are clear to dock at port three."

"Acknowledged control, we're coming in," Olivia responded. She then announced to everyone else, "We're cleared to dock. ETA five minutes."

"That's a fast dock," Vlasa noted.

"You complaining?" Serene asked.

"No, it's just we've never had to wait less than thirty minutes before."

Olivia adjusted *Seraph's* course to line up with docking port three. She fired the retro thrusters to decelerate until they were approaching the port at little more than a walking pace. She always found this the weirdest part of space flight. Giant hunks of metal orbiting the system's star at unreasonable velocities came together slower than she could jog.

Her comm panel lit up and Olivia accepted the call without looking, assuming it was more instructions from Hub control. Instead, she heard a gruff voice, slightly out of breathe, *"Ariana? You there?"*

"This is Olivia aboard *Seraph*. Who is this?"

"It's Jasper. I need to talk to Ariana. Now."

"We're about to dock. She'll be able to come see you shortly."

"Bah! Don't dock idiot girl! Put your captain on now!"

Olivia sighed. She didn't like Jasper, but Ariana got most of their work from him so she didn't want to antagonize him. She linked in Ariana to the channel.

"What's so urgent Jasper?" Ariana asked.

"I warned you not to come back here. As soon as you dock, you're going to be 'arrested'. And yes, I said that with quotes," Jasper wheezed.

"Gerald's dead, Jasper. He's not going to be a problem for you or us anymore."

"Ha. Gerald was just one symptom of a larger infestation. The Hub used to be a nice place to do business. Very few regulations and very little oversight. Good old-fashioned person-to-person business. But then unsavory types like Gerald have been making inroads. He may be dead, good job on that by the way, but he still has people here. And those people are planning to end you."

"We'll sort things out with Hub control," Ariana said.

"They are Hub control. Have you checked where this comm signal is coming from?"

At those words, Olivia checked the status of the transmission. She blinked in surprise, "Cap, he's calling from the *Glad Tidings,* not the Hub. Jasper never leaves the Hub."

"That's right. I like my comfort. But the Hub's not exactly welcoming anymore. So, I'm relocating. Minus a fair amount of my inventory I might add," Jasper said with bitterness. *"I suggest you do the same. If you need work, I still have that survey of J-25 for you."*

"You really want me to take that contract Jasper."

"I purchased it a few years ago. No one wants to do it. The option will expire soon and then I'll have paid those credits for nothing. I'm helping you avoid getting murdered. Help me out. I think we're both going to need the money. I doubt you're going to be welcome on many more PUG stations than I am."

There was a long pause from Ariana. Olivia neared the final capture point for the Hub's docking port. She reversed thrust without orders, bringing *Seraph* to a virtual stop relative to the station. She thought about everyone onboard the station she knew. If criminals like Gerald were taking over, she wouldn't want to be them, trapped aboard with no place to escape to.

"Captain, what if he's right? Our fuel is stocked. We still have another month or so of food. Maybe we should just take Sapik home and do that survey."

"I don't like the idea of being forced away from here. The Hub's become kind of like our second home away from the ship," Ariana said.

"It's always been my home. I don't like abandoning everyone I know to people like Gerald. I'd hate for the Hub to become another M-21. But I'd hate to become the first victim even more."

There was a long pause before Ariana answered, *"Back us away Olivia. Jasper, thank you for the warning. We'll take that contract. It will be like a vacation."*

"Good luck, Ariana. You can find me on Emay, probably. It's PUG but Captain Grimes tells me it's not too bad."

The comm channel ended and Olivia flew *Seraph* away from home.

Also by Wayne Basta

From Grey Gecko Press
Aristeia: Revolutionary Right
Aristeia: A Little Rebellion
Aristeia: Tree of Liberty
From Many Worlds Fiction
Worst. Book. Ever.
The Awesome Adventures of Max Power
Seraph's Gambit
Seraph's Bind
Seraph's Break (Coming December 2022)

Don't miss out!

Visit the website below and you can sign up to receive emails whenever Wayne Basta publishes a new book. There's no charge and no obligation.

https://books2read.com/r/B-A-DTNS-LSUWB

BOOKS 2 READ

Connecting independent readers to independent writers.

About the Author

Wayne Basta is a lifelong science fiction fan. Reading and watching it proved not enough, so he turned to creating his own universes. Aside from writing novels, he also loves games and works as the editor for d20 Radio.

Read more at waynebasta.com.